MAJESTIC MADNESS

By

Kyle A. Turk

BEST WISHES FOR A LONG
AND HAPPY LIFE TOGETHER !!

FOR TOMMY GRAPEFRUIT LEE
WALKER & NORIGAMI MIJA WRIGHT.

For Mom

Hope you enjoy !
xo Kyle

I

"Twenty years from now you will be more disappointed by the things that you didn't do than by the ones you did do. So throw off the bowlines. Sail away from the safe harbor. Catch the trade winds in your sails. Explore. Dream. Discover."

-Mark Twain

San Francisco

I say we do away with the lot of them...filthy bastards... Send 'em back where they came from, that's what I say," Sammy complained, taking another large swig of ale and slamming the glass down onto the table where the two men sat. "Filthy Chinks are always--"

"Hey!" interrupted the barkeeper, leaning forward and pointing intently. "Sam, there'll be none of that here," he declared. "--That goes for the rest of ya too," he added a moment later, a pointed finger slowly following his scan to the suddenly silent tables that were occupied by exhausted working men.

"Max," said Nep, Sammy's friend, "another man caught fever today. He's just upset is all...we all are."

Max was of Irish descent. His grandfather had emigrated from the famine in the 1820s and had moved the family more and more west, finally putting down roots in San Francisco as some its first settlers. Max's father had been fortunate to have been one of the first to arrive at the Gold Rush in the early Summer of 1848. He had been lucky. On his third day of panning, at a claim overlooked by other prospectors a few hundred yards off the beaten path, he had come upon a cluster of gold nuggets which filled his palm.

The nuggets weighed nearly four pounds, fetching nearly twenty dollars per ounce - about four hundred dollars per ounce in today's money. He worked the claim for only two more weeks, narrowly escaping starvation when a rock-slide knocked him unconscious and a sizable boulder pinned his right leg with the weight of a carriage. When he regained consciousness several hours later, he managed to reach his pickaxe and spent the next two days without food and water in total isolation, chipping away at the boulder until his damaged leg was freed. When patrons would later ask how he came to limp he would reply, "The good Lord might grace a man with luck, but he's quick to spit on his greed."

So with his coffers filled, he had made his way back to the city, purchased nearly an acre of vacant land adjacent to the docks, and leased all but a corner lot where he built and operated *The Prospector Saloon* until his death. Max had worked at his father's establishment his entire life, serving the droves of dockworkers who flocked there after a hard day's labor.

"Look, I'm sorry, Sammy. I didn't know. I'm just... It's my bar is all, and we've got rules," Max digressed. "I don't like things any better than you, but just...we gotta have rules ya know," he said apologetically.

Sammy nodded at no one in particular. "What are we gonna do, Nep," he asked solemnly. "What do they expect us to do, leave? To where? What are they gonna do, build a wall around them," he said slightly louder. "A goddam Great Wall of Chinatown so the *bastard* rats can eat all the *bastard* Chin--"

"ENOUGH!" yelled Max from behind the bar. "That's enough out of you, Sam! Nep, get him home!"

"Poor man...that poor, poor man. Bloody filthy bastards," slurred Sammy as he continued to lament into his beer.

In 1848 there were but seven, yes seven, Chinese residents in San Francisco amidst a population of around three hundred. By the mid-1850s, there were over seven thousand, and the Union

Pacific company was advertising in China for more. The Union Pacific had been contracted to build a railroad from the Missouri river west, to meet the Central Pacific outfit, which was to build eastward from Sacramento.

The problem was that the Union Pacific workers collectively quit in droves once the tracks reached the fertile and untapped mining opportunities in Wyoming territory, leaving the company with one-tenth its workforce. The few hundred Chinese who were mining in the hills near Cheyenne proved to be an excellent replacement: Loyal, hard-working, and organized into tight social groups with only one leader who spoke for the group. Now, a half century later, however, some residents complained of their overpopulation in the city. And with the plague onset, the anti-Chinese sentiment was escalating.

Nep stood and carefully helped Sammy to his feet, handing him the remaining gulp of ale as a consolation for the effort. The two men were around the same height, but Sammy outweighed Nep by at least twenty pounds, partially due to the strenuous work lifting heavy produce cargo at the docks, but arguably more so due to his steady intake of beer. And although he had an asthmatic condition, Sammy volunteered a few days each week with the fire brigade, more as a tribute to his late father than as a personal passion. The two men slowly made their way to the door, Nep turning his head enough to give

Max an apologetic glance. The remaining patrons slowly returned their attention to drinks and the flirtatious women around them.

As the sun began to fade and the streets outside the bar began to glow orange by the street lamps that lined them, Nep and Sammy walked toward their homes in what is now known as the Marina neighborhood of San Francisco. This night would've been no different from any other, but today's news had forced the entire city's attention toward matters of a more serious nature; namely a proposal being debated by the Board of Supervisors to quarantine a twelve block area due to a rising epidemic of bubonic plague that had come across the sea from China. Centralized in the unsanitary and overcrowded area known as Chinatown, the pandemic was threatening to infect the entire city. If the measure passed, nearly 15,000 of the city's 350,000 population would be isolated until the outbreak could be contained.

*

John Haley had turned thirty-six this Spring, a well-liked and patient man with a wife and young daughter. He was slightly taller than average for the time, with light brown hair and an easy smile to match his demeanor. He had been born to a young prostitute by an unknown suitor who had quickly passed through town on his way to Nevada for the Silver rush in 1870, her more than occasional opium use masking her pregnancy for the first several months. A few months after his birth, John's mother received an unexpected letter containing a marriage proposal along with paid warrant for passage from a childhood friend in Australia.

The suitor was the son of an officer, and she was certain he could provide her a good life, but she was well aware of the implications of her situation. The offer would surely be retracted if she arrived with a baby in tow. But the larger concern was whether her child would survive such a voyage in the first place, as infants were much more prone to infection.

She had been clean from the tar-like substance since learning of her pregnancy but had found only meager jobs running errands and mending the occasional garment, so regardless she would have no way to transport them both. She agonized privately, not telling a soul of her predicament, weighing her current life against starting anew. A few weeks after receiving the letter, a new mother approached the same storefront John's mother was shopping and the two chatted briefly, discussing the ages of their infants and admiring the window displays.

When the woman departed, John's mother stealthily followed the woman to her home and, that evening at dusk, placed John at her doorstep with a note pinned to his blanket which read simply: *John my love.* The resident's husband was first to discover the baby. He had been out for drinks and upon returning mistook the child for his own, clumsily cradling the baby and bringing it inside their home. When the couple realized the confusion they argued fiercely for two days, until finally Sammy's father had relented to his wife's constant pleading.

John grew up around the docks, helping the crabbers sort their catch and fishing off the wharf, while Sam spent most working hours at the market or on one of many pastures helping his father with his produce business. On one occasion as a teenager, John had saved a man from drowning. The man had been leaning over the side of his small boat, attempting to unravel the line to his crab pot when he suddenly capsized, his feet dragging netting overboard with him and tightly entangling both his legs.

John had thrown his fishing rod aside without a second thought and dove into the chilly Bay water, swimming furiously nearly a hundred yards, diving down as the drowning fisherman took a seemingly final gasp, furiously untangling the net from the man's legs. He struggled to drag the near-dead man to his boat, climbing in and pulling the man aboard with all his might.

When the man caught his breath and came to his senses, they returned to shore. A reporter recorded the man explaining that it was "as if Neptune himself rose from the bottom and lifted me out to safety," earning John the nickname *Nep* in the newspapers and the respect of the entire fishing community, along with a public promise by the man of "all the crab he could carry every Saturday for a year."

That day, Sammy had been approaching where Nep sat to join him as he fished from the dock when he witnessed the man capsize and watched Nep's brave rescue. The next day he had shown Nep how to lure some of the crabs into clamping onto his clothing by rubbing scented oils on them. With this, Nep would load up his arms and clothing with live crab, skip and jog along the wharf looking as if he was under some sort of ridiculous crab attack – sometimes acting the part by flailing his arms wildly – until he could round the nearest building, where Sam would help him carry half the bounty back to Sam's parents' basement. The boys were inseparable, growing up together and years later spending many nights drinking and gambling at Max's saloon.

As the two men walked from the bar, the sky grew dark and the sounds of laughter and singing could be heard in the distance. They made their way up toward the hill to Chestnut Street and parted ways. Sammy, now only staggering slightly, began to hum a melody as he made his way home. Nep paused briefly to watch his friend before continuing in the opposite direction, taking in his surroundings and the calm evening air, his gait swiftening at the thought of nearing his family after a long day at the docks.

*   *   *

II

*   *   *

As the street trolley came to a stop, the old man pulled his cane from beneath his arm and gingerly stepped down and into the brisk Winter evening. He turned slowly and pinched the front of his hat, a beaver-skin top hat adorned with peacock bullseyes, toward the Conductor. With a ring of the bell above him, the Conductor returned the nod to the old man and set the trolley in motion. The man watched and listened as the imposing machine seemed to magically move forward, marveling at the innovation of this new technology.

After a moment of thought, he pulled a silver flask from his breast-coat. As he fumbled to unscrew its cap, he glanced around for witnesses and, satisfied that he was alone, cocked his head back, and imbibed several gulps of the warming liquid. He let out a strong exhale, resealed the cap firmly, and set off further on his way. He had been looking forward to attending a lecture entitled "Decay of the Art of Lying," in which the popular author of the lecture had, among other things, suggested:

"The wise thing is for us diligently to train ourselves to lie thoughtfully, judiciously; to lie with a good object, and not an evil one; to lie for others' advantage, and not our own; to lie healingly, charitably, humanely, not cruelly, hurtfully, maliciously; to lie gracefully and graciously, not awkwardly and clumsily; to lie firmly, frankly, squarely, with head erect, not haltingly, tortuously, with pusillanimous mien, as being ashamed of our high calling."

Indeed, old frrind, the old man had surmised enthusiastically to himself in his eclectic tongue upon first reading. *What's not admirable about thett?* Although decidedly British both in accent and in birth, his time in Algoa Bay caused the occasional utterance to part his lips askewed, particularly when he had been drinking. The old man made his way toward his destination, a lengthy seven blocks to his east, pausing again to seal the nape of his regimental jacket for protection from the chill in the foggy night air and the drizzle of rain that had begun to accompany it. The streets downtown were nearly empty, bereft of the boisterous sounds of revelry that permeated most other neighborhoods at this late evening hour.

But he would fail to arrive at his destination. As he paused after only a few blocks to take another swig from his flask, his heart suddenly jolted. His eyes now flaring, he dropped the flask and desperately clutched at his chest, struggling to balance himself with his cane, managing to do so only long enough to collapse against a street lamp and slide toward the earth with a THUNK. A policeman who had just rounded the corner witnessed his duress and made fast to his aid. When he approached, he saw the dire state of the situation and ran quickly toward a busier avenue to hasten a carriage to convey the old man to the nearest hospital.

A young boy of about ten had also happened upon witnessing the collapse, but had awaited the policeman's departure for fear of being reprimanded for being outside after dark past curfew. The boy snuck quickly toward the old man, curious, shifting his gaze quickly to his left and right as he did. Convinced the coast was clear, the boy entered the range of the old man's vision, slowing his gallop and pausing several feet in front of him to stare. The old man, whose eyes had been closed, sensed a presence in his midst and now slowly opened them, blinking several times to attempt focus on the awkward figure in front of him.

He slowly lifted his right arm and gestured the boy toward him. The boy looked around him again, hesitant at the site of a struggling old man, cautious of worsening his already precarious situation.

"Boy," grumbled the old man, followed by a few coughs. "Boy, come hyah, come clohzah...don't be afreed," he continued.

The boy was confused at first. *What is this strange tongue?* He looked around again, hearing the policeman's whistle calls in the distance, seeing not another soul in plain sight. He inched closer and closer, shuffling his worn boots timidly along the cobblestones, as if ready to recoil at any sign of danger, until he was crouched in front of the man.

"Good lad," said the man, punctuating the phrase with several coughs and gasps. "Can you geep something safe foh me, lad," he managed.

"--Yes...yes, sir," the boy replied, now becoming nervous at the increasing volume of the voices and whistles in the near distance.

"Good lad," said the man as he strenuously reached into his breast-coat. "This has geeven me luck," he struggled to whisper to the boy, grimacing. "Geep it safe now," he stammered, coughing violently again.

The boy began slowly presenting his open hand to the old man. "I will," he said assuredly after a pause, "...promise, sir." The boy's head then quickly jolted upward from the sound of approaching hooves and voices. "I will," he repeated more assertively as he began to move. He grasped the metal piece and hastened his movement away from the approaching sounds. As he began to run, he peered back and noticed the old man's head wilt to the side, his eyelids slowly close.

The first policeman to arrive was now accompanied by several others as they came into view and the boy made haste toward the nearest alleyway and into the safety of the darkness. Once he rounded the corner he doubled back, crouching at the corner of the building. Peering only with the top of his head and eyes, he pulled down the brim of his chapeau as to avert any stray eyes toward his direction.

There was a sense of panic as he viewed the scene from a distance, realizing his selfishness at pausing more to ensure his safe leave than to witness the improbable rescue of the man. He waited only long enough to watch the old man being assisted into the waiting carriage, to hear the whip of the steeds who carried him before he turned and ran swiftly through the alley.

*   *   *

III

*   *   *

Emma grabbed her Teddy bear and ran from her room along the hallway of their third-story flat to the bedroom at the other end. She entered cautiously, tiptoed forward, and jumped onto the foot of her parents' bed, landing on her knees with an excitement that only a nine-year-old can appreciate so early on a Saturday morning. She launched her sixty-pound frame between the yet unmoved bodies resting there and nestled closely next to her mother.

"Mom-my?" she loudly whispered after only a few still moments as she grinningly jostled her mother's shoulder. "Is it time yet?" It was only nearing seven-o'clock but Emma was excited to go to the Baths near the ocean to be with her schoolmates as soon as possible. Her mother attempted to play dead, pulling her shoulder toward herself while pulling the covers up to her ear.

"Mommm-mmy?" she pleaded more slowly and a bit softer.

"Go sleep Emma, too early...sweetheart," mumbled her mother as she clumsily tapped Emma's hand, which had again found her shoulder. As her grin subsided, Emma rolled on to her back and heeled her feet down at the bed, letting out a purposeful sigh of disappointment. She looked at her Teddy.

"This is your fault," she said in a condescending whisper, "you said it was time and it's *not* time." She poked the inanimate bear on the nose several times to inflict seeming injury and looked at her parents with disgust at their apparent laziness. She let out another loud sigh and scooched her way like a caterpillar to the foot of the bed using her heels. She hopped off the bed and thumped out of the room and down the hall, hoping her clumsy antics would speed the process of getting her to the pool.

Emma Haley was small for her age, with dark, red hair and a bashful disposition from her mother Caroline's Scottish side, her pretty smile from her father's. She was cute in every sense of the word, with a small, button-like nose and big round eyes of green. She had freckles on both cheeks, which only added to her prettiness.

Her passion was swimming and today she wanted to show a boy at school that she could swim faster than he could. She had been awaiting today all week long with duplicitous anticipation. Firstly, she was going to prove that she was the best girl swimmer in her class. But secondly, and more importantly to her, Nathan was the best looking boy in school and had accepted her challenge to a race because she had made fun of his big ears.

"Ba-loney," Nathan had said with a downstroke of his arm. "Everybody knows I'm the fastest kid in school, knogh-ha-ha," he'd snorted.

"Emma'd beat you by a mile." Sara continued her taunting toward Nathan as Emma had noticed the group from a distance. "You don't even gotta give her a head start," she added.

"That's Applesauce and you know it!" replied Nathan confidently. "She couldn't beat me if I gave her an extra *ten*," he laughed, his cohort Floyd quickly laughing beside him.

Emma had overheard his dare on her way toward the group. "I'd beat you no problem with those flappers slowin' you down," she declared with her hands firmly at her hips, "bet you a half-dollar!"

Nathan had momentarily felt self-conscious and had moved his fingers toward his ears, but stopped before they made contact and lifted his gaze up from the ground abruptly. "You're on!" He pointed several times, his focus shifting to the easy profit the dare suggested. "This Saturday, *you're on*," he said again, beginning to shuffle his feet with excitement. In fact, he probably uttered the phrase at least fifty more times between bragging about how easy the task would be, and during his restless sleeps leading up to the weekend.

*

The Haley's lived in a typical three-story Victorian building near the corner of Chestnut and Mason Streets. On the street level of their building was a patisserie and below their flat lived its owner, a portly middle-aged man from Lyon, France, who would often spoil Emma with sweet delicacies if she would attempt to speak to him in French.

Precocious Emma would often sneak downstairs with her Teddy bear before her parents awoke to watch him prepare an array of treats in his kitchen, listening to him happily sing French songs and obliging him by repeating any French phrase he directed toward her in order to earn each one. Today Emma decided to quell her impatience by again stealthily creeping down to visit Monsieur Dubois. As she opened the side door to his kitchen she heard him humming and could smell the pleasing aroma of fruits and pastry dough emanating from his oven. "Bon jour, monsieurrrr," she greeted him softly and playfully.

Dubois stopped at once, dramatically raising and clapping the flour from his hands in a fury to suggest that his most important customer required his attention. "Ohhh, Mademoiselle!" he mused as she began to giggle. "Ca c'est un bon surprise!"

He vigorously wiped both hands on his apron as Emma took a seat on a nearby chair and began swinging her legs in anticipation. Dubois came near and whispered, *"Qu'est que vous desire au'jourduis, Madam,"* as he regally bowed toward Emma's blushing giggle.

"Je voudray a crassant sivou play, monsieurrrr," she replied while still giggling.

Dubois stood erect suddenly and changed his demeanor. "CWA-sont! CWA-sont!" he snorted sternly.

"CWA-sont! CWA-sont!" she retorted, unphased by his aggressive reprimand, and giggled again.

"Bien sûr," he mused. He pivoted and jovially went to the oven, within moments returning with the delicate pastry, one of its tips dipped in fine chocolate and still melting to the touch.

"Merci," said Emma, taking the delicacy with a ravenous smile.

Dubois returned to his work and his humming, happy to have her company. Emma offered little bites to Teddy, reprimanding him when his French was pronounced incorrectly and eating the bites herself; all the while swinging her legs under the chair and attempting to hum along with Monsieur Dubois.

After a half hour, the two friends bid each other *adieu* and Emma crept back up to her room. As she began to put on her bathing suit, she heard her mother arise and walk to the kitchen past her room. She quickly lay in bed and pulled up the covers, concealing her guilt and shifting her thoughts to the competition that lay ahead after she heard her mother pass. Soon her mother appeared in her doorway and Emma acted as if she was asleep.

Caroline walked in softly and sat on the side of the bed. "Emma," she said softly. "Emma wake up sweety, I made you some--" She stopped herself and swiped the chocolate from Emma's cheek with her finger, tasting it and sighing with a combination of enjoyment and disapproval. "--I've told you *not* to go down there, Emma, you'll end up fat and no one will play with you," she warned. "Come on, up you go," she ordered. Caroline arose and went back to the kitchen.

At around eight-thirty, Caroline and Emma said goodbye to John and headed down to the street to catch the trolley on California street that would take them to within a mile of the Sutro Baths, where they would then take a carriage the rest of the way, arriving nearly two hours after their departure six miles earlier. They waved to Mr. Dubois through his crowd of anxious customers and walked down the street to begin the long journey.

A visitor to the baths not only had a choice of seven different swimming pools — one fresh water and six salt water baths ranging in temperatures — but could also visit a museum displaying Sutro's large and varied personal collection of artifacts from his travels, a concert hall, seating for 8,000 and, at one time, an ice skating rink. During high tides, water would flow directly into the pools from the nearby ocean, recycling the two million US gallons of water in about an hour. During low tides, a powerful turbine water pump, built inside a cave at sea level, could be switched on from a control room and could fill the tanks at a rate of 6,000 US gallons a minute, recycling all the water in five hours.

Emma spotted some of her schoolmates and immediately rushed toward them. "No running," said her mother and the nearest lifeguard almost simultaneously. Emma's stride instantly transitioned into an awkward speed-walking one, inadvertently skipping when the frustratingly slow pace became too much for her excitement level.

The Baths consisted of an expanse shaped like an 'L' that measured five hundred feet in length and nearly half that distance in width. The remaining area was sectioned into six pools of standard size, nearly eighty feet in length with walkways in between each. The hundreds of glass panes that lined the sides and arched roof measured two feet wide by six long, giving one the sense of being inside of a greenhouse. Six hundred tons of iron columns, many in number, supported the massive structure. There were several toboggan slides, spring boards, thirty swinging rings, and the beautiful ocean view to her west. Caroline felt confident that Emma was safe here. The facility had been open for over ten years without incident and there were more rigorously-trained lifeguard attendants than she could count. She made her way upstairs to the relaxed viewing balcony and joined with the other parents in smiling broadly as their children began a day of leisure in the awesome structure.

*

Emma would later write in her diary -- I made my way over to the other end where all the other kids were as quick as I could manage. All the grown-ups seemed to be yellin at me to stop or slow down, but the excitement was almost unbearable! I could smell the salty ocean water and the voices echoed loud through the whole place. It was magical! Most of the kids were already wet and horsing around on the slide and in the pool. A few of the bigger boys were locked in some kind of arm wrestling contest in between two pools, one trying to knock the other into the water to impress the older girls. But my focus was on finding my friend Sara and plotting on how to beat Nathan.

I spotted her over at pool #3 and started running again, only to be told off. When I finally made it there, I saw that Nathan was in the water.

He looked much stronger without the baggy parka he often wore at school, and my confidence faltered for a moment until Sara calmed me down. He stopped his stupid splashing around with his friends when he noticed me and swam over to the edge where we stood. He asked if I was ready in a mean way, sounding foolish as he always did, but he does have a nice smile and teeth, and part of me was confused by my strategy, but he wouldn't pay me any attention otherwise...

He got out of the pool and, to my disappointment, made sure everyone was gonna get out of the way. I felt nervous and was easily half as excited as when Mama and me arrived. We argued about the rules for a while until we finally had them sorted:

I'd get to start first and Sara would count to ten before Nathan could dive in, and that if he dove in early his lanky, dopey friend Floyd would get socked in the face on Monday at school by Sara, seein' as how she was bigger than me... We'd go there and back and whoever touched the start first would give the other one fifty cents...also to be settled on Monday seein as we didn't have any pockets right then.

So we lined up at the start... I don't think I'd ever been so nervous. I could hear all the voices of the hundreds of people all at the same time! Then I managed to just hear the kids around me, there were at least thirty of them now who had emptied half the pool and were cheering. I heard my name called out a lot and that distracted me, but I'm not one to make excuses so I tried to ignore them too. Then I heard Sara sounding like a Big Top announcer, "Onnnn yourrr Marksss!" Everything went real quiet and I noticed my left leg shaking a little. I saw a few kids from the corner of my eye lookin confused and up at the ceiling, but I stayed focused. Then I heard "Get Settt!" And a moment later she yelled, "GO!"

I pushed off as hard as I could with my feet and dove in head first like Pa taught me last year, my arms locked and palms together, and I started swimming like crazy! I could still hear a lot of voices, but they sounded real distorted and almost louder than before I dove in. I swore they were yellin 'Emma's Great,' but now it's obvious that the second word wasn't "great"...it was "wait..."

I tore off to the other side of the pool, focusing on my breaths and reaching and kicking, all the things Pa taught me, and soon I could see the black paint on the far side approaching. Pa had taught me *how* to do a flip-turn like the real good swimmers could do, and I wanted to do it, I really did! But I was out of breath already from the nerves and decided split quick to take a peek when I reached the edge and see where Nathan was.

I reached out and kept kicking when I thought I was close and finally made it to the edge. I popped my head up and pulled my hair back as quick as I could. What I saw next was, well, it's hard to describe. I looked back and saw nobody at the other end where I had started! I was confused so I looked round and just as I spotted the piles of people clamoring at both corners of the building, a big piece of glass shattered almost clear on top of me! I heard my Mom's voice callin my name and finally located the source up on the stairs between the pool and the other level. She looked scared, real scared. I never saw her look so scared, but then she ain't never had a reason before I guess.

I didn't know what to do! People were screamin and carryin on, and I guess I panicked. So I took a big breath and went underwater and pushed off! I pulled and pulled with my arms as fast and as hard as I could to get back to the other side without comin' up for air, but when my breath ran out, I was still only about half way... So I started swimming again, all the while hearing Ma callin my name, gettin louder and louder. When I made it back I grabbed the hand that was extended and Momma nearly yanked my arm off getting me out of the pool! We were the last people outside the building far as I could tell.

*   *   *

IV

*   *   *

Joshua Norton was born in London in 1819. A few short years after his birth, his family moved to Port Elizabeth, South Africa with 4,000 other British settlers, a strategy by the British to strengthen the colony's numbers as it expanded eastward into native lands. His father was a shrewd and frugal man who poured over maps of all sorts throughout Joshua's childhood, investing in land, speculating that the area near Port Elizabeth would become a busy one and increase in value as hard times continued to beleaguer Britain and emigration increased. He was also an integral part of the creation of the town's library as a philanthropic portion of his commerce business. As there was little else to do, Joshua became an avid reader, spending hours of his free time reading whatever books arrived in Port.

His father's speculation was correct, affording him abundant wealth for his time. Seeing that there was no means for higher education in the commonwealth, his father made a sizable donation to England and eventually was able to send Joshua to the University of London, a newly chartered Royal school which afforded lodging and a transpose into the possibilities of a good education, even splurging for the posh cabin accommodations for the journey.

Joshua had mused that since his journey was backwards, beginning in South Africa rather than Britain, they were actually the *SHPO* cabins, as the original acronym was intended to signify *Port Outbound, Starboard Home,* allowing those who could afford them a view of coastline during a round trip voyage from Britain to its South African, Indian, or Australian colonies. His father had dropped his cutlery, wiped his hands on his serviette, and slapped Joshua solidly, chewing steadfastly as he returned to his cutlery and meal, and sneering at Joshua as he angrily cut his next piece of pork.

But only a few months after his arrival in London, a smallpox pandemic began back in Cape Town, the western part of South Africa. Wiping out a significant portion of its population, it spread east through South Africa rampantly, eventually infecting and killing Joshua's parents and sister. Devastated by the news, Joshua made the journey back to Port Elizabeth in haste to sort out his family's affairs and estate.

By this time, his father had amassed a sizable amount of land and a trading outpost. A new colony, tax collection had yet to impose itself in any stringent way, so his lucrative side dealings with mostly Dutch, Spanish, and Italian vessels went largely undocumented. During the following few years, Joshua learned the ins and outs of real estate and business, faltering only once early on before he had a firm grasp of topography maps:

A man had telegraphed an offer for a sizable parcel of land and Joshua had naively accepted. When the man arrived, they argued fiercely until a mediator was brought in from the local Council to settle the matter. Joshua had apparently agreed to sell what he had thought was a hillside lot for the equivalent of two thousand British pounds, when in fact it had been the larger developed lot that lay adjacent, ...on the ocean, ...fully tilled and containing several mills and irrigation ducts, ...valued at nearly *three* times as much.

The loss infuriated him of course, so he spent the ensuing years aggressively purchasing land and withholding it with contempt until the demand was so great that newcomers had no choice but to settle at his price. Needless to say, Joshua recouped his losses. Two years hence, at twenty-nine years of age in December of 1848, he read a newspaper headline that would change his life:

*

EL DORADO

of the

UNITED STATES of AMERICA

∞ ∞ ∞ ∞ ∞ ∞ ∞ ∞ ∞ ∞ ∞ ∞ ∞ ∞ ∞ ∞

The Discovery

of

INEXHAUSTABLE GOLD MINES

in

C A L I F O R N I A

Tremendous Excitement Among the Americans!

*

The California Gold Rush began at Sutter's Mill near Coloma, California. On January 24, 1848, John Marshall, a foreman working for Sacramento pioneer John Sutter, found shiny metal in the tail-race of a lumber mill Marshall was building for Sutter on the American River. Marshall brought what he found to John Sutter, and the two privately tested the metal. After the tests showed that it was gold, Sutter expressed dismay: he wanted to keep the news quiet because he feared what would happen to his plans for an agricultural empire if there were a mass search for gold.

However, rumors soon started to spread and were confirmed in March 1848 by San Francisco newspaper publisher and merchant Samuel Brannan. The most famous quote of the California Gold Rush was by Brannan; after he had hurriedly set up a store to sell gold prospecting supplies, Brannan strode through the streets of San Francisco, holding aloft a vial of gold, shouting "Gold! Gold! Gold from the American River!"

Although the men in San Francisco dropped everything and ran to the hills, the news traveled slowly in comparison to today, making its way by sea to the Sandwich Islands (Hawai'i) by June and north to Oregon by July. In early December, President James Polk made the announcement to Congress that gold had been discovered, and within six weeks the news had finally spread worldwide. Joshua had learned of the news within the month.

He hopped up from his chair with the newspaper and began pacing in a frenzy. "Aha!" he cried, pacing more quickly as he read. He had been growing bored and a bit lonely in the past months and felt his youth slipping away as he managed the day to day in the small port town. When he had finished reading the article, he stood dumbfounded and fixed his gaze out at the ocean from his home, literally half way around the world from San Francisco.

"There it is..." he said aloud as he gestured toward the sea. "My distiny handed to me on a gold pletter..." His servant, a young Xhosa boy – pronounced *Kosa* - from the abutting tribal land had stopped sweeping. Norton had looked around for anyone's approval and Toku obliged him with a grin and a nod. It mattered little that Norton was actually gesturing toward the South Pole; certainly not to Toku, who didn't understand much English at all. As he redirected his gaze to the ocean, he began laughing at the new and exciting prospect of the adventure that lay afoot.

"Surely there will be a mad dash to the place, the values will hit the sky!" he then exclaimed to Toku, who now mimicked Norton's excitement with his expression. "Six months or so by sea...or is it seven? Another to grasp the place and rub the right elbows," he said in a playful manner, twisting back and forth at the waist with his elbows raised. "And women, Toku!! Women from all over the world, hahaha," he bellowed. He grabbed the now frightened, frail boy and shook his shoulders vigorously. He beckoned another assistant to gather information and began furiously digging through newspapers and books for the ensuing weeks. His plan would be to sell his remaining property immediately, set sail for America, and invest in land when he arrived in San Francisco.

Cautiously hoping that few would see the opportunity in land rather than in gold prospecting, he began making estimates and calculations. He had seen this strategy work for his father and then for himself and was confident he would succeed. He began contacting everyone who had shown interest in his father's land, dating back to when he had first returned to Port Elizabeth. To the dismay of others, he eased prices and negotiated quick deals to unload his holdings.

Some began thinking he had lost his mind, and perhaps he had. Gold fever was a powerful force and Joshua had unmistakably caught the bug, they had surmised privately. Within a month, all that remained was the original three acre parcel on which his family had originally settled and the villa in which he stood...and the only reason he hadn't sold that was because he simply could not find the Deed for it. *Oh well*, he thought to himself, *the boy can tend to it while I'm away.*

He gathered all the information he could about California and America. There was very little, only what had been written in newspapers and what he could ascertain from ships that passed through Port Elizabeth and the books within the library his father had established. He had kept abreast of recent news regarding the rapidly developing nation, first with the war in Texas and a year prior the annexation of California into the Union. America now stretched across from one ocean to another. He knew that San Francisco was scarcely as populated as where he stood. Three hundred or so residents on a small peninsula as of an article from six months earlier, similar in climate and topography to South Africa and with little industry aside from fishing and agriculture.

He knew it would be dangerous...all of it. The journey itself would be a challenge, but there were other dangers: Disease, natives, a culture that the papers made out to be savage, and gold-hungry emigrants similar to himself, who would stop at next to nothing to strike it rich.

The distance between New York and San Francisco by sea was nearly 16,000 nautical miles and lasted between eight and a half and ten months. Those who could not afford passage by sea or were too impatient would attempt the 3,000 miles by carriage through largely unknown and hostile territories. That option would take between ten and twelve months, taking countless lives along in its path. Norton calculated that his 10,000 nautical mile journey would last approximately seven to eight months. But he had received the news three months after the rest. It would be a tight race, but he was optimistic. *After all*, he thought to himself, *I'll have a few months before the prospectahs who strike it rich return to San Francisco with their fohtunes to buy lehnd.*

*

He had booked passage for the following day, January 12th. With his affairs seemingly in order, travel chests packed, his holdings liquidated, and content that he was on the right path, he decided to visit the old cabin once more before setting off. The cabin was the original structure that his father had built when they had arrived. It lay at the far corner of the property atop the tallest hill, shadowed and protected from the winds by a large acacia tree that had grown so large that its branches obscured most of the exterior from plain view.

The cabin was quite small, a simple one-room structure with a fireplace at one end, a bed in which they all had slept, and a table for dining and knitting. The Nortons had moved into the larger home when Joshua was five, but he remembered running up the hill and playing here with his younger sister Elise throughout his youth, climbing the acacia tree when it was much smaller.

He fumbled with his remaining keys, cleared the overgrown brush and debris from in front of the door, unlocked the pad and pulled the heavy door open. He located a lantern on the old dining table near the entrance and struck a flint match from the box aside it. In twenty-five years the cabin had taken on a life of its own. Cockroaches scattered from the light and something slithered toward the far side of the room. There were thick spiderwebs covering everything and dust had blown leaves and debris through one of the small broken panes of glass in the only window, which faced the villa and the ocean beyond. There were old tools and a small, wooden rocking horse, a bicycle and old carriage parts.

He slowly and carefully negotiated his way around the four sides of the room. When he illuminated the back corner, he noticed a crate behind a stack of kindle marked *Fine Scotch Whisky* and *1814* singed onto the top panel. There was a crest he didn't recognize but the familiar plaid Scottish pattern criss-crossed the top of the crate. Probably, he had thought, part of the lot his father had brought on their original voyage to alleviate the boredom he must have endured. He swept an area of the table clear with his sleeve and set the box and the lantern down. He then located a pry bar among the many tools scattered around with which to open it.

He pried one side up, and then the other. When he lifted the lid, he was a bit surprised to see that there were a few bottles missing, as the top of the crate had been hammered down tightly. The remaining bottles were packed tightly with straw and looked surprisingly clean, as if they had just been packaged. The thought quickly passed as he licked his lips in anticipation and he proceeded to extract one of the remaining bottles. As he did, something clanked against the glass of another.

He shone the lantern closer into the crate and saw an object glimmer against the light of the lantern. He placed the bottle he was holding down at his side and reached into the straw carefully, moving it to the side to reveal what appeared to be a timepiece. As he picked up the object, he noticed the corners of a folded piece of parchment tucked under the other bottles. He removed the bottles from the crate hastily with his free hand, pulled out the note and unfolded it:

Dearest Julia,

Tis with a heavy heart and a head swimming in spirits that I scribe this. You have always stood by my side as a good woman, strong and beautiful. Our lives have been blessed with health, children, and wealth my dear. As I pen this I feel an illness growing in me and fear that I shan't see the morn of fortnight next. How I've strained against the conceal of my feverish condition from you and the children my love, but alas it is my lot to protect you all from the hardships of life. This small token of our lives together marks our anniversary, my sweet. Place it around your neck and keep me with your thoughts always, look within if hard times beset you and the children. Love of my life, you are dearest to me as none other. Be well my dear Julia and see our children through this time and beyond.

Your most humbled husband,

James

The hand which had held the note slowly descended to the table as he finished reading it, his gaze becoming blank as it rose to stare forward, emotionless, through the small window that faced the sea. A reluctant tear welled on his right eye's corner and sped down the side of his face. It occurred to him that after all of this time being back in Port Elizabeth, he hadn't grieved for their absence. In his defense, those who succumbed to smallpox were immediately disposed of in a blaze in an effort to control its contagion, so that by the time he had returned all that remained were inanimate bronze crosses in the ground.

After several minutes standing motionless, he raised the half-empty bottle and twisted the cork out, put it to his lips and took in a sizable mouthful, struggling its swallow against his choked emotions. Julia and Elise had befallen the fevers and subsequently the smallpox that had taken James only a week later, never receiving the locket, never finding the note. Their graves lay on the opposite hillside, a substantial distance from both where he stood and the villa, and he hadn't revisited them after his first return, nor would he do so now.

Joshua picked up the item again and briefly looked at it in the light, hardly taking notice of the details or inscription. *Idiot*, he thought to himself. *What sort of timepiece is oval...,* shaking his head slightly at himself and wiping his wettened cheek in disgust. His childhood began to retrace itself as he took another swig from the bottle.

He recalled the family's arrival, seeing the dark-skinned people for the first time, the heat and the smells, the cramped shed in which they stayed, the vast open spaces, the only slave auction he witnessed due to their abolition that year, his sister's hair, his mother's touch, his father's voice. He slowly replaced the bottles save the one he had opened, collected the note and locket, and made his way back down the long hill to the villa a few swigs at a time.

*   *   *

V

*   *   *

The boy hastily pulled the soiled scarf around his neck up over his nose, turned, and ran quickly up the alley away from the old man and the chaos he had just seen, the streets all but deserted, frequently looking behind himself to ensure he wasn't being followed. He made sure to keep to the alleys, going out of his way toward the Bay to avoid the streetlights and anyone who could implicate him.

As his pace slowed, realizing a safe distance between him and the scene, the boy began to recount the strange events that had transpired that evening, wondering whether it was fortune or fate that had imposed its hand and how it would inevitably come back to bite him in the ass. After all, the only reason he was out past curfew in the first place this particular Winter evening was to prove himself to the gang he hoped to join by robbing a trolleycar. Now he had to choose between returning to the wharf where they awaited him or to seek refuge and abandon any chance of becoming a member.

His sprint slowed to a trot as he checked left and right one last time before deciding to rest at the edge of the dark alleyway nearest to his refuge. He pulled an item from his pocket and unwrapped it from the cloth, revealing the rusted knife he had been given to rob the trolley. As he set it aside, he pulled the newly acquired item from his other pocket. Peering his head around the corner, the boy surveyed the street next to the alley where he sat to again assure his safety. He reached toward the light of the streetlamp with the item in hand and his heart began to race.

"Nep!" the boy heard as a whispered yell in the distance. "Nep, that you?" The voice was followed by an approaching shadow. Nep had recoiled upon hearing the first call, but now recognized the voice.

"Sammy?" he whispered loudly.

"Yeah, it's me," he assured and he ran clumsily to join Nep in the alley. The two sat closely together as Nep recounted the events of the evening.

"...and then he gave me this!" Nep showed the gold piece that nearly filled his entire hand, its chain hanging over one side and nearly touching the ground.

"Whooa," cawed Sammy, "Lemmee see!" Nep clenched it tighter and brought it to his chest, tightening his lips as he glared at Sammy, pondering whether he, or anyone, could be trusted. "C'mon Nep, it's me, lemmee see!" he pleaded.

Nep paused a while and then stood. Sammy followed suit quickly. Nep again scanned the street for signs of life and only spotted a stray cat who was searching for mice along the far end of the other side of the street. He moved cautiously out of the alley with Sammy close behind him and toward the nearest streetlamp.

"Okay," he whispered, still clutching it to his chest. "You can look, but the old man said I was the only one who can ever hold it, see," he said. Sammy nodded several times in agreement. Nep slowly presented it again and opened his palm. The locket was heavy for its size, but Nep had no frame of reference, so he omitted that fact. It was about two inches tall and nearly as wide, its thickness that of a railroad conductor's timepiece. There was a simple yet strong chain attached to the top and a clasp on the right side. It's face was worn down, but had the remnants of an ornate pattern around the edges.

Nep turned the piece over into his left hand and the boys examined the back. There was no pattern this time, but an engraving instead, which read:

PE-SA 1848

To my love

The boys looked at each other and shrugged. Then Nep returned it to his right hand and freed the clasp. He opened the locket to reveal two photos, one of a black dog with a crooked ear and a white stripe down its front, the other of a golden-haired dog with a large top hat and bow-tie.

"Huh," said Sammy in a peculiar tone.

"*Shhh*," warned Nep and looked around again quickly. Sammy covered his mouth with his hands. "Bummer," he whispered, looking at the scribbled handwriting across the bottom part of the photograph depicting the dog in the top hat. "Laz...Laza-- Lazarus," he managed, looking at the photograph of the skinny brown dog. The boys looked at each other and shrugged. After a few moments Nep closed the locket and sealed the clasp. "There," he said to Sammy decidedly, "you saw it. You can't tell anyone," he said, emphasizing *anyone* and beginning to take an authoritative stance facing Sammy, who was a few inches shorter than he at the time.

"I know," Sammy said defensively. "I won't! I promise, Nep," he said in a loud whisper.

"You better not, Sammy," Nep added, "I'm already gonna get a whoopin' from the Newbury boys for ditchin' the trolly robbing."

"No you ain't," said Sammy, happy to suddenly be off the defensive. "They got busted pickin' at thirty-three!" (Residents at this time often only used a number to refer to one of the forty-two docking piers that lined the city.) "Coppers took them an' the others they could catch down to jail!" he said in a relieved laugh. "That's how come I'm here! I ran as soon as I seen 'em coming and kept goin' til I got here. I figured you'd come this way after you chicken'd out," he said, suddenly hiding his smile as if he'd regretted saying it.

"What, you think I wouldn't do it?" he boasted, "I was *gonna* do it, but this old man croaked instead," he lied in a plea as Sammy looked at him blankly, "I had to help the old man! How ya think I got this piece," he said, jerking the locket upward next to his head with its chain hanging down. The two boys stared at each other for a few awkward moments until Nep finally grinned and burst into laughter. Sammy was quick to follow. Nep approached and put his arm around Sammy's shoulder as they began walking toward home.

"Guess I ain't fit for thievin' anyhow," he chuckled.

"Me either," Sammy concurred.

*

Nep awoke in a sweat much earlier than planned, the memory of the old man withered against a streetlamp fresh in his head. As the dream faded but the sun had yet to rise, he fumbled with his hand in the chilly and dark basement until he heard the distinct sound of a matchbox. He carefully struck a match and waited a moment for it to stay lit against the constant draft which blew in through the spaces between the foundation and the house. Inserting the match, he slowly turned the valve at its base and lit the cramped space, noticing a few small shadows scurry away from the light as he did.

Overall it was a large basement, but most of it was filled with the slatted wooden crates that Sammy's father used for his produce business. Stacked taller than Nep in most places, he had only a corridor to navigate past them along the wall until he reached the six by eight foot area he occupied. His bed consisted of a small mattress propped up by the same boxes that he saw stacked all around him.

Another box served as a nightstand when it stood on end, in the open side of which he kept a cigar box full of his valuables; a comb, his toothbrush (used sparingly), and a book called *Gulliver's Travels in Brobdingnag*, which, although orphaned from the other book in the series, he had read and enjoyed several times. At the foot of his bed were three more crates, two used as seats, the third turned on end as a table and draped with a burlap potato sack, where Sammy and Nep would play checkers or crack the crab they brought back on Saturdays.

Aside from that was his extensive wardrobe which, if you included what he wore to bed, included a jacket made of black denim, his boots, and a spare shirt. As the smell of the docks was nearly impossible to evade, plus for the fact that he had nobody to impress and little reason to go indoors for any length of time, he was okay with this.

He hadn't always stayed down here. He shared Sammy's room and was brought up as part of the family, except on the few occasions when the others would visit in-laws several hours away or vice-versa. When it was vice-versa, they would stow him with a friend across town and tell him they were taking Sammy to a special doctor.

Nep was never the wiser and Sammy didn't know the difference, nor did he care when they seemed to miss the appointment and his relatives would visit instead. In fact, even with their birthdays only a few months apart, Nep and Sammy had no idea they weren't biological brothers until a few years earlier, when Sammy's Uncle sent word that he was coming out from Chicago to stay for a spell.

It wouldn't have been a problem, except for the fact that this particular Uncle had wired Sammy's father some money to tide him over through the slow produce season and he'd be hard-pressed -pardon the pun- to explain the other mouth he was feeding. Nep had overheard Sammy's parents arguing, probably, he supposed, assuming that he was at the docks when in fact he was out in the yard just clear from view mending a trap, but either way he couldn't really make out what they were arguing about until he heard his name and inched toward the kitchen window.

"He can't stay there, it's too close," said Sammy's mother. "And the Johnson's boy is down with the flu!"

"There's no way around this," said his father, "you need to tell Nep the truth!"

"How's a boy that age supposed to understand something like that - that his mother dropped him on a stoop?! Abandoned him? --Hell, I'd have a hard time with that news at *my* age," she explained.

"Well that's what it is, you brought him in and he's our son but he ain't, so figure somethin' out and quick! He'll be here in two days," he resolved and closed the front door behind himself.

That evening, without discussion or provocation, Nep waited until Sammy was asleep and hauled his mattress outside, around to the small rear door leading to the basement through the misty dirt and grass, lit the lantern, stacked some crates as tall as he could around the perimeter, and went to sleep. The next day while she was doing wash, he simply said, "It's okay Ma, I won't be a fuss, just please don't send me off."

Flabbergasted, her arm outstretched, she tried to say something but Nep had run off as quickly as the words had left his mouth. After a few weeks, he was invited inside, but his pride interferred and he resisted, saying he preferred it down there on account of Sammy's tossing and turning waking him up. To avoid hearing the truth directly, he let several weeks pass before he even dared enter the house. And that's what that was.

He reached down and picked up the cigar box. Propping up his pillow and adjusting his wooly nightcap, he sat up and opened the box's lid, rubbing the sleep from his eye with his free hand. Inside the box, there was (not surprisingly) a cigar, two wooden bobbers next to a fishing lure and some silk line, six dollars and forty-seven cents, eight marbles, and a small but tall photograph of a man dressed in a fitted white baseball outfit wearing a white cap and clutching a bat. The cigar box's lid read *Cincinatti's Finest Tobacco*, which made sense of the letter 'C' woven onto the man's shirt.

But until he overheard a conversation through the floor from his basement dwelling between Sammy's uncle and father, Nep didn't realize how popular the sport had become. Heck, he didn't even know what or where Cincinnati was, nor did he really care. Later that year the Pacific Base Ball League would incorporate in San Francisco and several parks would be constructed throughout the city. And as for his latest acquisition, that remained to be figured out.

Nep trusted that Sammy would keep his secret,

so that wasn't an issue. He knew it was probably worth a lot of money because it was heavy, although he didn't know how much gold was worth. He couldn't sell it or trade it because the man entrusted him to *geep it safe*. So being resolved to these facts, there he sat, holding a shiny rock with two photographs of dogs he didn't know. He spent many nights with his rock in his dark, drafty basement dwelling, alone.

*   *   *

VI

*   *   *

Now listen, Toku," said Norton, "I know you don't undahstend a bloody wohd I'm sayin', yah? But you, my little frrind, take good keh of me propty, eh?" he said with a slow contempt.

"If I don't make it beck, it's your bloody lehnd, eh mate? Yah? All goes to Toku if 'Mista Noto' no come beck, got it, mate?" he tried to explain to the shirtless and clueless young boy as Toku himself uncomfortably nodded, fighting to evade the rapture of Norton's ghastly alcohol-ridden breath and invasive proximity as Norton again shook his shoulders. "You take keh," he added more sentimentally, "be a good lad...mind the villa." He removed a hand to point toward it. "Mind villa. Noto come back soon... Good lad." Satisfied he had made his point as best he could and realizing now that he was dehydrated, he tapped the boy's shoulders and turned away to walk aboard the *Margaret* and begin his long journey. The boy stood a moment processing the words, trying to make sense of them. They did not, so he simply waved at Norton's back as he boarded the massive ship. "Sobonana Missa Noto, sobonana!" he repeated until Norton was out of sight, "Sobonana!"

For this journey, Norton had created his own acronym: *POSF – Port Outbound, Seek Fortune!* His three trunk chests were loaded by the crew and contained everything he expected to require once he arrived at the gilded shores of what he had imagined would be a paradise beyond his belief: Maps of San Francisco and its surrounding lands, surveys and documents from local purveyors of land, values and data about current owners of land, addresses and references from those held in high regard in the local government. He had requested and received an assurance of entrance into functions that would mitigate questions of his person, age, origin, and yes, possibly his initial austerity as he rubbed elbows in the foreign land.

His purse was ample to say the least: Forty-thousand worth of American money, the equivalent of Eight-hundred-thousand in buying power toward his venture; enough to purchase and resell whatever he could find, he thought to himself. He knew that by the time he reached his destination the property values would already be on the rise, but he also knew that those who had struck it rich along the American River would be outmatched by his real estate acumen.

Norton had never been beyond the confines of London and South Africa, so when the *Margaret* made her stop in Rio De Janero his eyes opened wide. From the balcony of his stately cabin, he watched intently as massive barrels of spices - all colors of the rainbow represented - were being loaded onto the ship by fully grown local men, none of which seeming less frail than Toku.

In Rio he changed vessels and boarded the *Franzika* from Hamburg, Germany. The *Franzika* took port in Panama City, boarding several passengers who had opted to shave time off of the journey from New York and Europe to the west coast of America. Due to the newly imposed fees required by Panama City as a result of the sudden rise in demand, the vessel was detained for several weeks until money could be transferred to the travelers who lacked sufficient funds with which to pay it. The delay annoyed Norton, who at one point considered bribing the ship's Captain to leave sooner.

But he found the Americans interesting and energetic. Most were second-generation Americans who displayed an almost palpable optimism toward reaching the open spaces of the West, away from the vicissitudes of the tumultuous cities their parents had created. Norton spent several nights reveling in the cacophony of chaos that enveloped the burgeoning town. He had never seen drunks as belligerent nor prostitutes as aggressive. They were foreign to his immediate senses, but the time on the vessel had perhaps dulled them, he supposed... Oh, the smells...the new smells and tastes! He loved it, all of it! His thirst for adventure had seen its first meal, but it was to be an appetizer compared to what beheld him a few short months later.

At his behest, Norton obliged ship's Captain to lead the renditions of several British songs in the large gallery where the privileged passengers oft assembled, some to which he mis-remembered the words. Upon such occasions he replaced whatever curse word would fit, drawing cheers from most, but otherwise thinning the crowd many a night. He could discuss many topics in a serious manner one moment and captivate a small group with humor the next. He attracted steerage passengers and elites with the same ease.

His outward personality had won him the hearts of most who met him regardless of class or race. He was at ease with himself, partially for his departure from the familiar and his individualism with his loss of family, but mostly from his innate sense of adventure and his natural extroversion; one that seemed to keep vanity at bay whilst empathy at the ready. He was an anomaly: Young, ambitious, and wealthy. Curious, pragmatic, and engaging. He stood only slightly over five feet tall, but his cheerful and amicable presence was larger than life.

*

Eight months and three days later, on September 15th, 1849, Joshua Norton arrived in San Francisco Bay. To his initial dismay, there were literally over one hundred sailing vessels of all shapes and sizes moored offshore. Several had been refurbished into ferries which now actively carried men between the peninsula and the north or east coasts, and as he disembarked a flurry of people were lining the streets, eating and drinking, gambling and carrying on as if he was the last to arrive at a burgeoning party. He felt robbed, hoodwinked, and overwhelmed. As one newspaper had described the scene:

'In 1849, San Francisco was like a great anthill, when its busy creatures happen to be disturbed, and when all were visible, hurrying to and fro, out and in, backwards apparently in the most admirable confusion and forwards and cross purposes, as if every one were engaged in some life and death struggle.'

When he disembarked, however, it appeared that the ships were a decoy within his plot. Most had been abandoned and the rest were being used for storage. The town stood fanciful enough, but those he noticed milling about appeared to either be proprietors of a brick and mortar establishment or were quite young, less than five odd years past puberty. The others were either a mixed and downtrodden bag of women from all walks of life, or simple men who couldn't or wouldn't take the risk in the hills, the former he quickly decided to avoid...permanently.

The porters brought his luggage ashore and escorted him to the stagecoach that awaited him. The coach was freshly painted, ornate with careful accents of fleur de leis and colored in mahogany with bright orange detailing. Rather than the customary one or two horses, this carriage yoked four towering beasts, all of which looking worse for wear than the next.

"These ah used every day, these same hohses?" inquired Joshua.

"Yep, same ones," replied the coachman.

"Bloody amazing," he said about half way up the hill. "How many dimes do they bull this bloody thing up hyah, eh?"

"Mornin' til night, sir," the coachman replied dryly, "six or seven times a day I figure."

"That one's looking nyah to dead though, yah?"

"We feed 'em good, sir. They're tough mules."

Joshua relented his accusatory tone, leaning forward with his elbows on his knees and palms cupping his chin in enthralled amazement. The hill they ascended began at sea level and reached nearly

six hundred feet within a short distance. The
arduous journey lasted nearly forty minutes. Twice
during the trip the carriage had to pause when the
animal Norton had pointed out began attempting to
veer off track, stumbling as if delirious, bucking
several times in exhausted frustration.

After sleeping off the exhausting journey for
nearly twelve hours, Joshua awoke. He slowly arose
and sat at the edge of the bed, slid on his slippers
and picked up the robe that lay upon the chest at
the foot of the bed. He stood and made his way to
the windows of his ample two-roomed suite on the top
floor of the five-floored hotel and drew open the
curtains. From his vantage point atop the hill, he
looked north toward the hundreds of boats and ships
in the bay that lay deserted, a small island dotting
the landscape in the center of the Bay, and beyond
it the nearly vacant coastline a few miles across
the water.

He lowered his gaze toward the busier area
where he had arrived into port, watching the people
milling around with a sense of purpose, equal parts
business and pleasure as far as he could tell. A
grin came across his face for no conscious reason.
Perhaps his mind had sighed a sense of relief that
it had arrived at its destination and that the
beginning of something new was afoot. More likely,
however, it had become contented that dry land lay
below his feet, finally liberated from the long and

often monotonous months at sea. After a strong cup of coffee and a late breakfast, he decided to venture outside.

It was a warm late-summer's day, warmer certainly than he had anticipated for the time of year, forgetting momentarily that the seasons were opposite those of Port Elizabeth. As he departed from the ornate white facade of the hotel, he stood in the clearing of the cross-streets and spent several minutes assessing the land in all directions. To his east was downtown, with several two and three story Edwardian-styled buildings lining several blocks in every direction.

He could hear the hammering from where he stood from several different construction efforts, surely performed by men who were dividing their time between prospecting, he assumed. Beyond those loomed a tall clock tower with a pointed steeple. He could faintly make out the words of the sign on the long building structured below it: 'PORT OF' to its left, 'SAN FRANCISCO' on its right.

To his south and west, Joshua saw as he pivoted his stance to follow his shifting focus, was an obvious contrast containing vast open spaces of rolling hills and larger but more simply constructed houses and barns. Each was separated from the other by at least an acre, usually more. Particularly due southwest from where he stood were fewer than ten visible properties, larger homes yet, with storage barns and pens for horses, pigs, and other livestock, and divided by fences that stretched for what appeared to be miles in each direction around them. From the maps he had studied during the long voyage, he predicted the land in those areas would be his smartest starting point toward sound investments. Values, he had theorized, would increase fastest in the downtown district and along the coastline to the north and east, likely already fetching a hefty price, spreading inward toward where he stood and then toward the south and west of the peninsula that would become his new home.

*

It was nearing mid day this particular Saturday, so he knew that few, if any, land purveyors' offices would be open for business even in this frenzied atmosphere. He would be forced to await Monday to begin discussions and introductions with the men he hoped to befriend and deal in land. But there was no reason to delay his social entrance into this new society, so he thought, becoming overwhelmed at his lack of strategy toward that end.

He tempered his suddenly panicked anticipation by deciding to walk rather than hail a ride down the hill toward the wharf in the distance, and decided to use his time wisely to devise a schedule for visiting real estate companies he located throughout

the day. Sunday, he had planned, he would hire a
carriage to take him to the southern and western
parts of the peninsula to grade the land's
composition, its soil, and the general mix of
agricultural and industrial outfits that lay there.
But today he would simply soak in the day and let
happen what may.

As he made his way down the hill, steeper yet
at some stages than he had recalled it the previous
evening, he watched as the carriage and driver that
had brought him up to the hilltop hotel approached.

"Afternoon," was all the carriageman said in
his usual dry tone, tipping the brim of his
oversized hat. He turned away from Norton and spat a
sizable amount of dark liquid to the ground.

"Good day," Joshua replied loudly above the
sounds of the horses' movements.

"Pick ya up on the turn, sir?" he then asked.
"Least I can do," he said, referring to the gracious
gratuity Joshua had given him the previous eve.

"No, no," waved Joshua, "I'll do fine. Good to
get some aya and stretch me ligs."

"--Suit yerself then," said the man after a
moment, returning to his forward posture.

As he continued his walk down the hill and the
struggling horses and carriage passed him, the
sounds grew louder and the houses more compactly
arranged. He had passed a few locals, exchanging
simple greetings, and now stood on level ground a

few blocks from the water amidst the two-story buildings that had been constructed that year in a flurry. He turned east and began walking along a busier avenue, passing an array of pedestrians and businesses, most of which were closed. But up the way there was a more festive atmosphere and his growing thirst for a cold ale became justified in his mind after completing the long trek.

He realized that his initial perception of the place and population had been short-sighted. To be sure, there were many business proprietors and youths dashing around, but on this particular Saturday, many of the prospectors had returned from the river for the weekend, subsequently luring the more attractive women-of-call out from their confines and producing a cacophony of revelry in saloons and casinos that had sprung up that year.

Within the nearly two years since Brannan made his announcement in the streets of the sparsely occupied town, it had grown feverishly into a full-fledged city. The number of residents, estimated to be two thousand in February, three thousand in March, five thousand in July had increased to somewhere near twenty thousand by the end of the year, and all of these people had to have a place to live. The buildings in town were confined to an area of about one half-mile square and with a few exceptions were widely scattered. What was once less than a hundred buildings near the port had grown to become nearly a thousand, tightly constructed in tenementary rows, lining the now well-defined streets at the bottom of the hill he had descended.

*

"Good day," he said upon entering the card saloon and reaching its bar. It was approaching mid-afternoon and the place seemed quite busy to Joshua. A man sat at a piano, happily clonking an unfamiliar tune to Joshua's ears. Others cursed at losing a hand at cards, while others simply sat at the bar: dirty, odorous, emotionless.

"Yessir, what'll it be?" asked the bartender.

"My name is Joshua," he said, extending a hand, "Joshua Nohton from South Ehvrica."

The barman smiled crookedly, methodically wiping his hands on the soiled towel that draped over the waist of his apronstring and taking a moment to ascertain the strange man's character.

"Well it's nice to make yer acquaintance, stranger, Billy's the name--" he patronized, reaching to shake Joshua's hand briefly. "--What'll it be?" he repeated.

"A fine ale if you please, eh Billy," he said.

"You bet," Billy nodded and limped back to the glasses and beer taps.

"Quite a place you have hyah, eh?" said Joshua above the noise of the patrons when his ale was set in front of him. "Is it always like thess?"

"Yeah, lately it's been busier than all get-out," he said. "Some boys are startin' to give up in the hills and with the builders comin' in, there's plenty of work to be had 'round here."

"If yer lookin' you'll wanna talk to Red over yonder there, he'll set ya straight," he said. He pointed to the large red-bearded man at a far table, nodded again, and limped to the other end of the bar to field another order.

"Owns a bit of lehnd, does he?" inquired Joshua when Billy returned a few minutes later.

"Red? Naw, he don't own shit, he works fer Mr. Montgomery."

"Montgomery," repeated Norton, hoping for more information.

"Yeah, he's got some fancy place downtown, been buyin' up all kindsa land."

"Has he," stated Joshua, now feeling his anxiety rising again. "--Thank you, Billy."

"Best mind yerself, tho," he added. "Seems like you might got a satchel. Folks talk quick 'round here...they get to sniffin' it you might be sorry," he warned and limped away again.

"A *satchel*," he repeated the unfamiliar word. "--I see," said Norton. He placed some coins onto the bar and stood there for a while awkwardly, sneaking glimpses around the room, trying to avoid staring at the unusual clothing, songs, and language of the people who occupied the saloon.

Along with being small in stature even for his time, the eight months he'd spent in the confines of the ship had added several pounds to his frame, and he certainly was not prepared to defend himself in the event of an altercation, regardless of those facts. He had jet black hair that was combed back from the parting on the right side, giving way to its naturally untamed curliness presented lower behind his ears and at his neck. He kept a neatly trimmed moustache, unlike those of his counterparts around the room, who had seemingly ignored their general appearance completely.

His brows were thick and stern in shape, but his demeanor was mostly cheerful and his voice pleasant to the ear. In a conscious attempt to assimilate into this new world, he downplayed his adept command of the English language and dressed to conceal his wealth by wearing only the simplest of beige vests and a pale buttoned shirt. But his cleanliness and that of his attire in this part of town proved still to be obvious. He was conspicuously an outsider amidst the other saloon patrons.

"Red, is it?" asked Joshua to the unmoved men at the table when he had drawn up the courage to approach.

"Who wants to know," the large man grumbled as he layed down his draw cards.

"Joshua Nohton, pleased to meet you." He paused with his hand outstretched, retracting it after a few moments after realizing the man did not intend to reciprocate. "Um, yes. --Well, I'm told youah knowledgeable about lehnd and I'm in the mahket to puhchase," he said as he patiently watched the cards being dealt.

"So..." said Red flatly.

"Find another table, stranger. Can't ya see we're busy?" the lanky dealer interrupted as he set down the deck after dealing the last card.

"Apologies, gentlemin," continued Norton, "I thought yoh frrind here might know wheh I can find a Mistah Montgomery. It seems he may be able--"

"*Raise*," interrupted Red as he viewed his replacement cards, "two bucks!"

"Jeez, Red," the lanky man said, exalting Red's continued confidence that day.

"Able to what," grunted Red, taking his whiskey shot and obliging Joshua's distraction. "Monty's a busy man. Less you got a stack o' gold or wanna hammer some wood--" he said, finally lifting his gaze to Joshua, "--which it looks like you ain't...best mind yer busine--"

"--I'm interested in lehnd, Mistah Red," he interrupted, proceeding to pull a stack of twenty dollar bills from his vest and slapping them onto the center of the table.

"His address, please Mistah Red," said Norton

confidently after several moments of silent stares.

Red paused now, placing his hand of cards faced-down on the table in front of himself, the others pausing at Red's apparent disconnect.

The pot for this round had reached nearly ten dollars, a sizable sum considering that a decent meal cost less than a dollar, and Joshua's distraction had now clearly caught their attention. They looked at the addition to the pot and then looked at him now, not unlike a cat looks at a fieldmouse after inadvertently maiming it with an overzealous swipe.

"Well then," said Red. "Norton, is it?" He looked up at Joshua as he unexpectedly grabbed his hand and shook it vigorously with the grip of an ape. "Monty's down at the Tadich with the other rich folks most days, ya might find him there or at his lot next to forty," he said. "Where ya from, stranger?"

"Fohty, what's thett?" he asked, ignoring Red's question.

"--Forty's down by the basin downtown, the biggest dock that side of Market," said the lanky dealer, "--be there Monday for sure, but guy like you could probly talk his talk at the Tadich before then," he added, "snappy dresser like you."

"Taditch is it, eh?" said Joshua as he collected himself, pulling at the corners of his vest bottom. "Many thanks, mate, em--Red. --I'll

leave you now to... Apologies gentlemin... Red...
Gentlemin," he said with as much courtesy as he
could muster. He departed the table somewhat
awkwardly, bumping into an adjacent table as he
backed away. Managing finally to collect himself,
Joshua moved purposefully through the other tables
of card players and women toward the saloon's exit.

"Cheeahs, Billy," he directed toward the bar as
he waved on his way out, exiting the saloon a mere
twenty minutes after he had entered. He quickly
became cognizant of the blindly obvious departure
from his original strategy. He had planned to await
Monday before conducting affairs of business, but
the energy of the place had sucked him in... He
became more disoriented by his lustful impatience
than by his surroundings, quickly forgetting the
names of the men he had encountered in the raucous
place as he moved further away from it, but managing
to notice the name on the parapet of the saloon as
he looked back at the place several paces later. *The
Prospector.*

*

Now you've done it, Joshua thought to himself
as he strode along the waterfront which curved
eastward and then southward along the Bay. *If thess
bloody Monty is the man we suspect, you've saved the
week's end, mate,* he congratulated himself. Norton

wasn't outwardly arrogant, but the bundles of money that burned a hole in his mind and pockets along with the months of anticipation toward its use projected a confidence in his personality which seemed artificially heightened to him.

His placement toward a higher education, curtailed by the death of his family, had hardly been earned. His placement into the University of London, seemingly a ruse by his father, who had donated a sizable sum to the establishment. What he knew had mostly been learned through trial and error upon returning to Algoa Bay and Port Elizabeth by his own accomplishment, fortunate enough to have had the reserves of his father's estate to more than make up for his lack of business acumen and experience.

Forty-five minutes into his walk, Joshua reached the downtown district and located the place in which he hoped to continue his ambitious destiny. He withdrew the linen cloth that rested in his pants pocket and wiped the perspiration from his brow, looking at the unlit neon sign adorning the front of the Tadich Grill. The downtown buildings were largely two-story brick structures, with evenly distributed windows and tiled roofs. Most were deserted this Saturday, but a few, including the tailor a few doors down and the rug importer, acted as if it were any other day of business.

As he approached the door to enter, a couple

exited. The woman was gorgeous and delightful, with perfectly cured hair and long nails, dressed regally in a fitted black dress which hugged her bosom with pleated overlaps, extending sleekishly to the frills at its end, a few inches above her heels. The man whose arm carried hers wore a silk tuxedo and top hat, was quite tall and wore a full, brilliantly manicured moustache with twisted tips at its sides.

"Oh, Monty," laughed the woman, "you really mustn't keep telling that awful story."

"On the contrary, my dear, it's the only one I know that allows me to curse splendidly," he cajoled as they began walking east toward Montgomery's dockside abode.

Joshua, whose courtesy after holding it had gone unnoticed, released his grasp of the large wooden door's brass handle and allowed it to shut by its own weight. Now sensing that he was under-dressed, he paused momentarily before gaining the courage to seize the opportunity that lay before him.

"Mistah Montgomery?" he asked, flattening his hair and attempting to iron his vest with his palms before the man he addressed could bear witness.

Montgomery slowed to a halt and angled his head leftward abruptly, continuing his playful laugh and correcting his top hat with a free hand as it shifted from the sudden movement.

"Yes?" he asked loudly over his shoulder, still

smiling from his jovial mood.

"Might I hev a moment of yoh time, sir," Joshua asked in a determined, purposeful voice.

Montgomery circled the couple playfully in a dance until they both faced the man who had distracted them. He was a bit stoned, but a man of Montgomery's intellect was never far from sobriety when it called. He was easily Joshua's senior by ten years in truth, but his rigid exercise regimen and lack of gray whiskers concealed that fact from plain view. He looked Norton up and down now, considering the man's purpose.

"Pardon me, darling," said Montgomery, nuzzling at her nose lovingly and then releasing his arm from her waist, placing both hands in his fancy pockets and beginning to sway on the heels and toes of his polished black shoes.

"Yes? --Well? --Were you expecting a gratuity, young man?" he questioned jokingly, to the audible enjoyment of the woman beside him. "Because if you were, that would be the funniest--"

"--I'm interested in lehnd, Mistah Montgomery," said Norton dryly. "Apologies, Miss," he digressed quite seriously, bowing slightly toward her. "I was told you hev some holdings, sir... If it's not an inconvenience, I wondah if we could discuss thim privately," he finished with conviction. "Joshua, sir, Joshua Norton," he offered, lifting his head slightly with each word.

Montgomery's demeanor shifted from aloof to serious as he studied the man standing before him with curiosity. He whispered something to his female companion and stepped forward several paces to within a short distance of Norton.

"What exactly do you suppose I should say right now, young man," he stated in an angered hush. "Yes? --That I have land? --Let's go look at some maps together immediately?" He began to chuckle. "Do you know how many *simpletons* with a few coins to rub together I deal with every day? *Do you*? Can you not see that I am with the company of a lady at the present? You have got some nerve--"

"--Not et all," interrupted Norton, pleading with the palms of his hands as he stepped backward. "I'm heppy to await Monday, sir. I just, --I simply wanted to mek your acquaintance and thett is it, thett is all," he quickly blurted against Montgomery's affronted reaction, looking now at the ground. "I hev a sizable, em--satchel," he then added more timidly under his breath. He waited several moments, beginning to consider turning and walking away in the awkward silence.

Montgomery finally spoke. "Did you strike it rich in the hills yesterday or something, Mister...Norton, was it?" he asked as he again started swaying on his heels. "Find a few nuggets, did you?" he mocked arrogantly, rubbing his thumbs across his fingers. "Do you have any concept of land values these days? ...or any idea for that matter about anything at all?" he said in an irritated tone.

"I beg your pahdon, Mistah Montgomery," Joshua said apologetically. "I have no intention of whesting yoh time. I'm newly arrived hyah from South Ehvrica with a sizable sum," he explained. "I'm an honest businessman and would like to make some strong investments hyah... Whatever you'll considah at whatevah juncture you please, sir."

"--I see," said Montgomery after a moment. "And what, may I ask, is your definition of *sizable*," he inquired.

"I would prefeh to discuss mettahs of that nature privately, Mistah Montgomery," he said after a pause. He glanced toward the gorgeous woman, now sensing Montgomery's piquing interest and regaining his initial confidence.

Montgomery looked behind himself toward the woman. They grinned at each other before he turned back toward Norton. "...Very well," said Montgomery after some deliberation. "Do you see the building over there with the black awning?"

"Yes," replied Joshua, trying to contain his excitement.

"Meet me there at eight o'clock this evening. --If you arrive one minute late, or you turn out to be *wasting* my time," he warned with a finger, "you will quickly become sorry that you ever set foot in this place... Do we have an understanding, Mr. Norton," he stated firmly as he turned to reaccompany his ladyfriend.

"Yes, sir, eight o'clock it is... I wont be lett. Thank you, Mistah Montgomery. Eight o'clock shahp," he said with a broad grin which masked a much larger elation.

"Not a moment after," said Montgomery over his shoulder.

As Joshua made the journey up the long hill to the hotel, he marveled at his good fortune, laughing aloud to himself as he looked into the distance in every direction with fevered anticipation. That evening, dressed in his best clothing, Joshua had made his way to Montgomery's building by carriage, arriving a few minutes prior to eight o'clock.

*

Heston Montgomery's father was Captain John Berrien Montgomery of the American Navy. On July 9, 1846, Captain Montgomerey disembarked from the U.S. Sloop-of-War with about seventy men under his command. Stepping ashore, Montgomery marched up Clay Street to Kearney and, at the plaza subsequently named Portsmouth Square, the American Flag was hoisted with no resistance from the Mexicans. Yerba Buena was now under American rule. One year later, in 1847, the name would be changed to San Francisco in honor of Saint Francis.

Heston, or *Monty* as he preferred to be called by friends, was part of his father's crew during the conquest and was placed in charge of the largely uninhabited peninsula's military. A short time after his arrival, he retired from the military and subsequently created a vast real estate empire with the help of the large commission of land his father had received. He built factories and dealt heavily in imports as the population grew and became a popular figure within the circles of the wealthy elite, helped by the fact that one of the few main thoroughfare's bore his surname – thanks to his father's conquest.

Joshua was greeted by Montgomery's butler and escorted into the study of his two-story mansion. The simple, yet elegant room was warmed by a large fireplace, crackling softly. Wooden-paneled walls and book shelves lined the surrounding walls of the small but cozy room from floor to ceiling. A large carved desk and a large leather chair faced a red, velveteen fainting couch with tall undulating sides.

Above the mantle of the fireplace hung a self-portrait of the stern, balding blonde-haired man wearing a regal tuxedo and top hat. He was seated in an ornate armchair with the thumb and fore-finger of his left hand twisting one of the tips of his long moustache. Although he had dabbled in a few different ventures before the gold rush began,

Montgomery's proudest tale regaled the few thousand dollars he had invested to assist an acquaintance a year earlier. The investment had returned a sizable sum in only a few months:

Levi had initially meant to set up a tent fabrication business, but the wrong material had arrived instead. He had quickly sewn a pair of trousers together for a prospector friend in order to stay afloat until his proper textile shipment could arrive, but the warm and very durable trousers turned out to be a favorable fluke, becoming the envy of every prospector who encountered Levi's friend in the hills. The incredible demand in June and July grew so large that Mr. Strauss was forced to seek outside investors and to part with a large percentage of his business.

He had happened upon a conversation with Montgomery and lamented his story, to which Montgomery quickly drew up papers and procured the investment capital. When Monty had sold his share back to Levi only a few months later near the end of the 1848 year, it would prove to net him just over eleven thousand dollars. Seeing the droves of men arriving by ship every week, he subsequently began purchasing even more of the inexpensive land. He currently owned more than half of the land on the peninsula, but Norton hoped to change that as quickly as possible.

When he had become comfortable with Montgomery and was prepared to reciprocate with the details of his life, Joshua began tracing his own family's history. He detailed the beautiful landscape and people and traditions of Port Elizabeth, eloquated his father's success in real estate, and lamented of the tragic epidemic that had ended their lives. Once both men had become acquainted to a comfortable degree, the discussion shifted to land investment.

A fifty-vara lot, the smaller of the two common sizes of city lots, sold once for twelve dollars now could command thousands, and if very well located then tens of thousands of dollars. Interest rates that year had climbed from eight to fifteen percent per month. Bricks cost a dollar each and lumber rose to five hundred dollars for a thousand feet. San Francisco was booming, and Monty knew it. He took an immediate liking to Norton, deciding that their encounter had offered both a timely opportunity to take advantage of the current climate, and to create an ally as it continued to grow.

Realizing his haste was warranted, Norton immediately purchased ten thousand dollars worth of land from Montgomery that evening, site-unseen as it were. Within a few weeks he had purchased as much as he could afford from Montgomery with another twenty-five thousand, reserving the remainder for development and for creating a luxurious lifestyle with which to enter San Francisco's elite society.

VII

*   *   *

Caroline was a few years younger than her husband John. She was the youngest of three daughters of Scottish emigrants, growing up poor in the ramshackle tenements that lined the streets in the South of Market Street (SOMA) neighborhood. Like the rest of the women in her family, she had dark auburn hair and bright green eyes. She was a slight creature with somewhat plain features overall, but she had a wonderful laugh that she displayed often. Like most girls at the time, she grew up working in the textile factories, manipulating the large looms in sweatshop conditions and sewing the finishing touches onto various items of clothing.

She had seen John, Nep as he was then known, for the first time when she was fourteen years of age on a Saturday while accompanying her mother to the docks. Her mother was collecting a shipment of linens, while Caroline waited patiently. She had watched as the boy danced along the wharf crazily, covered in crabs, giggling with excitement between the occasional grimaced reaction to being pinched. She laughed loudly from the wagon in which she sat, and Nep had enthusiastically overheard, heightening his act for the enjoyment of his newest fan. After that day, she often thought of the silly boy at the docks during her monotonous job in order to distract herself, a few times being reprimanded for giggling aloud to herself at the thought. On the few occasions, she had revisited the docks and had hoped to see him again, but the encore never occurred.

Ten years later, when Nep was accompanying Sammy to the bank on Market Street where she happened to work, she had recognized him. Sammy had been nervous to enter the world of well-dressed folks and had asked Nep along for moral support.

She had said that he reminded her of a boy she saw dancing with crabs one day, that the boy had a similar face. He and Sammy had laughed and explained the Saturday crab deal at the docks. The boys had finished their business and exited the bank, when Sammy had begun taunting Nep, calling him a chicken by simply flapping his elbows. Realizing his ignorance, Nep built up his courage and re-entered the bank. Two years later, Emma was born.

*

Caroline sprang to her feet with the rest of the frightened parents on the balcony who had begun screaming their respective childrens' names. "Emma!!" she shrieked, "Emmma!!" She jostled her way among the other parents toward the stairway, like cattle all of them bottle-necking the narrow route. The balcony they occupied swayed again suddenly, forcing one man to bump into another and over the railing and into one of the pools below, while forcing the others into a compact sea of frightened parents against it.

Once steadied, the group collectively began shoving their way down the narrow stairs, each yelling louder than the person next to them. Caroline had been watching Emma the entire time and was dismayed that she was still in the pool, screaming in a frenzy and waving her arms recklessly, her handbag clipping several people around her unapologetically. "Emmaaa!" she yelled repeatedly until Emma finally appeared to see her.

Emma raised her hand out of the water to signal the connection to her mother and began thrashing furiously to reach the side of the pool. In truth, she was an awful swimmer. It had taken her nearly four minutes to reach the far end of the pool, and Caroline was desperately hoping she could even make it back before the entire building collapsed. When she reached poolside, Caroline desperately crouched and thrusted her arm as far toward Emma as she could, her hand shaking with intensity. She pulled Emma violently out of the water with unusual ease and yanked her soaking daughter to the exit as quickly as she could.

*

At the same time, Nep and Sammy had been walking along the wharf toward Max's to grab a bite for lunch. Suddenly, they felt a slight tremor below their feet which grew into a strong rumble lasting about five seconds, but caused a nearby window pane to crack and shatter to the ground. A horse drawing a wagon bucked wildly and jolted to its side, pulling the wagon sideways, toppling it and throwing its driver from his perch. In the distance, a faint plume of smoke began to rise from over the hill toward the south.

The men steadied themselves, confused, their senses alerted to whatever might happen next. They stood still for a moment and looked at each other blankly. Suddenly they dropped their gear and began running up the slope toward their homes. Nep stopped suddenly after they had been running for a block or so.

"Dammit! God Dammit!" he yelled to Sammy.

"What is it," Sammy puffed while slowing to a jog, his asthma clearly affecting him.

"They're at the Baths today, dammit!" Nep

slapped his knees and pivoted to face downhill. Sammy had stopped and was catching his breath.

"I'm sure they're okay, Nep," he said with his arms outstretched, as if annoyed at Nep for causing him to break stride. "There's nothin' out there...probably didn't even feel it."

"Aww, bullshit, Sammy. Goddammit," he disagreed. "You know what that place is made on? *Do ya*?" he asked in a hushed whimper, "It's on the edge of a goddamn *cliff*. --And it's made of *glass*, Sammy! Christ almighty, oh geez..." Nep crouched and palmed his forehead with both hands.

Sammy dropped his arms back to his sides and jogged toward his friend. "I know, Nep, I know," he consoled. "We'll get... We can't do anything from here, right? Come on," he directed, "we'll head to the police station first and make sure they're okay, alright?"

"Right," Nep agreed somberly and nodded into his palms. "You're right... Dammit! Okay--alright, let's go," he said as he stood.

The men resumed their pace and ran several blocks to the nearest police station. As they ran the local fire brigade passed them, a few recognizing Sammy and slightly waving to him.

"Guess it's - a big deal - down there," Sammy managed to say between gasps. "Our turf - stops - at Powell," he explained. Powell served as both a main thoroughfare and an unofficial line of demarcation for the eastern edge of Chinatown. "Guess I'll - find out - tonight," he added, his thirty-six hour shift at the fire station beginning later that evening. Surprisingly, there was little noticeable damage to any buildings they passed as they ran. Several other people were disoriented, the trolleycars and carriages had stopped, and the barking of dogs could be heard from several directions in the distance. But other than the smoke that could be seen rising in the distance and a few toppled crates of vegetables along the street, the scene was not unlike any other day. When they reached the station, there were a handful of others impatiently awaiting return telegraphs from various parts of the city.

A deputy recognized Nep and acknowledged him with his eyes while trying to calm several people who were concerned for their loved ones. "Listen. Everyone! Listen, please," he finally said above the commotion, figuring he could quell the rising tensions with an announcement. "I need you all to quiet down and listen, I'm only going to say this once," he warned.

"Okay," he started once the voices had begun to subside, "I know you're all worried about your loved ones. The following neighborhoods have reported serious injuries: Downtown, Chinatown, Central Basin, and Ocean Beach. If you do not--"

"--The Baths?!" interrupted Nep. "Where on the

beach, Jimmy. The Baths? Jimmy! --*Dammit*..." The man remained steadfast in his speech, determined to remain professional.

"If you *do not* have loved ones--" he elevated his voice to adjust to the renewed commotion, "--*in those areas*, please return to your homes," he resolved. The crowd thinned slowly as some comforted others who were affected by the announcement.

"Jimmy, what about the Baths?" asked Nep as he reached the counter behind which Jimmy had spoken. Jimmy looked down toward his telegraphs and dryly said, "One dead, four injured, Nep."

"Jesus, Jimmy, Who? Men, women, children? *Who*?" he pleaded, banging his fists soundly on the desk.

"Nep, try to calm down," he said, "I don't have names, but it says a man and wife, and a mother and son. The man who died was hit by a shock or somethin' workin' on the tracks nearby or somesuch," he explained. "The other one collapsed from overexertion and his wife was knocked over trying to aid him. The mother and son were injured in the commotion while trying to exit the Baths. That's all I got Nep, I'm sorry... But I think yours are okay. Best thing you can do is head home and wait for them, I'm sure they're just as concerned about you as you are about them."

Nep eased his tight grip upon the counter and exhaled in frustration, looking over at Sammy, who was sweating profusely. "Okay... Thanks, Jimmy."

Sammy and Nep departed the Station and went in separate directions; Nep to his home to await Caroline and Emma, Sammy toward his to check that his mother was safe. Neither mentioned returning to work, silently assuming their absence from the docks would be excusable considering the odd circumstances.

"Come by the station later if they get stuck and we can get to the bottom of it," said Sammy as he began jogging home. Nep simply nodded and began in the other direction, still concerned for the safety of his wife and child. Sammy returned home to find his mother seated in the kitchen, calmly knitting. She was fine, she had said when he asked, but was upset that one of her decorative porcelain plates that hung on the wall had jarred loose and crashed into several pieces on the floor. She asked briefly about his day as she fed her son, but quickly resumed her regular routine of nagging him about settling down with a good woman as if nothing significant had occurred that day.

Caroline and Emma finally returned several hours after the tremor. They were exhausted from the journey, shuttled by no less than three carriages for what seemed an eternity. The group embraced outside of their home and discussed their fright, recounting the damage to the Baths and their concern for those who had been injured. But today would pale in comparison to the events of the following day.

VIII

"There are two times in a man's life when he
should not speculate: when he can't afford
it, and when he can."

-Mark Twain

*   *   *

Within a few years of its discovery and
Brannan's announcement in the streets of San
Francisco, most of the gold that could be panned
easily from the riverbeds along the American River
in northern California had been extracted.

Investors, some of whom who had struck fortune
on the same river banks a few years prior, would now
sink many thousands of dollars into purchasing and
transporting machines and equipment to the hills.

They planned to build extravagant mines using
the latest available technology in an attempt to
unearth whatever remained below ground. Pioneers who
had originally worked for themselves or in small
groups now opted to accept a nominal wage under
investors rather than to continue to prospect on
their own. In all, nearly five-hundred million

dollars worth of the shiny metal was extracted between 1848 and 1855, when the California Gold Rush had finally run its course.

By 1852, Joshua's real estate fortune had grown six-fold to nearly a quarter-million dollars in value, thanks in large part to Monty and the other men with whom he had rubbed elbows. His wealth and prominence had not only given him access to the elite and intelligent businessmen of the City, it had given him access to valuable information.

His personality and natural skill at creating lasting friendships, his presence within the community and good will toward its residents - both rich and poor, young and old - made him welcome everywhere he went. His business acumen was sharp and respected, his generosity consistent and applauded.

Men of prominence who were members of the exclusive Pacific Club often discussed business opportunities and trends at the swank parties that were often held at the Pacific Hotel and other grand ballrooms located downtown. Recently, talks had begun to swirl regarding a shift from individual prospecting along the river to industrialized shaft building and mining. Some predicted the end of the gold reserves approaching, others thought that the majority had yet to be unearthed and that the businesses that had invested in such pursuits would reap even more yet.

One evening, Joshua overheard a man complaining that a lot he had hoped to sell atop Russian Hill, a mere block from some of Joshua's more valuable holdings, was poised to be sold for a loss. Norton became nervous, wary that the time was near to adjust his strategy and hedge against the possibility of a decline in property values. He decided to seek the counsel of the man who had helped grow his fortune.

*

Norton was again kindly greeted by Monty's butler and led into the comforts of his favorite room. As he entered, Monty was at his desk. *A bit late in the evening to be working*, he thought to himself, *for a man who needs not lift a finger...*

"Working on your next million, eh Monty?" he said coyly.

"Ha! Indeed, Joshua... Indeed. Please," he slightly looked up as he gestured toward the room, "make yourself comfortable my friend."

"Seems there is talk of the possibility of a shift, eh?" he said vaguely as he poured two glasses full of wine, attempting to extract clues from Montgomery's wisdom.

Monty sensed Norton's serious tone and paused, impressed by the intuitive observation. "Yes, Joshua," he said as he joined Norton in the warmth of the center of the room. "I've recently been made aware of the same concern," he said, accepting the crystalline glass from his guest. "However, several good men, Joshua, some of whom you know well I might add," he reminded, pointing a finger from his glass, "believe that the bulk of gold still rests under the ground... Only time will tell if they are correct, but no sense in worrying about things of such a speculative nature," he added, bringing the glass to his lips.

He was aware of Monty's bias toward the chess match that was finances, knowing well-enough that he would eventually reveal the strategic insight Norton sought if he only persisted long enough. *After all*, Joshua had thought on a few similar occasions, *I'm the man who improved his wealth ten-fold within a day of first meeting him...*

"I *am* worried," insisted Norton. "I just overheard some min talking about tekking a loss on the lehnd next to mine, Monty," he said flatly. "--I'm not going to bloody well wait foh the newspapers to tell me what to do, eh? Am I?" he chirped, drinking a large swig of wine.

Monty sighed and placed his glass on the table next to him. "Very well," he finally said and leaned forward in his chair. "There is a famine, Joshua," he said carefully, "in China... The Chinese have banned the export of rice. But, my friend, as we speak a cargo from Peru sits aboard a ship that rests in the Bay... Two-hundred thousand pounds of rice," he said. "As far as we know, that's all of it, since China's cutting us off," he said. "I know that may sound like a lot, Joshua, but it's hardly a substantial amount to feed merely the Chinamen here for even a few weeks, let alone the entire city," he explained calmly. "I had planned to liquidate some parcels and make them an offer toward it, but the damn buyers backed out on me yesterday...moved their money to the hills, as you deftly pointed out. If you were to give me, say...three cents per pound, Joshua, I'd be inclined to make you privy to the deal." Montgomery grinned and reached for the carafe to refill his emptied glass.

"Easy as that is it, eh mate," Norton laughed suspiciously. "Surely you have enough resehrves to make the deal, yah?"

"I wish I did, Joshua," said Montgomery with a sigh. "The price was at four cents a pound just last week... Now it's nearing fifteen... Hell, it'll likely reach thirty cents by next week," he added with intensity.

Joshua silently calculated his potential profits as he began pacing. He was aware of the obvious risk involving the purchase of the entire supply in order to assure control of the price and corner the market, but Thirty-thousand dollars for two-hundred-thousand pounds of rice was a sizable investment, one that would leave him very exposed.

"You say it was fohr cents last week, eh," he asked rhetorically, still skeptical. "Who else knows of thess?"

"Look, Joshua," said Montgomery, "nobody is going to cut in ahead of you. Shake my hand on three cents at fifteen and I'll set it up this night... But we have to move *quickly*," he urged. "By this time next week you'll have doubled your money...or better," he said convincingly.

"Two cents at twenty," offered Joshua flatly toward Monty's outstretched hand.

"Two and a half at eighteen," countered Monty, now smiling broadly... Norton paused momentarily and reached out his hand to shake on the deal.

If all went as planned and the demand for rice caused its price to rise above eighteen cents per pound, he would owe Montgomery five thousand dollars. There was no thought given to the contrary, and why would there be? Between the influx of gold fortunes and the exponential growth in land values, there simply was no space for pessimism. The men enjoyed another glass of wine and discussed the details of the transaction.

That evening, Joshua followed the instructions delivered to him by Monty's assistant and met with the Captain of the *Glyde* at the saloon next to Pier twenty-three. With the help of the ship's interpreter, the men negotiated for over an hour. They finally settled at twelve and a half cents per pound, unload included, and drew up papers. The entire cargo of two-hundred thousand pounds of Peruvian rice was in Norton's possession and he was beside himself with anticipation of the quick profits it would purportedly bring. The cargo had cost Norton twenty-five-thousand dollars, nearly all of his savings.

*

The next morning the Chronicle printed the story on the front page of its newspaper with the headline: *Famine in China, Rice Shortages Expected!*

Norton was beside himself with joy. Three days hence, the price had risen from fourteen to a staggering twenty cents per pound. In another three days, it had reached thirty cents, and Joshua stood to profit nearly forty thousand dollars in one week if he could sell all of it. He began visiting purveyors the following day, pitting one against another as the price and demand continued to rise rampantly.

The first offer he had received had been thirty cents per pound for the entire load. Another had been thirty-two cents for half of it. Yet another had been thirty-six cents for fifty-thousand pounds! He continued to negotiate diligently, shuffling between potential buyers in an attempt to attain the best possible outcome. When a comparatively smallquantitied offer presented itself that day, he quickly sold fifteen thousand pounds at the incredible price of forty cents and paid Montgomery the five thousand owed to him, plus a fine bottle of Scotch. The following day, however, disaster struck.

Another Peruvian ship arrived in port carrying one hundred fifty thousand pounds of rice. The evening edition headline sent Norton into a panic: *Rice from Peru Arrives!* The article went on to explain that ships had been re-routed to San Francisco to mitigate the rice shortage.

By the next day, the price had dropped to twenty cents per pound. In the following three days, two additional Peruvian vessels arrived carrying another four-hundred thousand pounds of rice. By the end of the week, the price had plummeted to three cents per pound, reducing the value of Norton's remaining hundred-eighty-five-thousand pounds to a mere Fifty-five hundred dollars...

He dashed around the city in a frenzy, desperate to unload his remaining rice holdings, but to no avail... None wanted to buy from him now, showing contempt as if Joshua had known of the other ships all along. He then returned to Pier Twenty-three and argued fiercely with the *Glyde's* Captain, attempting to void the rice contract. The ship's Captain was unmoved. Frustrated upon his arrival by the *Glyde's* disappearance from the Bay the following day, he hired an attorney and filed papers to sue.

For the next four years, from 1853 to 1857, Norton and the rice dealers were involved in protracted litigation. Although Joshua prevailed in the lower courts, the case reached the Supreme Court of California, which ruled against him. A few months later, the Lucas Turner and Company Bank foreclosed on his remaining real estate holdings in North Beach to pay most of his remaining debt. When he sought to receive benefits from the Insolvency Law, his finances were listed as follows: Liabilities $55,811; assets stated at $15,000, uncertain value.

*

"You bloody *pirate*!" Norton denigrated Monty angrily. "You knew they were coming hyah and you bloody-well fohsed me to meet with that *schtupid* Peruvian *tit* and take this deal!" He paced heatedly with his hands at his hips behind the couch next to the fireplace. His head and gaze followed his boots between utterances, his mind focusing on the next inflammatory segments of his unrehearsed beration.

"Joshua please," pleaded Monty, "I had no idea about anythi--"

"BOLLOCKS!!" Norton snarled as he continued pacing, his head unmoved as he angrily swiped the excess spittle from his lip.

"Why would I do such a thing--"

"--Because you are bloody *greedy*, *Monty*... You

bloody, greedy, bastahd," he yelled furiously, pausing briefly to pound his fists into the cushions below him. "...Because you haven't a *soul* in that *empty, vapid, pitiful* skeleton you call a *pehson!"* he accused in a forceful staccato, glaring intensely toward Montgomery but quickly returning to his furied pacing and fixing his eyes again at his boots as his tongue reloaded. "I made you *rich*, Monty, from the *moment* we met," he exclaimed. "Or don't you recall..."

"I was wealthy long before we ever met, Joshua," Monty bragged in a commanding retort. He had grown impatient of being chastised by the desperately distraught man in his home. "--What," he chided as he laughed raucously, "do you think that I am indebted to you in some way, you simple little fuck?" he said with disdain. Montgomery stood from his chair and pointed a finger, focusing his words. "I've done nothing to deserve this, Joshua. Now *please...* Calm your temper and let's figure out this mess."

Norton continued to pace, slightly less petulantly. "I thought I was more to you than simply a pawn," said Joshua sadly. "You've ruined me, Monty," he lamented more softly. "I'm bloody ruined..."

The room fell silent as Norton's pacing began to subside. He turned away from the couch and leaned his forearms on the mantle above the crackling sounds of the fireplace. Montgomery waited a moment for Norton to calm himself, then cautiously strode toward him, placing a consoling hand upon his shoulder.

"Listen to me, Joshua," said Montgomery very calmly. "I am a friend...your dear friend. I knew of only one other ship arriving after this one, I figured the price--"

Joshua quickly recoiled from Monty's touch. "You see?!" He backed up a few steps. "You see? I knew that you could not be trusted--"

"--Please, Joshua," Monty interrupted quickly, his hands raised in supplication, "I simply expected prices would hit twenty-five and we'd both be happy," he pleaded. "I had no idea that more of the damn things would arrive, Joshua. You must *believe me*, I'm your friend. I would never purposefully hurt you," he resolved.

Joshua stood motionless for over a minute as his emotions rose and fell sharply against his adrenaline. He felt devastated. He had nowhere to turn and had now damaged his relationship with a man he thought was his best friend.

"Very well, Monty," he conceded. "Issue me a note for the five thousand and we can put this mess behind us," he said calmly.

"Yes, of course Joshua," said Monty in a patronizing tone. "Um, let's see," he said as he walked toward the desk at the corner of the room.

"I believe I... Oh, nuts," he said in feigned disappointment as he shuffled the papers on the desk. "It'll have to wait until Monday if that's alright, my friend," he said, grinning sheepishly toward Norton.

Joshua was deflated now that the adrenaline had worn off. He managed to lazily raise his slouching head and nodded toward Monty.

"Very well, then," said Monty, relieved and chipper. He clapped his hands and fetched another bottle of wine to lighten the mood.

The two men reminisced their first encounter and laughed about its awkwardness. They discussed their previous dealings and Monty advised Joshua on possible investments using the five thousand dollar reimbursement when he received it. The following Monday, Norton went to visit Montgomery, but Monty was long gone. He had been planning on following a lead on some investments in Chicago and saw this escalating predicament as the perfect catalyst to flee. Montgomery never returned to San Francisco. And Norton never heard from him again.

*   *   *

IX

"Keep your fears to yourself, but share your courage with others."

-Robert Louis Stevenson

*   *   *

When Sammy arrived at the fire station later that Saturday evening, the full brigade was present. It was an unusual sight to him, as there were normally only four men on duty during any of the thirty-six-hour shifts for which he was accustomed to volunteering. With only six beds in the room upstairs his first thought was where he and the other eleven men would sleep. It had become standard procedure since the city's most recent fire ten years earlier in 1896, when the men on duty at the time had been unable to contain a small chimney fire in SOMA that resulted in razing several adjacent tenements.

"I'm glad he's on the mend, but quarantine or no quarantine, I ain't goin' to goddamn Chinktown if it spreads there. They can kiss my ass," declared one of the men.

"Me neither, they can burn for all I care, rats an' all!" yelled another.

"Hell, I ain't even s'posed to be here tonight, Chief," said yet another. A few other men chimed in with equal sentiment aimed at the brigade chief.

"Okay, alright, settle down," he said. "They got this one isolated, anyway. Turns out it wasn't nothin' to do with the tremors in the first place," he said. "So let's just sit tight, tend to the work around here, and get some sleep."

The Board of Supervisors was poised to make a decision regarding the outbreak of bubonic plague the following Monday that had raised the question of quarantine. Two of the firemen from their brigade had been afflicted with a strong fever a few days earlier, after a routine call to Chinatown had forced them to enter the most unsanitary section of the district. One of the men had died from the ravaging onset of the plague. To the relief of the rest of the firemen, the wife of the other man, for whom Sammy had been lamenting days earlier, had sent word that afternoon that her husband's fever had broken and that he was improving.

Since it had first been settled, San Francisco had suffered serious fires on six separate occasions. The City had since created several safety precautions, organized fire brigades throughout, and upgraded fire stations with the latest technology. Now, in 1906, the Fire Department of the City and

County of San Francisco was composed of of forty-four engine houses, two corporation yards and repair shops, two drill towers, the Department stables, corporation yard stables, and battalion chief headquarters - Fifty buildings in all.

Equipment included thirty-eight steam fire engine companies and ten hook & ladder truck companies; eight chemical engine companies, one water tower company, and two monitor batteries, with a unformed force of over five hundred men.

In addition to the above were the following apparatus for relief, emergency, and other purposes: Fourteen steam fire engines, sixteen hose wagons, two cistern water towers which held one-hundred thousand gallons each; two monitor batteries, four hook & ladder trucks, fourteen officer's buggies, six hydrant carts, ten delivery wagons, two supply wagons, one crane-neck truck, an oil tank wagon, a horse ambulance, and a hay wagon.

Even more impressive, everything was automated in the firehouse. The lights would illuminate on the first strike of the bell. By the time the men upstairs were dressed, the stable doors would have automatically opened and the horses moved out under their collars. The drivers would then snap the collars, jump into their seats on the carriages, and be out on the street within moments.

*

"...and then this huuuuge piece of glass almost hit me square on the head!" Emma continued. "So I saw Mama and swam back as quick as I could! ...I guess that means I won the race, huh Pa," said Emma as she swung her legs under the table.

"Hmm. I guess it does, but I doubt Nathan will see it that way Emma," said Nep.

"But he never even made it half way and I went the whole way," she pleaded.

"That's true, sweetheart, but it wasn't his fault, now was it," Nep said in a lecturing tone.

"Well I say he owes me a half-dollar! ...Or Floyd should get socked by Sara," she resolved.

"Honey, that's not nice. We don't do that," Caroline scolded. "We don't hit people, do you understand me young lady?"

"Yes, ma'am," Emma obliged with her head down.

"Now come on, let's get you washed up for bed."

"But Maaaam, it's only--"

"No lip, Emma," said Nep firmly. "Listen to your mother and go get washed up," he ordered.

When she had cleaned her teeth and showed her hands to Nep for his approval, the two entered her bedroom and Nep began reading Emma a bedtime story from his now complete series of Gulliver's Travels:

"They bury their dead with their heads directly downwards, because they hold an opinion that in eleven thousand moons they are all to rise again, in which period the earth (which they conceive to be flat) will turn upside down, and by this means they shall, at their resurrection, be found ready standing on their feet. The learned among them confess the absurdity of this doctrine, but the practice still continues, in compliance to the vulgar."

Emma began to giggle. "Why did they think the world was flat, Papa?"

"Well, they didn't have the big boats like we have now, so I guess they couldn't see far enough into the distance find out," Nep explained.

"That's silly," she concluded. "But everyone knows the world goes around and around now though, right?"

"Yes, Emma, everyone knows now," Nep explained with a grin. "Technology lets us see into the future, so that we can see what's coming next... Okay, that's enough for tonight," he said. Emma began to whine and plea.

When she had finally relented, he kissed her forehead lightly and tucked her snugly under the warmth of the blankets.

"Good night, Papa."

"Good night my dear, sleep well."

*

Early the next morning, Monsieur Dubois awoke at his usual early hour of four o'clock. He washed up and put on his chef's jacket and apron, along with a red scarf and black beret and made his way downstairs sleepily with methodical steps.

He had been a chauffeur for a wealthy couple on the outskirts of Lyon as he studied the culinary arts in the evenings, and had saved enough money for transit to what was then being advertised as the 'Paris of the West.' He had been in San Francisco for three years and had opened the patisserie within months of arriving. A loyal base of customers paid him visits several times each week and business was good, but he missed his homeland and it showed in his ever-growing waistline.

His specialty was his delectable raspberry religieuses. Similar to an eclair, they consisted of a fluffed pastry filled with a unique raspberry cream - the recipe for which he held closely secret - and topped with an almond-hinted frosting. In addition to this, Dubois added a dollop of melted Ghirardelli chocolate on the side. Customers lined up to select a treat from his large glass display case and then sat at one of the linened tables near the front of the store.

Emma had fallen asleep more quickly than usual and thus had arisen early, well before her usual time. Knowing her parents would sleep for several more hours because neither worked Sundays, she crept downstairs once more to pass the time with her friend and watch him prepare for the crowd on this, his busiest day.

Dubois stopped humming as he sensed the odd trembling below his feet. Pans began clanking loudly together, a few falling from where they hung. Baking trays rattled and flew off their shelves, scattering around the floor with a frightful noise. Emma was covering her ears and began to shriek as Dubois leaped into action, grabbing her small frame by the waist and curling her under his arm like a baguette. He staggered unevenly into countertops and the wall several times, trying to brace himself by lowering his stance as he moved forward to the exit of the kichen and into the front of the store.

From the doorway between the kitchen and front area of the store, he moved haphazardly through the narrow path next to the display case, between the chairs and tables, faltering and tilting with every step. As he passed the foremost tables, a ceiling beam crashed dangerously near to his back; then another, which crushed the glass of the display case with the force of a crashing ocean wave.

Emma was still covering her ears and was now screaming for her parents at the top of her lungs, tears streaming down her face as she did. As they finally exited the patisserie, Dubois was hurled forward by a jolting shift of the earth below him and landed clumsily on his side, fumbling Emma from his grasp above his free hip and launching her several feet into the air. Moments later, the surrounding buildings began crumbling with an audible roar.

As their eyes reacted, Emma let out a shriek and resumed her sobbing screams atop the deafening rumble. "Ma-*ma*! Pa-*paaa*! ...Mam-*maaa*!!" She scooped her teddy bear from the ground tightly to her body and began running toward the door of the building. Ma*ma*!!" she continued to scream. Suddenly, just as she approached the entrance, an explosion erupted on the top floor, halting Emma's stride.

Moments later, the remaining wooden frames began creaking more loudly in an awful cacophony of sounds. Noticing her perilous advance, Dubois yelled as loudly as he could as he lunged and grabbed her when she came within his reach. He turned and stutter-stepped quickly away from the deafening sound. The planks and studs of the building swayed abruptly and contorted in unison once more. As Emma turned to face the building from the safety of Dubois' shoulder, she watched in horror as it collapsed, imploding toward the earth in a frenzy of noisy dust and smoke.

Nep and Caroline had been sleeping soundly when the earthquake began. Ten seconds hence, when the shaking roused Nep from his sleep, he shook Caroline awake and attempted to make his way to Emma's room. He fell to the floor as he left the bed, then ricocheted against the walls of the hallway like a pinball, nearly falling again in the yet darkened apartment, but eventually found himself at the entrance of her room.

"Emma!" he shouted, fighting the darkness of the early morning to ascertain that she was no longer in her bed. "Emma! Where are you!" he yelled again. Nep entered the room and opened the nearby door to the closet, using its doorknob as an anchor against the violent shaking of the building. "Emma!!" he yelled continuously, desperately scanning the room, but hearing nothing from his little girl.

He managed to exit her bedroom, again bouncing against the hallway walls toward the kitchen. He opened the door and saw broken glass and plates laying scattered across the kitchen floor. The brick chimney had crumbled from the force of the quake, blocking the rear door completely. He faintly recognized a box of matches under the kitchen table when he was finally knocked to the ground.

Flailing wildly back and forth across the shards and debris, he managed to grab and pull open the box, clumsily grasping a few matchsticks as the rest were strewn across the floor. With a purposeful motion, he struck the matches against the sandpapered side of the box and perished almost instantly in the resulting explosion of odorless gas that had accumulated in the kitchen.

Caroline had been knocked unconscious when the large brass frame of the painting above their bed was jarred from its hanging hook and fell squarely onto her head and arm, pinning her motionlessly in bed. Instants after the kitchen explosion, the building caved into itself and Emma became one of many newly orphaned children.

*

At the first tone of the alarm, the lights shot on and Sammy was wrenched from his deep sleep, disoriented and confused. His bed and those of the others were shaking violently, some even careening around the room like kites in a violent gust of wind. For several seconds, the men could do no more than to brace themselves on whatever their hands could find and exchange terrified glances.

The few who were able to leave their beds stumbled and fell clumsily around the room as they attempted to collect their heavy clothing from the wall hooks and floor, where most of it had fallen. Sammy did his best to arise from his bed and dress himself, but the task proved nearly impossible. When the tremors finally gave a slight pause, the men began consecutively sliding down the fire-pole toward the horses and fire engine wagons.

When he reached the ground floor, Sammy grabbed the nearest horse, one of several frightened beasts which bucked its front-quarters wildly in frightened confusion after having been released from the confines of its warm, sleepy stall. He yoked the animal with all his strength, finally controlling the animal enough to calm it down as the brunt of the force that had moved the earth began to subside. The other men did the same in concert and began boarding the steam fire engines. The brigade collectively stampeded and motored toward downtown and the smoke that began to fill the air in the distance, none uttering a single word.

The shock had snapped gas mains and toppled hundreds of chimneys. Entire blocks of wood, brick, and even steel structures had twisted and collapsed within minutes from the sheer force. Fifty fires broke out simultaneously, centralized in the Financial district and SOMA, but the destruction was only beginning.

One hundred or so miles in both directions along the San Andreas faultline - north to Santa Rosa and south to San Jose - the crust of the earth slipped as much as twenty-one feet. Fences, rail tracks, and buildings all suffered in its wake. The equivalent of six million tons of dynamite, twelve times the power of an atomic bomb, mangled the city. Hundreds of homes and buildings fell like dominoes, crushing thousands of helpless victims as they became trapped or slept through the horrific event.

The steam-powered fire engine truck which Sammy had boarded carried four men plus a driver. The mens' uniforms were made of thick denim, their porcelain helmets shaped much like the ones from ancient roman times. Each firefighter carried a large axe on their belts and several wet cloths to protect against the fumes.

The engine itself contained a large cauldron of water and several fittings for attaching hoses. When a steam engine arrived at a location, the horses were separated from the engine to avoid ash that would be created by the coal fire that was then lit. The coal fire heated water in the cauldron above it and created steam. The steam gathered in a chamber where pistons would then react to its pressure and begin pumping water inward from an outside source.

The collected water then entered a large air chamber to equalize it against the choppy pumping action of the pistons. Another set of pistons then pumped water out through another hose, which had arrived on a separate wagon. Once connected to the engine, the hose was rolled out away from the engine wagon by two men and toward the foot of the blaze.

*

As the fire engine approached downtown, the extent of the damage caused by the quake became clearer. All along Market Street dust filled the air from the collapsed and maimed buildings that lined it. It was still early morning, but hundreds of people could be seen walking the streets in a confused daze, wondering what had just happened. The fire engine made its way further along Market Street until it reached the Call Building.

The Call Building was one of America's first skyscrapers and the only one of its size in San Francisco. The new 18-story Call Building was 315 feet from the street to the tip of the lantern on its dome, easily the tallest building in San Francisco, on the Pacific Coast, and west of Chicago. The impressive structure dwarfed the surrounding landscape and gave the City great pride, so the brigade chief had deployed several wagons to attempt its salvage.

When Sammy's engine arrived, the men quickly snapped into motion. They lit the fire and connected to the nearby fire hydrant. While the men on the ground worked, Sammy and several others made their way up the stairs of the nineteen story structure. The men had stretched the hose until it would extend no more, nearly a hundred feet above the ground to the seventeenth floor at the base of the impressive dome.

After ten minutes the engine began pumping out water to where the men stood. It flowed out the hose and toward the flames and smoke as the men began shifting its nozzle to several hot spots. But a moment later the pressure suddenly faded, the flow of water reduced to a trickle. The men stood confounded and began angrily calling down to the others through the window and smoke that permeated their surroundings.

The water main had broken during the quake. In fact, literally all of the water mains had broken throughout the entire city. There was no water, save the 100,000 gallons in each of the two cisterns in the city. One was located in the nearby SOMA neighborhood, the other within a few blocks of the Call Building.

The men spent the next two hours transporting water from the nearby cistern into a series of troughs they had procured from a supply store, where it could then be pumped up through the hose. Sammy and the others returned to the upper floors and began trying to quell the growing spread of the fire.

Suddenly and without warning the fire seemed to explode and magnify in intensity. The already damaged gas main under the building had snapped from the continued pressure of its weight, seeping the flammable gas through its interior and upward. The elevator shafts acted as vacuum flues, sucking the flames of the fire back downward and emblazoning the rest of the floors. They were trapped. Within moments, Sammy and six other brave men had been incinerated near the top of the building.

The explosion had been caused when someone a mile westward in the Hayes Valley had lit a fire outside his house to cook breakfast. His was one of hundreds of chimneys that had been damaged beyond use. The *Ham & Eggs* fire, as one newspaper coined it, ignited the broken gas mains throughout the city one by one in furied succession.

The fires that burned for the next three days would eventually destroy 250 city blocks, transform 28,000 building into rubble, leave 250,000 of the city's 350,000 population homeless, and kill over 3,000 residents. According to a meter housed near Stanford University's powerhouse used to track generated voltage, the jolt had reached a magnitude of 7.8 and lasted a full twenty-eight seconds. Thirty years later, with the invention of the Richter scale, the quake's magnitude was estimated to have been 8.5.

*

Major General Frederick Funston, who was in command of the Presidio of San Francisco, was the highest ranking officer in the city. By eight o'clock that fateful morning, he had quickly assembled nearly two thousand troops and volunteer recruits. Their orders were to fight fires, evacuate citizens, and prevent crimes.

Immediately after the earthquake, he demanded authorization from the Mayor to order looting be punished summarily with execution. Mayor Schwartz conceded, urging newspapers to print and distribute the proclamation immediately. Funston ordered his troops to kill on sight anyone caught looting, but in the chaos that ensued, even many of the soldiers were seen doing so. Children who were caught looting were spared, but humiliated in public in the ensuing days by being forced to stand at the busiest of streets wearing placards proclaiming their crimes, such as *I Am a Junk Thief,* and *So Am I*...

As one survivor had recounted - "One man made the trooper believe that one of the dead bodies lying on a pile of rocks was his mother, and he was permitted to go up to the body. Apparently overcome by grief, he threw himself across the corpse. In another instant the soldiers discovered that he was chewing the diamond earrings from the ears of the dead woman... The diamonds were found in the man's mouth afterward."

By ten o'clock, Funston had become aware of the breakages of water mains and directed men to dynamite several buildings to create fire breaks. The effort was largely ineffective, instead demolishing the interiors of the buildings and causing more fires. Finally, the desperate, last-ditch strategy finally worked at the wide avenue of Van Ness, where a successful fire break was created, but only after the residences of many city elite were demolished by the dynamite to enhance its width. A newspaper writer named Jack London had tried to explain the scene:

> "I knew it was all doomed. I walked for miles and miles through to empty blocks. In the intense heat of the city, two troopers sat on their horses and watched. Surrender was complete."

By eleven o'clock, two-hundred fifty city blocks had gone up in flames. Many residents walked to the tops of the many hills throughout the city and watched helplessly as the SOMA and Financial districts, Chinatown, and the Barbary Coast burned throughout the night. The next morning, people had a collective look of irritated apathy, as if someone had cheated them. Word traveled inland from the coast that ferries were taking people across to Oakland, so thousands made the long trek down to and along Market Street to the embarcadero.

Although the Board of Supervisors had not held session to vote regarding the quarantine of Chinatown, and although the city had burned and crumbled, sentiment toward Chinese residents remained largely unchanged. Wagons near the perimeter of Chinatown reluctantly offered rides for Twenty dollars to Chinese residents who earned just Fifteen dollars per month.

When they reached the waterfront, they were treated as second-class citizens, forced to wait most of the day for the non-Chinese residents to be accommodated before being allowed to board and cross the Bay. Many who were able-bodied took jobs aboard ships heading west toward their homeland or southward toward Panama, where the United States had recently acquired France's concession of the mosquito-infested area with the hopes of completing a canal. Those Chinese who remained courageously prevailed and helped to rebuild San Francisco and what would become the largest Chinatown in the Nation.

Men and women could be seen pushing huge trunks or carrying their remaining belongings down Market Street in wheelbarrows. One man was even seen rolling a barrel of whiskey, the clothes on his back his only other possession. But when the masses arrived at the waterfront, the ferries would allow only what each passenger could carry, leaving the dock strewn with thousands of half-emptied trunks and cases.

Drinking water became a precious commodity and men were seen scavenging for food cans from the debris. The city was a blackened wasteland of checkered blocks of ash and debris. The financial lines of demarcation and the disparity of classes had all but vanished, as men, women, and children who remained spent the ensuing days waiting in long lines for food rations and camped in one of the several parks that dotted the City.

Within days, nine-hundred thousand rations arrived from military garrisons in Seattle and Portland. Congress sent one million dollars of relief funds. Those whose homes had been damaged but survived were asked to cook on the streets outside of them. Men who were seen idle were handed a shovel and followed the dumptruck five or six blocks until another man could replace them. With the heightened threat of the plague by dislodged rats, a bounty was offered for their disposal at City Hall.

To encourage residents to stay and assist with the efforts, lofty wages were paid to laborers. Carpenters could earn four dollars per day, more than double what New York City lawyers made the same year. Within weeks, buildings and homes were being erected and residents were looking to the future. Within a year, nearly four-hundred thousand would inhabit an entirely new San Francisco.

*   *   *

X

"An aim in life is the only fortune worth finding."
         - R L Stevenson

                    *   *   *

Well then you shouldn't have trusted him in the first place, Joshua...

"I am aware of thet now, Mother, but I thought that he was my frrind," said Norton as he looked at the photograph.

Friendships and business dealings should never commingle, my dear son.

"Yes, that has become abundantly cleah, Mother. No longer will I trust any man, let alone one who propohses such a fantastic bahgain. When he finds his way beck we can sohrt things out prohperly..."

Norton had made his way to the large forest near the opening of San Francisco Bay and found refuge in an abandoned fur trader's shack in the northwest corner of San Francisco's peninsula known as the Presidio, named as such in 1776 when New Spain made it the military center of their colonization of the area. Years later it passed to Mexico and then to the United States in 1848.

The shack was a remnant of years past and a place where nary a soul would disturb his privacy. The simple structure lay near the edge of a hundred-foot cliff which overlooked the entrance to San Francisco Bay and was surrounded by several freshwater creeks and a plethora of trees clustered densely in places; oaks, magnolias, hawthornes, maples, pines and redwoods, plus acacias similar to the one he remembered from home.

Surely you must have a few coins to reserve passage? Perhaps you should return home for a while until things settle down, dear. No reason to let things fester inside... A nice long trip like that will--

"--We've discussed thess to exhaustion already, Mother," he asserted. "The courts have instructed all ships to deny my pehssage until the remaining debts are paid. I cannot leave! It's bloody hopeless," he lamented.

Well then you ought make the best of it, Joshua...and mind your tongue. Perhaps there is a place for you in the Parliament there... You're quite intelligent and popular, I'm certain they would be delighted to have you as a--

"--There is no Parliament hyah, Mother," he interrupted disdainfully, "they have one min who is refehrred to as the President and several min below him who enact the laws... Incompetent min at thett."

Well then there you are. Speak to the people in the town and convince them that you should be their leader, the... President is it?

His father's photograph stared back at him idly as he spoke to his mother, and Joshua didn't dare ask his opinion. He sensed that his father was extremely disappointed with hearing of his recent financial irresponsibility, envisioning his father's arms crossed in disdain below the border of its frame. His father's visage had remained silent for the entire three months since Norton had shifted from an inner dialogue to one of confiding in his inanimate parents, who lived now inside the locket at which he gazed. The financial devastation had flipped a switch in Joshua's head, leaving him disillusioned and disoriented, leading him to take refuge in exile from the predicaments of the real world.

He had existed scantily in the cold and dilapidated shack for nearly a year, sneaking every so often back into town for supplies... But he would only dare venture into Chinatown cloaked in secrecy, so as not to be noticed by past contemporaries and the like. The once fanciful attire he wore was now threadbare, much like the increasingly unkempt man who wore it, and he had not engaged anyone aside from his parents in nearly a year.

His only comforts were what he had been able to carry back from his outings. They consisted of a dozen books or so, a small home-made chess set with three pieces missing, a few spare items of clothing, and a journal in which to store his ever-distorting thoughts. He sometimes scavenged during twilight hours near the garrison buildings at Fort Point, nearly a mile's trek from his shack. When one of the night watchmen had noticed him skulking around on a cold night, he placed a tattered army uniform, along with several cans of rations next to the garbage bin.

The next evening, the uniform was gone. When Joshua returned the next month, he happened upon a rusted sword in its sheath and an official Army hat. When he returned to the shack later that night, he excitedly adorned the full regimental uniform and proceeded to deliver what would be the first of numerous impassioned speeches toward the vastness of the ocean below him. He became more and more detached from reality, conjuring scenes where he acted as the ruler of the cliffs of San Francisco or re-enacted one of the many plays he had seen as a wealthier man. He played all the roles of course, only once successfully coaxing his mother into reading for a small female role.

The thought wasn't a bad one; of becoming President, that is. He *was* popular to many people in the City, or at least he had been at one point, and he disagreed with many of the government programs and laws, largely regarding the men who held political office with contempt. He was hesitant to re-enter society and to face his financial predicament, but his thoughts of returning to power and prestige grew into an obsession rather quickly.

As his newly found zeal and enthusiastic fascination with its prospect became an increasing reality in his mind, he flew away further into delusions of grandeur. The voice of his father began regularly stoking Norton's ego with rousing monologues of pride for his son's regal attributes. Joshua would often sit on the few animal hides and bed sheets which covered a small area on the floor, leaning against the wall of the shack with his eyes closed, grinning and stroking his beard, and assimilating every ounce of whatever delusion was concocted into his head through the voice of his father.

*

Since all of his properties had been liquidated to mostly satisfy his oustanding debts to the banks, Norton's only remaining possessions sat idly in a trunk held by his previous residence, the elegant Metropolitan Hotel, which had since stowed it downstairs in the basement. When he emerged from asylum after more than a year, he was indistinguishable from a vagabond for his wear and tear. His curly hair had grown quite long and his moustache had grown into a full and bushy beard.

He offered salutations to a few women he recognized, who simply looked at him awkwardly and slightly recoiled, only conjecturing after he had passed whether it could possibly be the affable gentleman from South Africa.

He continued down Market Street, adorned in full regimentals, including the stunted and tilted hat, the likeness of which becoming synonymous with the impending Civil War. He arrived at the Metropolitan in elated spirits and greeted the bellmen and porters, who seemed surprised that the stranger called them by name. For this, they allowed the haggardly man to enter the hotel without incident. He passed through the grand lobby and toward the stairs of the three story building, but was intercepted by the receptionist.

"May I help you, sir?" she politely asked.

"Good day, Rebecca," he said with a large grin.

"Mr. Norton?!"

"Yes my deah, I've come beck! I've returned with big, big plans to repair this great nehtion," he proclaimed happily as he began walking up the steps.

The young lady paused in awe. "Yes, I see," she said timidly. "Oh, um, Mr. Norton?"

"Yes, my deah...just heading up to collect my--"

"--Sir, your room has been cleared out," she

interrupted apologetically. "I'm very sorry, but we hadn't a clue where you had gone... But we do have your trunk downstairs," she added, "would you like me to have the porter fetch it for you?"

Norton halted his ascent. "Cleahed out, you say... When did this heppen?" He was more confused than irritated, simply wanting to collect his identification and clean up so that he could begin campaigning.

"Um, about a year ago, sir... Sir, you've been gone a long while and, well...and we're a hotel you see," she explained. "I'll just have a porter collect your trunk Mr. Norton." She walked swiftly toward the entrance of the hotel.

Norton stood spellbound, contemplating the duration of his absence, trying to make sense of things in his cloudy mind. "Yes, very well," he uttered softly under his breath as he turned slowly, reluctantly descending the stairs to the lobby.

Rebecca dispatched a porter who departed and reappeared in the lobby several minutes later with Norton's trunk. Norton opened and inventoried it, lifting a suspicious eye to Rebecca and the porter. He then simply dragged it outside and began towing it down the street. *Bloody pirates*, he mumbled to himself as he exited. *They'll receive no favors from me when I'm elected...*

Dusty and tired from the five-mile hike to the Metropolitan from the shack in the Presidio and the additional three-block trek with his heavy trunk in tow, he finally arrived at the Eureka Lodge. The dingy lodge was a flophouse on Commercial Street, between Montgomery and Kearny streets. The room that became his new home was nine feet by six, roughly the same size as the shack in the Presidio, with a rickety-springed iron cot, a lopsided chair, a sagging couch with soiled upholstering, a washbasin, and a simple nightstand.

There was no closet, so he hung his clothes on the rusty nails that protruded from the walls. His accommodations at the Metropolitan had cost ten dollars per night, twenty-fold more than the fifty cents per night he would pay at the Eureka for the next seventeen years. But in comparison to the musty, cold shack, it was a paradise. Now he would set his sites on the task at hand. He gingerly opened the locket and perched it against the small bedside lamp.

*

The next morning, having bathed properly for the first time in over a year and after shaving the sides of his beard, he adorned his regal regimentals and began attempting to reconnect and hobnob with his old cronies and business associates. He visited men who still held leases at the properties he had once owned and visited several of his regular stops.

Norton's lowly financial status and his strange attire made matters increasingly difficult and awkward for seemingly everyone except Norton himself. But in contrast to his outward appearance was his jovial persona. His ease of purpose and light-hearted demeanor seemed to soften the discomfort of those he encountered.

He began attending synagogue on Saturdays and a different church each Sunday. A guise perhaps, but it proved to grow his circle of popularity. When he did as such, he wore the more ornate regimental jacket he had found a few days prior to his departure, with stunning epaulettes and brass buttons. He viewed its discovery as a sign that the powers that be requested his return to the City.

Though largely abstemious, he frequently visited bars and saloons to discuss politics and garner interest from what he hoped would be his constituency. But he refrained from openly divulging his plan to run for President. This was due in part to the perception that his father would advise Norton when the timing for action was right. His father had insisted that Norton first regain the trust and friendships in what his parents reiterated was *his* City before making such a bold announcement.

He visited Universities and libraries, debate societies and lectures, and theaters when the money he regularly won playing the wags in chess was ample enough to do so. If asked where he had vanished for the past year, he would simply say that he had taken a trip west that had opened his eyes and refreshed his soul.

Near the end of 1859, Norton's father had led him to believe that the Presidential election was to be held the following year and advised Joshua to enact his plan swiftly. Joshua immediately strolled proudly along the busy streets to City Hall in the fancier of his regimentals. With his sword at his side and the regal intent to register his name on the ballot for consideration in the upcoming primaries, he strode proudly toward officially launching his campaign. When he arrived at City Hall, Joshua made his way to the Office of the City Clerk and approached the young man behind the desk.

"Yes, sir, what can I do for you today?" the young man said brightly.

"Good day young min, my name is--"

"Yes, sir, Mr. Norton, I know who you are," the young man chimed. "My father rents your warehouse over on Kearny. The cigar factory?" he reminded.

"Ah, yes, of couhrse..." He omitted the fact that he was no longer the owner of the property, encouraged by the ignorance of the young man.

"Yes, sir," he replied cheerfully. "It's a pleasure to meet you, Mr. Norton."

"Likewise, good lad," he said as they shook hands briefly. "Well, now. Yes... To affairs of business, shell we?" Norton smiled and excitedly wrung his hands together in anticipation. In his proudest voice, he cleared his throat and proceeded to finally make the declaration he had been rehearsing for several months...

"I would like to hyah-by announce my candidacy and to pless my name foh considerehtion on the ballot for the Presidency of these fine United Stehtes of America! I hev great plans to repaihr the damage that has been inflicted onto this nehtion by the incompetencies and inadequacies of this administrehtion and those villainous thieves and pirates of the past whom have damaged its reputation, hyah and abroad!" As he had made his declaration he soundly thumped the desk with his fist to punctuate his inflections, grinning enthusiastically all the while.

The clerk sat erect at the first boisterous notes of the small man's speech, and now sat dumbfounded as he wondered how to reply. His initial thought was that he had become the victim of some sort of prank put on by one of his co-workers, his gaze searching around the room to each of them for signs of guilty pleasure. Seeing none, he returned his gaze to the man standing before him.

"Um, sir? Well, um, we already have a President, Mr. Norton... President Buchanan, sir. And besides, the next election isn't for another few years," he said rather bluntly.

"No?" asked Norton. "I'm certain youah mistaken

young min."

"No sir, that's a fact. Um, the election is a few years out, but anyway you'd need to visit Sacramento about that. And besides, there are rules about who can run for office--"

"--Well then the Vice Presidency will have to do," Norton interrupted enthusiastically, pointing upward in triumph.

"No, um... Mr. Norton, you see there are rules that would make it difficu--"

"Rules? What rules?" Norton interrupted again, becoming irritated. "I have greht plans foh thess nehtion!"

"Well, sir, you have to be born here in America for starters," he said. "And, well... I don't mean to make assumptions, but sir it sounds like you're from other parts," he added uncomfortably.

"Yes, yes, but what does that hev to do with enathing, young min?" Norton asked with effrontery.

"And plus, sir, only the President can pick his Vice President," he explained. "Here, hold on." The young man held up a hand as a signal for Norton to pause and began searching some papers in the side drawer of the desk. When he had located it, he presented a document to Norton. "It says right here, sir. If you want to go ahead and read it, I think it'll clear things up."

"Very well, very well," Norton said impatiently as he snatched the document from the young man's grasp and brought it toward his face.

"It's in the second part I believe, sir. The part about having to be born here and all is around...here," he said as he pointed.

Section I, Article II

No person except a natural born Citizen, or
a Citizen of the United States, at the time
of the Adoption of this Constitution, shall
be eligible to the Office of President;
neither shall any Person be eligible to that
Office who shall not have attained to the
Age of thirty-five Years, and been fourteen
Years a Resident within the United States.

"*Preposterous*," exclaimed Norton, beside himself with disappointment.

Seeing that the man who stood before him maintained a serious demeanor, he consoled, "I'm very sorry Mr. Norton, I wish there was something I could--"

"--The Senate then! This priffle says nothing about thett, eh young man?" he insisted, shaking the documents at the clerk.

"Sir, the Congress has the same rules I'm pretty sure... Best you could hope for is Mayor, but you're just a bit--"

"--Fine! Mayor will have to do," Norton

conceded flatly. "When is thet bloody election then, young min," he asked blamefully, wishing silently to himself that he still owned the warehouse so that he could evict the boy's father as his first act upon departing City Hall.

"Gosh, I'm really sorry Mr. Norton," he said fearfully. "The election is next month, but the cut-off date to register was back in August."

"Blast! Rat bloody *scoundrels*," he exclaimed, loudly enough to rouse the attention of those in the office who hadn't already been disturbed by his boisterous ramblings.

"Sir, I'm really sorr--"

"--Good day, lad," said Norton as he tossed the papers in the air with fiery stare in his eyes and a cold demeanor. "... *Good day*."

Norton turned and hung his head, stomping away from the young man's desk and through the exit feeling deflated and upset, eager to confront the visage of his father to offer petulance toward the embarrassment he had caused by his idiocy. He uncharacteristically snubbed the greetings of those who now recognized him on the street, isolated in a world of self-deprecation, murmuring insults to himself in practice for the deluge he planned to hurtle toward his father.

As his gaze shifted upward from the ground as he walked angrily, he began to notice the names of several businesses on the buildings along the street. He began bitterly complaining to himself. *Empire Grain, Imperial Lumber, Empire Textiles! Imperial Fashion!* he thought to himself... *If this is such a bloody empire, where is the bloody Emperor?!*

He stopped sharply in his tracks.

Moments later he trounced toward home, his gait fervently swiftening and the broad grin returning to his face. He rushed back to his room at the Eureka to discuss his revelation with his parents.

"No mother, I cannot become even a member of the Congress, you see. But there is a vacancy for a much *loftier* position," he declared with a laugh.

After consulting his parents for a few moments more, he closed the locket and scribbled onto a blank but soiled page he had torn from his journal. He folded and tucked it into his jacket and hurriedly made his way to the offices of the nearest newspaper. When Norton arrived, he proceeded to storm past the receptionist and into the office of the editor. He demanded that the editor print his announcement immediately, reiterating much of the oratory which he had shared earlier with the young man at City Hall.

Once the maniacally enthusiastic man dressed in full regimentals had departed, the editor of the *Bulletin* joked with his colleagues as they shared it, laughing at its absurdity and repeatedly reading parts of it in mocking voices. The editor eventually returned to his office, chuckling to himself every so often.

The next morning, however, and with a rich sense of humor, he decided not only to publish the proclamation, but to feature it on the front page of the newspaper, in all apparent seriousness:

PROCLAMATION

At the peremptory request and desire of a large majority of the citizens of these United States, I, Joshua Norton, formerly of Algoa Bay, Cape of Good Hope, and now for the last 9 years and 10 months past of S. F., Cal., declare and proclaim myself Emperor of these U. S.; and in virtue of the authority thereby in me vested, do hereby order and direct the representatives of the different States of the Union to assemble in Musical Hall, of this city, on the 1st day of Feb. next, then and there to make such alterations in the existing laws of the Union as may ameliorate the evils under which the country is laboring, and thereby cause confidence to exist, both at home and abroad, in our stability and integrity.

NORTON I, Emperor of the United States.

The citizens of San Francisco rejoiced the obvious ruse. The next day, several citizens who knew him paused to jokingly bow obsequiously at the newly appointed presence of His Majesty. Norton was ecstatic. Enveloped in his own warped sense of worth, oblivious to the notion that he was being obligingly humored, he made his way to a busy intersection on Market Street and declared that by unanimous acclamation, he humbly accepted the fine citizens' confirmation of his newly appointed position as their Emperor. This was met with a mixture of entertained laughter and explosive applause from the large group who had stopped to listen.

*   *   *

XI

*   *   *

Six days had passed since the earthquake had taken the lives of Nep and Caroline Haley. Sammy and over three thousand others had also perished in the largest natural disaster the country had ever witnessed. The subsequent fires that had decimated the City were all but extinguished and the smoke had begun to give way to clearer skies in the temperate Spring climate in San Francisco.

Dubois had taken personal responsibility for Emma's well-being after saving her life from the collapsing building in which they both had lived. They made an odd pairing; a rotund middle-aged Frenchman next to a slight, auburn-haired girl. But it seemed they were all one another had for the time being, and had kept each other in close sight since the dreadful morning that lingered vividly in their minds.

They had joined the thousands of other displaced citizens who had begun camping in Civic

Center Park, one among several of the parks around the City that had been infiltrated with tents and masses of displaced people. As with many restaurateurs, Dubois was selected to cook breads in a makeshift oven, which had been constructed using a fraction of the six million bricks that had formed buildings and chimneys just days earlier. Emma and others played games nearby to pass the time, delighted that school had been canceled indefinitely. Emotions were largely subdued during the daytime, but at nightfall an audible murmur of grieving could be heard drearily emanating throughout the camps from the huddle tents of survivors, both young and old.

Emma vacillated between appearing calm and erupting into convulsive fits of sobbing for much of the ensuing nights, as the recent memory of the frightening collapse of her house and the sudden loss of her parents resurfaced again and again. Dubois had done his best to console her and explain that her parents were only gone for a little while, that they were hurt and someone was fixing them, but to little avail. She eventually grew exhausted and her sobs descended into whimpers as she fell asleep, awakening in the mornings confused and disoriented.

When they awoke the following morning, Dubois joined the large groups of people who began their newly assigned activities while Emma joined the other young children in the clearing nearby. As the day progressed, people watched in awe as hundreds of men on horseback arrived with rations, clothing, and supplies into camp. Their arrival was met with cheers and many ditched their places in line to assist with unloading the wagons and horses.

A well-dressed woman carrying a clipboard walked toward where Emma and the other children played. Her dark hair was medium in length and beautifully wavy, covered by a lace-embroidered hat with a large ribbon and wide brim. Her voice was playful and pleasant and her gait was light and certain. Her skin was pale and soft like the dress she wore and she had an air of intelligence about her.

"Good morning, children," she said happily as she approached a sizable grouping.

A few of the children echoed her greeting while others acted oblivious to her arrival.

"Could you all come over here please, I'd like to speak with you for a moment," she said.

Several children moved toward her rather excitedly while others were slow to transition away from their activities. Once they had all arrived she asked them to sit. They were all under the age of twelve, which seemed an unspoken age at which they were expected to contribute to the overall effort in a more meaningful way.

"My name is Miss Rose and I help children find toys that they've lost," she said with a smile.

The girls and boys erupted into cheers and began shouting the names or descriptions of their dolls or toy boats respectively. She raised her hands and began fanning them over the children until they began to calm down.

"Now," she continued. "Raise your hand if you can't find something that was very special to you." All of the children raised their hands playfully and kept them in the air. "Very good," she said applaudingly. "Please lower your hands... Now raise your hand if you can't find your dog or your cat or you bird." Many of the children raised their hands.

"What about my frog?" one boy asked anxiously.

"Yes, or your frog," she laughed. "Any pet that you've lost..." Relieved, the boy's hand shot up quickly, his head tilting sideways as he smiled broadly.

"Very good, children... Please lower your hands," she said again. "Now, please raise your hand and keep it way up in the air if you can't find your Mommy or Daddy," she said more seriously.

Thirty or so children raised their hands, several of them calling out which one, most others sensing nothing strange about the line of questioning. "Very good! Now, would those of you with your hands raised please follow me?"

The children looked around at each other, those with hands raised feeling special for being part of a select group. The others frowned in disappointment as if they had lost at the game that had been played. Eventually the remaining children dispersed and the selected group followed Miss Rose toward a table which stood in front of one of the hundreds of tents that dotted the park.

"Okay, children. Now I would like you to *quietly* organize into two lines. The girls' line begins here on my left, and the boys' line begins here on my right," she gestured.

Before she could finish the sentence, the children began quickly jostling each other for the best spot they could manage, still clueless as to what was about to happen. For all they knew, the nicely dressed lady was about to dole out knuckle sandwiches to their innocent little faces and administer wedgies to boot... It did not matter to them. Being closest to the front of the line did.

Another slightly younger woman sat in one of the chairs, which now faced the line of boys. Miss Rose sat in the vacant seat aside her which faced the line of girls. Without explanation, the ladies motioned the child at the front of each line and began inundating each with questions about their lost loved ones. Soon some of the children had been sent back to play, having only lost one of their parents. A few others began crying and were escorted away from the line by one of the other women who stood behind Miss Rose.

The line stopped six feet or so from the table

and Emma was sixth in line with the girls. As she advanced her position, she began overhearing some of the questions and became increasingly anxious. After a few minutes, it was her turn to approach. She stepped gingerly up to the desk and stood nervously before Miss Rose, cradling her teddy bear tightly. The questions were organized in a way that would allow the children to feel at ease, so as not to frighten them into reticence. Miss Rose finished making notes about the previous girl who she had interviewed and looked up at Emma with soft eyes.

"Hello young lady... My, what lovely red hair you have," she said sweetly. "And what is your name?"

"Emma," she said shyly and nervously.

"Well it's a pleasure to make your acquaintance, Miss Emma," she said calmly. "And how old are you, Emma?"

"Eight," she replied softly.

"Emma, do you know where your house used to be, or what your address might have been?"

Emma began feeling the urge to flee, but feared the possible consequences of doing so. She felt that she was being held against her will and the memories of the events from that horrible day began rushing back to her mind. She fought back her emotions and began looking around for Mr. Dubois among the grownups.

"Um, no," she said in a whimper. She had

spotted him between a few of the surrounding tents, busily rolling out dough and chatting with people in line. She wanted desperately to call out to him to come to her aid, but it was too late. She began to blush nervously as she heard the next question.

"Did you lose one of your parents, Emma?" she asked more softly. Miss Rose tried to ignore the obvious stress of the child. She had worked at the orphanage for nearly two years and was well-trained in child psychology from the University of Stanford, but it was always challenging. Each child was different and to say that this situation was unique was a vast understatement. Emma's face began to contort as her emotions suddenly waved over her. She began convulsing and crying loudly, her head swelling pink and her clenched eyes welling up profusely with tears.

I want my Papa!" she yelled as she inhaled several gasps. She convulsed more tearing cries. "I want my Mama and Papa! They're *gone* and I want them *back*!" she screamed in anger and continued to sob as she stood in place at the foot of the desk. Many of the other children now began crying too, sensing that this game might not be as fun as they had hoped.

"Where are they?! I want to go *home*," Emma pleaded, throwing her teddy bear to the grass forcefully and crossing her arms as she convulsed. Miss Rose glanced behind her and saw that the remaining staff were tending to other children, so she left her seat and made her way around the desk to where Emma stood sobbing.

"Okay, Emma," she whispered softly as she crouched in front of her and gently put her hands on Emma's arms. "It's okay Dear, let it all out sweety... I'm here to help you, Emma. Everything is going to be okay, I promise," she said in a motherly voice.

Emma continued to sob for several minutes until one of the aides returned from consoling another child. Miss Rose picked up and gently handed the teddy bear to Emma while instructing the young lady to escort her back behind one of the tents and away from the crying and the glaring eyes of her peers. When she finally became calm, Emma explained the details of the earth shaking and the house collapsing, of how Mr. Dubois saved her and how she *tried to save Papa and Mama from the house falling down like an elephant.* She wiped her tears away several times with her wrists as she sat in the folding chair.

"I'm very sorry to hear that Emma. You're a very brave girl. Very brave indeed," said the young woman. "We're going to make everything better, okay? --Emma?"

"Okay," was all Emma said. She sat slumped over, batting the back of her teddy bear's head onto her knees. Her dangling legs hung limply, not finding the energy to swing themselves on this particular occasion.

"Do you know your Mama and Papa's names?" the young lady asked.

Emma grimaced toward the young lady smugly at the seemingly rhetorical nature of the question.

"Emma, do you remember your Mama saying your Papa's name? Think hard, Emma," she asked carefully.

Emma thought for a moment and could not.

"Who is taking care of you?" she then asked.

Emma pointed to Mr. Dubois. The young lady lifted her gaze to follow Emma's hand. "The fat man making bread," said Emma. "He doesn't know English very good, though, so you have to speak French," she said snidely, assuming the young girl could not.

"I see," she replied. "Okay, well I'm going to go speak with him for a moment. Will you be a good girl and stay right here, Emma? I promise I'll be right back and everything is going to be fine, darling."

"Okay," said Emma as she continued looking downward and batting the bear. She again thought of fleeing... But to where? What would she do? Where would she sleep?

The young lady departed and strode toward Dubois. When she snuck glances a few moments later, Emma could see him looking over toward her a few times as the woman spoke. Then she could see him gesticulating the story in a very animated way, with many of the spectators swaying their heads in sympathy. The lady made some notes on her clipboard and then turned to walk back toward Emma.

"Your friend Mr. Dubois says you're a very smart and brave girl, Emma. So I'm going to explain something to you because you're smarter than the other kids and can understand, okay?"

Emma nodded, feeling slightly less anxious at the flattery. "Okay," she said.

"Your parents went, um, to Heaven when your house fell down. Do you understand, darling?" she asked. Emma nodded complacently, feeling her emotions beginning to return. "They're in a new place, a wonderful--" she stopped herself, noticing Emma's adverse reaction. The young lady skipped ahead to divert Emma's attention. "We have a special place where children like you can stay. It's a very beautiful place, with toys, and games, and books. Doesn't that sound nice, Emma?" she asked.

"Okay," frowned Emma, again wiping the tears that began quietly streaming down her cheeks.

"It's a great big house with lots of rooms and a garden and you'll make plenty of friends! So what do you think, Emma? Would you like to come live in the big house with the other children?"

"What about him?" She pointed to Dubois as she sniffled with a downward gaze.

"Mr. Dubois can come visit you anytime, Emma, so you'll see him very soon," she promised.

"Can I still play with my friends?"

"Of course you can," she replied cheerfully, "and you'll make new friends too," she added.

"Alright, but I get to bring Teddy."

"Certainly, Emma... Now I want you to go to your tent and collect your clothes and other things, alright?"

"I don't have any things," Emma said flatly.

"Oh, I see," replied the lady solemnly. She realized her misstep and suddenly felt an overwhelming sadness for the little girl. "Well then, let's follow the others to your new home, shall we? It's going to be fine, Emma, I promise. We have plenty of toys and clothes there, okay?"

She coaxed Emma off of the chair and they walked toward the street to join several of the other children who had become newly orphaned, many of whom still emotional. Dubois saw Emma from the distance and wanted badly to run down the hill to hug her and say *adieu*, but he could only wave and smile, having been warned that doing so would cause more harm – and tears – than good.

Now several adults had begun waving to the children for whom they had briefly cared. All were displaying a thin and contrived facade of joy, while oceans of sadness welled inside them. The children were boarded onto the wheeled street trolley and it departed, heading west along Market Street toward the hill in the distance. Emma sat quietly, looking back at Dubois and the remaining children who had resumed play in the park clearing. Several of the children were still sobbing and confused, feeling as though they were wrongly being punished. But Emma sat resolved, she had decidedly shed her last tear that day.

                              *

Twenty minutes later the trolley approached a rather imposing brick building located several blocks west of Van Ness, on Buchanan and Waller streets. Van Ness was the wide thoroughfare that had been successfully utilized as a fire break few days earlier, saving many of the sparsely situated homes and buildings that were west of the inferno. It had suffered structural damage to its exterior during the quake, but because it lay west of Van Ness, the San Francisco Orphan Asylum was not destroyed and all of the children who were inside during the earthquake had escaped safely.

The orphanage resembled a sort of medieval castle, with gables on all four sides and an assortment of metal spires poking upward from its peaks. The building's wooden frame had become exposed near the tops of the walls in many places which, in combination with the spires, only added to its ominous appearance. In the center of the roof was a pointed steeple with a bell inside, which rang loudly to alert the children when it was time for recess, prayer services, or mealtime. As the children began stepping from the trolley, Emma noticed some children playing in the large yard and spotted Sara among them. She perked up immediately and began running toward her, yelling Sara's name and waving happily as she ran. Sara was equally thrilled when she noticed Emma and ran toward her. The two girls embraced gleefully once they met.

"What are *you* doing here?" asked Emma.

"My stupid house fell down and my Auntie is gone now," replied Sara, less than enthusiastically. "I hid under the bed and then ran out the door like crazy, Look!" She raised her arm to show Emma the long scrape that ran across her forearm. "You shoulda seen all the blood, it was gross," she said in a strange giggle. Sara's mother had succumbed to cholera when Sara was an infant and she had never met her father, so the loss of her Aunt had not affected her to the same degree as the other children.

"Eww," said Emma in disgust. "Yeah, me too," Emma said sadly. My Mama and Papa fell down in the house. I *tried* to save them, but the fat baker man who lives downstairs pulled me away before I could..." she said emphatically.

"Ugly, huh," Sara digressed toward the building.

"Yeah, what *is* it?"

"It's like a school but you sleep over," Sara said plainly. "I got here a few days ago. It's okay I guess, at least when we don't have to do chores, that is..."

"Where do you sleep?" asked Emma.

"Up there. We all do." Sara pointed to the windows near the top of the large structure, where wooden joists showed through spots where missing bricks had been jarred loose and tumbled.

"With the boys?"

"Of course, silly, but they sleep on the other side of the curtain," laughed Sara. "It's not so bad... And Nathan's here," she teased flirtatiously.

Emma began to blush. "So," she said bashfully.

"Come on, I'll show you around." Sara took Emma's hand and led her toward the entrance of the daunting building. The staff allowed the children to orientate themselves at will but kept a watchful eye as they darted between the floors and rooms. Sara pointed and explained the different rooms vaguely, describing the various members of the all-female staff in her perceived wisdom after being there all but a day. They went through the main hall and dining area and up the wide staircase to the second floor. She showed Emma the bunk beds in the sleeping room and the lesson room and where the toilets and showers were. She was relieved to have her friend Sara by her side and Emma quickly began feeling comfortable in her new surroundings.

Sara was among the tallest of the girls, nearly a foot taller than Emma, and she often used this fact to her advantage to intimidate some of the boys who had yet to develop. She had bright blue eyes which angled slightly upward at their corners and long blonde hair which often made Emma jealous, although she never admitted to it. Her eyebrows were slight and her nose and mouth seemed too large for her face, but overall she was very pretty.

The girls had met that year in school and had become close friends when a boy had been bothering Emma and Sara intervened. She had grabbed the boy by the ear and punched him in the stomach with all her might. The boy buckled to the ground in agony and Sara was swiftly chided and sent to the school headmaster. When Sara was released from detention, Emma had given her a silver hair barrette for *saving my life* and the two became quickly inseparable.

At lunchtime, the bell atop the roof began to sound and the two hundred or so children gathered at the massive wooden tables in the grand dining hall. The sound was deafening as children milled around tables and argued over where they would sit. The massive fireplace at the far end of the hall was deemed unusable due to damage from the quake. This wing of the orphanage encompassed roughly half of the main level, the other half being reserved for two classrooms and the offices of Miss Rose and the other staff.

There were four tall windows draped with red curtains on its long wall, with two more on each of its shorter side. The children ranged in age between four and fourteen, with the former grouped tightly at their own specified table. The rest commingled as they pleased, eventually claiming permanent seating surrounded by new and old friends.

Once seated, Miss Rose quieted the children by launching into prayer, her head bowing and eyes closing sincerely after the first few phrases. Those who had recently arrived showed the newest orphans by example, leaning their elbows onto the edges of the table and pressing their foreheads into their hands. After a collective *Amen*, the staff of twenty women began slopping the mushy brown stew into bowls that lay in front of each of the children. It was a pleasant atmosphere overall, with laughing and taunting pervading the room. When the volume would reach a certain level, Miss Rose would loudly say *Chil-dren* and the crescendo would commence anew from a murmur.

After lunch, Emma and the other newly arrived children were assembled separately and assigned beds and a chore schedule, while the others began carrying out their duties or enjoying their free time playing ball games, marbles, or skipping rope out in the grassy lawn. Once they had received their assignments, they ran upstairs to acquaint themselves with their new sleeping quarters.

Emma's was the last bed at the farthest end of the room, far away from the boys' side of the room, and next to one of the tall windows that lined the upper floor in the same arrangement as the dining hall. While several of the other children in the room began chatting and testing the comfort of their thin mattresses, Emma began gazing out through the window near hers.

The window faced due east toward the largely barren wasteland that remained of San Francisco, a blackened reminder of how quickly her life had transformed in a matter of days. In the far distance, she could faintly make out the encampment where she had stayed and where Mr. Dubois was probably still busy cooking for the hungry masses. Further yet, she could see the remains of some of the buildings and the tall metal skeleton of the skyscraper that had taken Sammy's life. She was sad, but her tears had dried and she decidedly composed herself.

Her gaze then focused downward to the sprawling orphanage lawn, where about fifty children engaged in assorted activities. She crept up closer to the window and zeroed her focus, snooping around the yard trying to see if Nathan was anywhere to be found. Some of the children were playing baseball with a stick and a rubber ball, while others were jumping rope or playing Tag. Some of the girls braided each others' hair as they sat in a circle on the lawn, while others skipped on a hopscotch made from chalk.

It was an insular oasis, far and removed from the destruction that lay so near to it. She thought it peculiar that two boys were sitting off in the corner of the lot, quite a distance from the other children. They appeared to be looking curiously at something on the ground. She recognized Floyd by his terribly matted black hair and large nose, but did not recognize the other boy.

"Oh man, you shoulda been there Floyd, it was swell!" said Randy in a flurry of excitement. Orphans often socialized with the neighborhood children and it was not uncommon for them to play on the orphanage lawn together.

"Where'd ya find it?" Floyd asked in amazement. Both boys were eleven and had known each other their entire lives. As with most children at the orphanage, the two boys had never discussed the events of the earthquake in detail. It was an unspoken taboo.

"Me an' Ian were out fishin' by thirty-two, and on our way back we saw this reflection comin' from some rubble, see," he began. "We snuck up there and dug around a little, and bam!" Randy exclaimed. "Wouldn't ya know it, by golly, I pulled away some busted mirror glass and it was right there lookin' at me, haha!"

The large mirror which had hung in the living room of what had once been Sammy and Nep's house had smashed along with everything else that had crashed to the ground. The glass shards had apparently formed a shield against the flames and protected the item through the duration of the fires. In the basement, long forgotten, Randy had discovered Nep's cigar box.

"Geez, Randy, that's *real* swell," agreed Floyd. "Whoooaa," he said in awe as he picked up the lure gingerly. It was meticulously carved and sanded from bone into the shape of a minnow, painted black with a bright yellow underbelly, and had tri-hooks attached at its midsection and tail.

"I can't *wait* to try it out tomorrow with my Pa... Um, I mean, I bet it works, um, real sweet," he trailed off. Suddenly wanting to mask his discomfort from the mentioning of his father around his orphaned friend, he began pointing out the details of the lure. "See! It's got three hooks on each one--"

"What's this thing?" Floyd asked as he pointed to something else.

"Heck if I know, haha. Looks like something for girls if you ask me," he said. "You want it?"

Emma had moved away from the window and set the toothbrush and washcloth she was provided on the small, single-drawered side table. She opened the drawer to see what was inside and discovered a small

black book with red fringes that had the words 'Holy
Bible' written on its cover. She shrugged, placing
her items in the drawer and pushing it shut. Nep and
Caroline had taken Emma to church on several
holidays each year, but did not consider themselves
pious. Regardless, Emma was currently more
interested in getting back downstairs to Sara and
searching for Nathan.

As quickly as she began her stride, she
suddenly stopped, curious as to the identity of the
girl would be sleeping in the bunk below hers. She
went toward the small table at the other side of the
stacked bedframe and cautiously opened the drawer.
Inside she saw an identical book to the one in her
drawer, a toothbrush, a hairbrush, and among other
items the barrette she had given Sara. She gasped,
smiling excitedly. She quickly closed the drawer and
rushed to the other end of the room and down the
stairs to the lawn.

When she arrived, she joined Sara and met a few
of Sara's new acquaintances. She snuck glances
around the lawn in an attempt to locate Nathan, not
convinced that Sara had been telling the truth. As
the girls chatted idly, she suddenly spotted the
backs of a few boys walking toward the far corner of
the lot. She recognized Nathan as one of the boys
who was approaching Floyd and the other boy, but the
other boy with Nathan was a bit larger and Emma
didn't recognize him from school.

"Oh, that's Harry," Sara said in a foul tone when Emma had asked. "The boys call him *Slug* because he's a good stick man, but we just call him that because he *is* one."

Nathan was average in height and scrawny, with light brown hair that nearly covered his eyes and a strong chin. By contrast, 'Slug' had clearly reached puberty and stood taller than the rest of the boys and most of the women on staff at the orphanage by the age of twelve. Prior to the quake, the two had been part of a gang of pickpockets who called themselves *The Gophers,* based loosely on the fact that they would *go-fer* anyone's pocket, no matter what. Nathan had never officially picked a pocket, but had come across some abandoned booty and rationed it to the gang, so Slug felt obliged to befriend him at the orphanage.

"Well what do we have here," Slug said authoritatively as he snatched the box off away from Randy and looked at it. There were singe marks that ran diagonally across most of it, with two of the corners severely burnt and missing, but the inside walls and items in the box appeared mostly unscathed.

"Hey give that back, you *bully*," yelled Randy automatically.

"Yeah, and what are you gonna do if I don't," said Slug, confidently smiling as he peered into the box.

Randy stared at him angrily from below, weighing his options as Slug began rummaging through what had been his prized box. "Let's see... I want...this," he declared playfully. Slug removed the baseball card and began stuffing it into clumsily into his vest pocket.

"I'm gonna tell Miss Rose and you'll get in trouble," threatened Randy, who was visibly upset. "I don't even live here, they can't do nothin to me!" His lips were quivering with anger.

Slug lifted his gaze from the cigar box and locked eyes with Randy. He shoved the box into Nathan's chest and lunged down, grabbing Randy with both hands above his shoulders and wringing the boy's shirt toward him. Nathan instinctively took hold of the opened box and stood wide-eyed next to Floyd, who had scurried to his side when Slug had advanced toward Randy. Suddenly the whistles of the ladies on duty began blowing and three women began running in heavy dresses toward the scene.

While Nathan was distracted, Floyd reached into the box and snatched some of the marbles and darted away. Nathan felt the movement of the box he held and decided to follow Floyd's lead. He grabbed the necklace and a few of the remaining marbles and dropped the box to the ground, its remaining contents emptying onto the grass as he ran away. Slug was shaking Randy violently and cocked back his right fist. Just as he did, the three women grabbed him and wrenched him away from Randy with all of their strength. Once the boys were separated, Slug covered himself with his arms as the women swatted him like a swarm of bees until they were convinced he was under their control.

"I *told* you," screamed Randy from his back as he supported himself on his elbows. "I *told* you, you rat! I only wanted the lure anyhow, ha-ha-*ha*," he jeered confidently.

"*Fooey*," snarled Slug, "I'll get you! --I see you around here again I'll get you, that's a promise!" One of the ladies began swatting him again to contain his outburst.

Randy swallowed hard and scurried to his feet. He grabbed the box and the items that had strewn around it, stabbing himself on the fishing lure as he fumbled to return it to the box. He ran away down the street as fast as he could and never returned to the orphanage. Slug, Nathan, and Floyd were sent to Miss Rose's office immediately to explain themselves.

"Harold, this behavior will not stand under my watch," Miss Rose reprimanded. "I will not have you bullying the smaller boys, is that clear?"

"Yes, Miss Rose," mumbled Slug. He had been at the orphanage for less than a week, but had already managed to make his way into Miss Rose's office on three separate occasions.

"Unfortunately, I believe I must make myself
clear in a more convincing way if we are to have an
understanding," she said. Slug became suddenly alert
of her change in tone. He watched as Miss Rose
removed her hat, walked to the tall bureau behind
her desk, and procured a long wooden yardstick.
"Place your hands on the desk please, Harold," she
ordered sternly.

Slug looked at the other boys and then at Miss
Rose. "But--"

"Now!" Her newly assumed demeanor conflicted
greatly with her elegant look and Slug was suddenly
terrified. He slowly presented his hands facing
downward and reluctantly reached toward the desk.
"Turn them upward, you pestilant child, as though
you were begging God's forgiveness!" The boy was
beside himself with fear and the looks on Nathan and
Floyd's faces did nothing to ease his fright. He
slowly gazed up at Miss Rose as he turned his palms
to face upward. Just as his wrists became visible,
the ruler cracked down hard onto them. Slug let out
a loud scream as his wrists instantly reddened.
Before he could complete his cry, the ruler cracked
down again, and again in quick succession.

"You will behave yourself, do you understand?"
said Miss Rose as she continued the whipping with a
crazed look in her eyes.

"I'm sorry," Slug whimpered, pulling his wrists
to his chest in pain. "I won't, I won't do it

again," he trembled.

"Put your damned hands back onto the desk this instant young man!"

Slug had tears in his eyes now, averting the petrified gazes of the other boys, who were nearly wetting themselves with fear. His forearms bled slightly as he presented their quivering flesh once more. *Smack! ...Smack! ...Smack!*

In all, she administered twelve blows to the boy's wrists, one for each year of his pathetic life, as Miss Rose had explained it. "Now," she said as she calmed herself, "if you behave yourselves there will be no need for this sort of *discussion* in the future."

Nathan and Floyd nodded fervently, hoping that this was not simply an intermission between beatings from the chameleon standing over them. Slug sat hunched over, leaning to his side in silent agony, limply cradling his bloodied and bruised wrists against his chest.

"Consider this a warning," she said to Nathan and Floyd. "Next time you will endure an equally severe punishment."

"Yes, ma'am," they said in unison.

"Yes, Miss Rose," she ordered.

"Yes, Miss Rose."

"You will transcribe the first twenty pages from Gospel of John prior to Bible studies tomorrow," she demanded. "Failure to do so will warrant the same punishment as your friend Harold, here."

"Yes, Miss Rose," they agreed in unison.

"Very well, then, off you go."

The boys slowly exited the nightmare they had just witnessed and hurriedly ran upstairs to collect their Bibles to begin the lengthy process of their assignment. Slug was sent to the resident nurse's office and was bandaged, but complied with Miss Rose's punishment to avoid another beating.

By the time they finished their transcriptions and made it to bed, it was nearly midnight. Nathan, Slug, and Floyd flopped their exhausted bodies onto their respective beds and lay motionless. The rest of the children slept soundly, uninterrupted by the boys' late entry into the sleeping hall. Nathan had closed his eyes in exhaustion only moments before noticing the lump in his pocket. He fished out the item and laughed to himself at forgetting about it so quickly.

Aside from the glimmer that shone in from the nearly full moon through the curtains across from his bed, the long sleeping hall was ominously quiet and dark. He turned onto his side and peered over the edge of the bed at the locket, which he held down a few inches from his mattress and into the dim, gray glow. He used his thumb to lift the clasp that held the two halves together and pried the weighty piece open. His head moved closer as he squinted, trying to make sense of the photographs he saw. In his exhaustion, he simply laughed through his nose softly at the two dogs. He opened the drawer next to his bed, deposited the locket quietly in the back behind his other possessions, and fell asleep.

*   *   *

XII

"O, dear, it was always a painful thing for
me to see the Emperor begging, for although
nobody else believed he was an Emperor, he
believed it."

 -Mark Twain

            *   *   *

In the days and weeks that followed his Royal
Declaration, Norton I - Emperor of the United
States, rose quickly into celebrity. The pretensions
of Norton were fully encouraged by the masses and as
speedily humored by the press. He took himself and
his position extremely seriously, approaching his
duties with vigor and enthusiasm. He continued the
rigorous schedule he had begun upon first returning
to civilization several months prior, attending any
and all functions of society in full regalia.

With the encouragement and support of the
masses, and the delusional whispers of his parents,
he felt unstoppable. Where he was once a young
businessman with a 'satchel' and a sense of
adventure, he was now a well-respected yet quirky

and unpredictable figure, who magnanimously spread his convictions of equality and justice throughout San Francisco. The people loved him and would stop at nearly nothing to support him. He became an instant icon, recognized by name if not by face in the ever-growing population of the American West.

Throughout the 1850s, the issue of slavery had drawn a division between the eastern states. The South relied on its free labor to ensure profits while the North, who were more readily quickened to industrialism, increasingly found the practice to be antiquated and inhumane. In 1857, the Dred Scott Decision of the Supreme Court ruled that blacks were not U.S. Citizens and that slaveholders could move their slaves to the free parts of the country.

In October 1859, tensions escalated when abolitionist John Brown attempted to start an armed slave revolt by attempting to seize the US Arsenal at Harper's Ferry in Virginia. When General Robert E. Lee surrounded the small building later referred to as his 'fort', Brown yelled an array of several different voices as he scurried around the small shack to give the appearance of many armed men inside. When Lee captured Brown, he suggested that Brown was insane. And when news reached Norton of Brown's pending trial, the Emperor issued a proclamation in Brown's defense:

PROCLAMATION

It is represented to us that the universal
suffrage, as now existing through the Union,
is abused; that fraud and corruption prevent
a fair and proper expression of the public
voice; that open violation of the laws are
constantly occurring, caused by mobs,
parties, factions and undue influence of
political sects; that the citizen has not
that protection of person and property which
he is entitled to by paying his *pro rata* of
the expense of Government--in consequence of
which, WE do hereby abolish Congress, and it
is therefore abolished; and WE order and
desire the representatives of all parties
interested to appear at the Musical Hall of
this city on the first of February next, and
then and there take *the most effective steps*
to remedy the evil complained of.

October 1859

During the trial, Governor Wise of Virginia
concurred with General Lee's accusation that Brown
was indeed insane. However, instead of
institutionalizing Brown, he sentenced him to death
by hanging. As a strong proponent of equal rights,
and endemically empathetic and somewhat ironic in
this instance, Norton issued a proclamation

extricating Governor Wise from his position as Governor of Virginia and appointing the sitting Vice President to its post:

PROCLAMATION

DISAPPROVING of the act of Gov. Wise of Virginia in hanging Gen. Brown at Charlestown, Va., on 2nd December;

AND CONSIDERING that the said Brown was insane and that he ought to have been sent to the Insane Asylum for capturing the State of Virginia with seventeen men;

NOW KNOW ALL MEN that I do hereby discharge him, Henry A. Wise, from said office, and appoint John C. Breckenridge, of Kentucky, to said office of Governor of our province of Virginia.

December 1859

"I don't rightly know, father," said Norton as he lay in bed looking at the locket. "I suppose these things tek time, but I will remain adamantly steadfahst and stay the couhrse to ensure that we correct the wrongs of this nehtion. I have called all leaders of the Stehtes to congregate under my counsel February next and will be mehking some announcements toward a multitude of things."

Is it not possible to simply banish them from the Republic and take their lands, son? You are the Emperor, are you not?

"Father, there is a certaihn protocol for these things," he said. It had been several months since his proclamation was printed, yet Congress had failed to disband.

Perhaps you should move to utilize your infantrymen, Joshua. Have you not a suitable Navy or Army Brigade at your disposal?

"Excellent idea as always, Father! I will assemble my Armies and forcibly remove those wretched, intransigent cowards," he said emphatically.

Darling, please don't encourage our boy to acts of violence, said his mother. *Surely there must be a more diplomatic method to disband the Parliament.*

"*Congress*, Mother," he corrected. "It is refehrred to as the *Congress*. And no, father is correct. If they will continue to ignohre our peaceful authority by means of the written wohrd, then *We* must call in the Army to tek action."

The next day he stormed into the offices of *The Bulletin* once again with his usual regal and purposeful determination. His proclamation would again appear on the front page the next morning:

PROCLAMATION

WHEREAS, a body of men calling themselves the National Congress are now in session in Washington City, in violation of our Imperial edict of the 12th of October last, declaring the said Congress abolished;

WHEREAS, it is necessary for the repose of our Empire that the said decree should be strictly complied with;

NOW, THEREFORE, we do hereby Order and Direct Major-General Scott, the Command-in-Chief of our Armies, immediately upon receipt of this, our Decree, to proceed with a suitable force and clear the Halls of Congress.

January 1860

By this time, Emperor Norton's interruptions at the offices of *The Bulletin* and other newspaper publishers throughout San Francisco had become an almost daily occurrence. But they were always met with a jovial sense of excitement and anticipation, namely for two reasons: Firstly, they offered a pleasant, if not entertaining distraction from the daily monotony of office work... Here was a small, strange, yet seemingly intelligent man dressed in full – but unkempt – regalia playing a part on the stage of life that only he believed to be real. And secondly, his whimsical offerings sold papers. Lots of papers. In fact, everywhere the Emperor made an appearance seemed to benefit from his presence.

Tourism had grown tremendously throughout the 1860s with the completion of the transcontinental railroad and shopkeepers jumped at the chance to sell figurines, photographs, and pins with images of their favorite Emperor in windows and upon shelves.

A few days prior to the meeting scheduled for February 1, which Norton had requested to be held at the Musical Hall, the building coincidentally burned down. Undeterred, he quickly had the meeting rescheduled for February 5 at the Assembly Hall nearby. But when the Emperor arrived that evening, the doors remained locked and the streets surrounding the Hall were virtually deserted.

The *Bulletin* printed Norton's speech in its entirety, however, which stated in part, "...Nothing will save the nation from utter ruin except an absolute Monarchy under the supervision and authority of an independent Emperor." A few months before Abraham Lincoln would be elected President, Norton issued the following:

PROCLAMATION

WHEREAS, it is necessary for our Peace, Prosperity and Happiness, as also to the National Advancement of the people of the United States, that they should dissolve the Republican form of government and establish in its stead an Absolute Monarchy;

NOW, THEREFORE, WE, Norton I, by the Grace of God Emperor of the Thirty-three states and the multitude of Territories of the United States of America, do hereby *dissolve* the Republic of the United States, and it is hereby dissolved;

And all laws made from and after this date, either by the National Congress or any State Legislature, shall be null and of no effect. All Governors, and all other persons in authority, shall maintain order by enforcing the heretofore existing laws and regulations until the necessary alterations can be effected.

Given under our hand and seal, at Headquarters, San Francisco.

July, 1860

The legend of Emperor Norton continued to grow rampantly. In 1861, a play entitled "Norton the First" debuted on a San Francisco stage. When Norton arrived to occupy his Royal seat - one of the best seats offered at the theater which had been reserved for His Majesty - the attending crowd broke into boisterous applause and the orchestra played a fanfare. His ego was enthralled by the attention as he graciously bowed to the crowd.

Rumors began to spread that Norton was a direct descendant of Emperor Napoleon Bonaparte. This was possibly due to his diminutive size, standing barely over five feet in height, but perhaps additionally due to the intensity with which he manifested the duties of his regal position. In 1862, the nephew of Napoleon Bonaparte, Napoleon III was attempting to expand the French Empire. Using as a pretext the Mexican Republic's refusal to pay its foreign debts, he planned to establish a French sphere of influence in North America by creating a French-backed monarchy in Mexico, a project that was supported by Mexican conservatives who resented the Mexican Republic's laicism.

The United States was unable to prevent this contravention of the Monroe Doctrine because of the Civil War; Napoleon hoped that the Confederates would be victorious in that conflict, believing they would accept the new regime in Mexico. But his imperial dreams would not be so easy to achieve.

In Mexico, the French army suffered its first military defeat in fifty years. The under-armed Mexican army had defeated a much better-equipped French army. The defeat not only surprised the world, but served to revitalize the national spirit of Mexicans. To this end, Norton amended his title to Norton I - Emperor of the United States and Protector of Mexico, dispelling the rumor of any French lineage and, in theory at least, expanding his Empire.

He always carried a cane and also an umbrella during days of inclement weather. When his uniform began to look shabby, the Board of Supervisors, with a great deal of ceremony, appropriated enough money to buy him another, for which the Emperor sent them a gracious note of thanks and a patent of nobility in perpetuity for each Supervisor.

*

A stray dog began to accompany Norton on his daily walks and royal visits to eateries throughout the city. The dog was known as Bummer, due to his habitual begging and bumming of meals. He was welcomed inside several saloons due to his skills at killing rats, and Norton often shared his free meals with the canine. Bummer was a shaggy Newfoundland cross, black with white paws and a white stripe that stretched from his forehead to his underbelly.

One evening, Bummer had intervened during a fight between two dogs over some scraps in an alley. A larger dog had been fighting a slighter one and had maimed it to a point of near death. Bummer chased the bullying dog away with veracity and tended to the maimed dog, bringing it rations of the scraps Norton would share and huddling next to it during the night for warmth. Within days, his new friend was following Bummer around town on ratting and scavenging missions, as a team once finishing off nearly one hundred rats in twenty minutes as one saloon proprietor had noted. Due to his miraculous recovery against seemingly improbably odds, locals collectively decided to refer to him as Lazarus.

Although he never claimed ownership of the dogs, Norton, Bummer, and Lazarus became a constant fixture on the streets and in saloons around the city. When Lazarus was naively snatched by a new dog-catcher, a mob of angry citizens demanded his release, petitioning to have the pair declared city property so they could wander the streets unmolested. The city supervisors released Lazarus and declared he and Bummer were exempt from the city ordinance against strays. And so it went, the Emperor and his two sidekicks filling the local newspapers with entertaining headlines and stories.

On one occasion, Emperor Norton took lunch at a local eatery away from his usual stomping grounds. As with anything involving finances, it was customary for Norton to issue his royal receipt, to be accounted against the imaginary levies of taxes, which he had imposed on his subjects and collected regularly as his regular income. When he had finished his meal, Norton attempted to offer one such receipt to the proprietor of the restaurant.

But the man had refused it, explaining that since Norton's royal visit the previous week, the sales at the establishment had doubled. To the audience of diners in the establishment, Norton stood abruptly and declared, "By Royal Decree and appointment of His Majesty, Emperor Norton I, We hyahby deem this estehblishment Royal in status!" The following week, Royal proclamations began appearing as permanent fixtures in storefronts and restaurant windows throughout San Francisco:

BY APPOINTMENT TO HIS IMPERIAL MAJESTY, NORTON I.

- or -

HIS IMPERIAL MAJESTY, NORTON I,
EATS HERE WITH BUMMER AND LAZARUS.

On the rare occasions when Norton's proclamations became scarce, many newspapers would fabricate stories to provoke him into action or create ongoing pranks by having falsified telegraphs sent to him from other parts of the country. One such stunt portrayed a man in New York as claiming to also be an Emperor. This infuriated Norton to no end. He marched again into the offices of *The Bulletin* with his newest Royal decree:

PROCLAMATION

Down with usurpers and imposters! Off with his head! So much for cooking other people's goose! The legitimate authorities of New York are hereby commanded to seize upon the person of one Stellifer, styling himself King or Prince of the House of David, and send him in chains to San Francisco, Cal., for trial before our Imperial Court, on various charges of fraud alleged against him in the public prints.

NORTON I - Emperor of the United States and Protector of Mexico.
S. F. 6th day of Nov. 1865.

"The nehrve of this bloody *infidel*, attempting to usurp me from my given right to the throne, eh?" he complained to his parents as he paced his tiny room at the Eureka Lodge. "To think thet someone would be so brehsh and arrogant to us! It's unthinkable--"

Joshua, I have something serious to discuss with you--"

"Please Mother! Allow me to finish befohre you congratulate my retaliatory strehtegies," he interrupted. "I've published a retohrt that will allay any quehstion toward my authority! It reads as follows..." He cleared his throat and began pontificating in a lofty tone. " Down with--"

Joshua, please! --I have some rather difficult news to share...

Norton stopped reading his draft and lowered his gesticulating arms to his sides in frustrated impatience. "Oh? --Whet is more impohtant than an *imposter* in our midst, eh? --What is it, Mother? Is it Mexico? Whet's heppening thyah that cannot wait?"

My darling, please calm yourself and listen... Your father has fallen ill with some sort of dreadful fever. He's in agony and I feel helpless. The sound of her imaginary weeping gave Norton pause.

Norton's demeanor changed drastically. He sat on the edge of the bed and picked up the locket, bringing it close to his face. "It's alright, mother," he said solemnly. "Father will perheps not endure in his state of illness, but please... Please, Mother. You must take leave from Port Elizabeth immediately. I implohr you!" he pleaded. "Leave Father in the care of the physician and make haste away from thyah on the earliest vessel! Take Elise and return to England swiftly, I beg of you."

No Joshua, I cannot leave your dear father, don't be ridiculous. I must remain by his side and take care of him. Your sister and I are well, let your concerns lay with the health of your father.

"Please Mother, no," he begged. "Please heed my wahning, you must listen to me! Take Elise and go far away or you will suhrely succumb to the same wretched fate as father!"

Joshua, you are frightening your sister, please refrain from this horrible ranting. Your father will surely recover, my apologies for concerning you, my dear. His fever will pass, darling, he likely needs his rest is all.

"I beg of you Mother, take leave immediately. Immediately!"

I must go now, dear. I must tend to your father. Be a good lad, Joshua...

He beckoned her several more times, but the voice refused to reciprocate in his head. Norton began pacing furiously and tugging at his goatee. He was panic-stricken, his mind confusingly twisted into a demented re-enactment of events past for which he had no remedy.

A hidden part of his brain was controlling this, but to Norton it felt as real as on the day the news had arrived in London at his University. Days passed, and then weeks of silence from the visages in the locket. He became reclusive, worrying constantly and sleeping only upon exhaustion, pacing his tiny room and continuing to attempt to beckon the voice of his mother for a reply.

Finally she spoke. *My dear Joshua, you were correct. I'm afraid your father has passed on, my dear. And now your sister Elise and I have also fallen ill. I fear we may have the same condition. We should have listened to you, my darling boy. Your concerns were valid, how ignorant a mother can be to the words of her son... I fear this may be our final discourse my wonderful son, as I have not the energy to bring words to my mouth. But please know that you will always be loved, my dear son. Be a good boy, Joshua.*

"No... No, Mother, please say something more," he said in a deeply sorrowed tone. "Please do not leave me, Mother. Elise? No... This cannot be," he lamented.

Joshua could say nothing now, he knew what fate had befallen them. His pleas had not been heard, and he simply sat and wept loudly for their loss. He grieved for several weeks before finding solace and emerging from his lodgings. Some had begun to speculate that he had departed San Francisco again, as the banks which had shown patience with Norton had recently renewed their efforts to collect on their remaining debts.

But when he did re-emerge, he was as sprightly and more determined than ever to make his parents proud. A newly found freedom had washed over him and he was finally his own man. Norton, Bummer, and Lazarus became the royal 'We' he referred to in his continuous string of decrees and proclamations.

*　　*　　*

XIII

*   *   *

Four years had passed since Emma had arrived at the orphanage asylum, but she had made little progress toward attracting the attention of Nathan in any meaningful way. This was largely due to his - and all of the boys for that matter - lack of reciprocal interest in the opposite sex. And it had not helped that the genders were largely separated during most of the day, only seeing each other substantially during lunchtime recess. Added to this was the fact that her growing crush had heightened her level of timidity around him drastically.

As she predicted, Nathan had grown into his skin, and big ears, and was increasingly becoming an object of her obsession. Her attempts at passing flirtatious glances toward him or the pithy greetings she could manage to utter had made no difference in the slightest. She had kept her crush secretive from Sara and the other girls for the better part of a year, mostly for fear of being ridiculed and embarrassed.

But the tension in her head and heart had
finally reached its limit and in recent months she
had begun pointing out his physical attributes to
Sara and her other girlfriends; How his hair looked,
or his eyes, or how well he played baseball, or how
fast he could run, or how he was taller than Sara
now, or--

"Emma, geez!" Finally Sara had grown tired of
listening to Emma's frail voice carry on about him
and walked up to Nathan confidently that day on the
lawn.

"Hey Nathan, watcha doing?" she asked.

Nathan had turned fifteen that week. He was
nearly a year and half older than Emma and Sara,
having grown to the same height as the latter, with
a newly deepened voice and confident swagger. Like
the rest of the boys, he wore laced leather boots,
khaki pants with either a beige or navy buttoned
shirt without a collar – sometimes accompanied by
suspenders - and a typical coppola cap similar to
those worn by newspaper boys.

In warmer weather, the boys wore shorter
knickers and shirt sleeves, while Emma and the other
girls wore simple, yet pretty dresses of a solid
color and ribbons or barrettes in their hair year
round, adornin knit sweaters and scarves in
inclement weather. He swept his long bangs under his
cap and turned to face her. "Um, nothin' much. We
were just fixin' to--"

"--Emma likes you," she interrupted.

Nathan glanced over Sara's shoulder and became uncomfortably reddened. He had known Emma was standing there because he had noticed everywhere that she stood with great curiosity. The petite, red-headed creature was becoming a regular fixture in his mind.

"So," he said defiantly.

"Well you should, ya know, go talk to her... You like her too, right?" she asked bluntly. "I mean I see you looking at her all the time and--"

"No I don't," he deflected in a nervous laugh.

"Aw come on, Nathan. Just go talk to her," she pleaded. "I know you like her..."

"*No way*," he said in a frightened voice. "Not with all those other girls around... Uh-uh, no way," he said flatly as his head turned back and forth.

Emma's expression visibly changed at seeing this and her heart sunk at the rejection it implied.

"Fine," said Sara with her hands now on her hips, "I'll just go back and tell her that you're a big chicken." She flapped her elbows a few times with the threat.

"No. --Um... I mean, okay. But away from the others," he pointed. "Over there. Tell her to meet over there around the side in um, five minutes...or a little while," he uttered nervously.

"Are you gonna meet her there if she does, or are you gonna chicken out?"

"Yeah, --I mean No! I'll be there, geez," he said bashfully. Sara turned and strode smilingly back to where Emma and the other girls were standing. He could see Sara bouncing excitedly as she shared the newest juicy developments and the group collectively looked over to ogle him. *What am I doing*, he thought to himself as he realized the gravity of his impending doom. *Aw, geez, what am I supposed to say...*

Emma jumped once and then tried to contain her excitement when she heard her instructions. With her hands laced demurely in front of her, she shyly made her way to the far edge of the lawn and around the side of the building, biting her upper lip to keep from smiling. Her heart was racing with the intensity of a galloping horse and she stood fixing her hair as Nathan rounded the corner sheepishly.

"Hi," he grunted as he waved from a safe distance.

"Hi," Emma replied. The two stood in silence for what seemed like an eternity to both, the blood pumping toward their faces as they struggled to make eye contact.

Nathan finally spoke. "Is this about the race? 'cause I never even--"

"No, silly. --I just... I," she paused and slowly walked over to the corner of the building where Nathan now leaned. He stood sweeping the grass with his right shoe, his head drooping lazily, staring blankly at the ground with his hands in his pockets.

Emma lifted herself onto her toes when she reached him and pecked his cheek quickly. "There," she said with a smiling blush.

Nathan lifted his head, startled. "What, what was that for?" The words parted his lips with no conscious thought.

"Don't you like me?" Emma sulked.

"Sure... You're swell, I guess," he said as he came to his senses.

"Oh, good," Emma sighed in relief. She grabbed his wrist and pulled his hand out of his pocket taking it into hers and now smiling broadly. She began leading him around the corner to display their new mutual adoration, but Nathan recoiled from her grasp, scurrying backward quickly around the corner to where they had stood hidden from the sight of others.

"Wait," he said in a hushed whispered, "shouldn't we keep it a secret?" As he spoke, the bell began to chime, indicating that recess had ended.

"Oh," said Emma in dismay. "Okay, I guess." Her arms straightened and her hands folded and her fingers laced in front of her again as she grinned, happy enough for the victory of knowing they were finally together. "Meet here tomorrow then?"

"Yeah...swell," Nathan said in a sigh of relief. As they peered around the corner to see whether the coast was clear, they saw the backs of the others as they were heading inside the building.

*

The next day, Nathan had met with Emma as promised at their special location and the two had stood quietly facing one another for several minutes. They were both petrified of the new situation, not knowing what to say or do, if anything. Finally, Nathan worked up the courage and began to lean in to connect their lips, something he had rehearsed the previous night in his mind over and over again.

When he was within inches, however, Nathan recoiled and stood up quickly, flinging Emma's hands away from his grasp as his name was called loudly from behind him. Floyd had tracked him down and was beckoning him to take over as catcher in the ongoing game. Another boy had apparently caught the ball with his forehead instead of his glove.

"What are you guys doing?" he asked, perplexed by their coupling.

"Nothing, um, see ya Emma," he said abruptly and ran toward the field and took his place behind Slug at the plate. Emma stood motionless and in shock, slightly deflated and upset at Floyd, momentarily sad at her misfortune. But then began running and skipping swiftly back around the corner and toward Sara, excited to fabricate gossip about her first kiss with Nathan.

As Emma improvised the details of the story to Sara and the other girls several minutes later, Floyd stood nervously on the mound contemplating his next pitch to Slug. His first two had sailed into the dirt well out of range, an obvious result of his fear. He knew he had to throw a hittable ball, but Slug could hit almost anything and further than any other boy, so Floyd just closed his eyes, wound up his arms, and threw the ball as hard as he could toward the looming figure at the plate.

Slug stared intensely at the approaching ball with wide eyes and pursed lips. He swung forcefully at it and made solid contact, sending the ball high into the air and toward the far end of the field, nearly the same spot at which he had harassed Randy several years earlier. A boy back-pedaled toward the distant edge of the lawn, but could not reach the ball before it bounced heavily on the ground behind him and continued bouncing and rolling away from his pursuit and into the stone wall.

Slug had rounded second base before the boy had even touched the ball and now lumbered his stocky frame around the bases as quickly as he could manage. As the boy in the outfield released the ball, Slug had nearly reached third base. By the time the shortstop caught it, he had rounded the final turn and was heading toward home plate.

When the ball reached the small infielder, he turned quickly and hurled the ball toward the catcher as hard as he could. Slug dove head first with his arms outstretched as the ball entered the small leather glove of the catcher. His torso made contact with the dirt and he slid several feet, touching home – a small, sand-filled bag made of canvas - just as Nathan's glove met his back.

"*Out,*" one boy yelled hopefully from the outfield.

"I'm *safe,*" insisted Slug as he began to get up.

"No way, he was *out,*" yelled the shortstop who had thrown the ball to Nathan.

"I'm safe and that's that," Slug said as he stood and wiped away the dust from his newly soiled shirt.

"You were out by a *mile,*" insisted the shortstop confidently to Slug's back.

Slug turned to face the boy, whose demeanor quickly changed. He pursed his lips and began marching toward the small and now fearful boy.

"Slug, *no,*" warned Nathan from behind the plate. He knew Slug was right. The boy's throw to him had been accurate, but if anything it was a tie, and Nathan knew that a tie always goes to the runner. He ran quickly around and in front of Slug, trying to slow his angered momentum and talk sense into him.

"Get out of my *way*, Nathan," he snarled through his clenched teeth as he continued to move purposefully forward.

"You were safe, Slug, okay," he pleaded and then warned, "Leave him alone, or you'll get it from Miss Rose again."

"I wanna hear it from *him*. Get outta my way!" He shoved Nathan aside and marched toward the boy as the boy moved quickly toward the mound to hide behind Floyd. When Slug was near, the boy turned to run, but Slug had pounced toward him and grabbed the back of his sweater. Floyd had been whipped around behind Nathan, who was now within reach of Slug and the boy.

"*Let him go*, Slug," yelled Sara from the sidelines. "Pick on someone your own size!" She was the only one near to his size, but he chuckled at the notion. The boy fidgeted against Slug's grip.

"*Say it*," he demanded. He swatted the back of the boy's head with his free hand.

"*Slug*," yelled Nathan. He grabbed Slug from around his waist and began attempting to pull him away from the boy. As the momentum began to pull all three backward, Nathan raised his head just as Slug's elbow whipped around, inadvertently connecting solidly with Nathan's nose.

"*You were safe, you were safe,*" the frightened boy said desperately as Slug released him and shifted his focus to Nathan, who was cupping his bleeding nose in pain.

"*Hey,*" yelled Emma. She and Sara had been watching and now ran toward the boys on the field. Emma put her hands on Nathan's as Sara kicked Slug in his shin as forcefully as she could.

"*Oww,*" he cried loudly. Now Slug was hopping in circles on one leg as Nathan paced around aimlessly, covering his bloodied nose as Emma followed his every step.

"I told you to pick on someone your own size," said Sara with her hands on her hips.

Whistles began to blow, but were outmatched by the large steeple bell that began to ring as they approached the scene.

"Harold, this *will not* stand," Miss Rose paced behind her desk once Nathan and Slug were brought before her.

Slug had tried to explain the situation, lying about how he had politely asked the small boy to change his stance on the ruling and how the boy had pushed him, causing his elbow to inadvertently strike Nathan's nose. "It was an accident, Miss Rose... Promise!" he had pleaded.

"Is this true?" she asked Nathan.

Nathan slid his eyes toward Slug, fearing further repercussions from saying the wrong thing.

"Yes ma'am, he was safe," he said in a clogged and muted voice, holding a bloodied cloth to his nose.

"Well fortunately for you, Harold, I have made arrangements to transfer you to an apprenticeship," she began to explain. "You need to learn discipline and a trade, and Mr. Logan has agreed to take you on as his pupil," she said. "But let me make something abundantly clear, young man," she added with a pointed finger and her other hand firmly at her hip, "You will not be welcomed back if you misbehave, you will be left to rot out on the streets. Do I make myself clear, Harold?"

"Wha-... What am I gonna be doing, Miss Rose?"

"It's a biscuit factory, Harold," she chided condescendingly, "so I would assume you will be making biscuits."

"Oh," lamented Slug. "Well can I come play base--"

"No," said Miss Rose. "It's time you grew up young man," she stated sternly toward the fifteen year olds. "Now pack up your things and be down here within the hour. I've telephoned Mr. Logan and he is en route as we speak. Chop, chop now, Harold. Off you go." She attempted to dismiss Slug with a wave of her hand.

"But what about my friends and--"

"--You don't have any friends, Harold...believe me," she condemned. "Now off you go, we don't want to keep Mr. Logan waiting when he arrives."

Slug looked deflated and confused. He reached down to rub his shin once again and looked at Nathan for sympathy. Nathan simply shrugged.

"Go, Harold... Now!"

"Yes, Miss Rose," he complied. He arose from his seat and walked out the door with his head hung low, muttering that he was safe under his breath as he did. Once Slug had left the room, Miss Rose turned and walked toward the front of her desk.

"And as for you, Nathan," she said dryly, "there is absolutely no reason that a young man with your potential should be lollygagging around with the likes of that bully."

"Yes, Miss Rose," obeyed Nathan.

"Anyway, I have made similar arrangements for you. A man named Mr. Clifton will also be collecting you within the hour," she said with a grin. "This is a very important time in your life, Nathan, a grand opportunity for you to become something in this world. Now go to the clinical room for a fresh cloth and tend to that awful mess on your face," she waved with a disgusted grimace.

"But I--"

"Nathan? ...*Go*," she said sternly as she pointed toward the door.

Nathan reluctantly stood and exited Miss Rose's office on the ground floor of the orphanage. He, like the others, had felt a certain attachment to the place. Like all of the other children, he had seen it as a new beginning, and the last five years in the company of others had grown strong ties to the orphanage. He was saddened as he swapped the bloodied cloth for a fresh one and made his way upstairs to pack his things.

"See you around, Nate," was all Slug said as he angrily stormed past Nathan and out of the large sleeping hall toward the steps. Nathan did not have time to reply before Slug was well past him and was lost inside of the thoughts in his own head at that moment anyway. "Sorry 'bout your nose," Slug added as he descended the stairs.

The large sleeping hall was vacant and Nathan stood blankly for a moment, still fidgeting at his nose with the cloth as he approached his bed. Dropping to his stomach and hands, he reached under the space below the bed and found the canvas bag he had been given years earlier after the quake. He stood, tossed the bag onto the bed, and walked over to one of the many rickety clothes bureaus that lined the wall.

As he opened his drawer, he looked through the nearest window and noticed Slug as he sadly made his way onto the carriage in which Mr. Logan had arrived. He could faintly hear the mocking jeers of those children who had fallen victim to his violent outbursts throughout the years, but he sympathized with Slug's trepidation as he was experiencing his own. Logan was a large Russian man, middle-aged and with a large head and forearms the size of a newborn baby. Nathan realized why Miss Rose had chosen him, Slug would be no match for a man of his size.

He scooped up all of the contents of the drawer at once and walked back to the bed, shoving them carelessly into the bag. He then sat and opened the drawer of the small desk next to his bunk, grinning slightly when he saw the Bible that he had begun associating with punishment since his first transcription assignment. He realized he would no longer be forced to transcribe passages or listen to lectures from it, so he removed it and placed the Holy book under his bunk with rebellious pleasure.

He gathered his comics, playing cards, and marbles, throwing them all in with the clothes haphazardly and began to close the drawer. But as he did, he heard an odd sound, like a coin in its final stages of spinning before it comes to rest. He pulled the drawer open again and lowered his head to peer further inside. There, in the back corner of the drawer, was the necklace. *What the--*, he mumbled. He had forgotten altogether about it since stashing it there behind his collection of comic books and drawings, which had hidden it from him for years.

He grabbed the necklace and flipped the attached locket over and over several times in his hand, grinning at the recollection of the day it had come into his possession. As he began to open it, he heard the steps of heavy wooden shoes and quickly stuffed the item deeply into the bag, below his other possessions.

"Nathan?" Miss Rose asked in a booming voice.

"Yes, Miss Rose."

"Mr. Clifton has arrived to collect you earlier than expected. Have you packed all of your belongings?"

He looked out the window and saw a large vehicle. "Is that him?" he asked with sudden excitement. Although many of Henry Ford's model-Ts could be seen driving in the distance, Nathan had never seen one up close, and had certainly never thought he would be riding in one any time soon. Only men of prominence could afford such a luxury, so Nathan became wild with anticipation. Now he cared nothing about where he was going and everything about *how* he was going.

"Yes, Dear. Now listen to me," she said in a motherly voice. "Mr. Clifton is a very influential man and an excellent engineer. This is a rare opportunity for you, so I want you to treat it with a great deal of respect, is that clear young man?"

"Yes, Miss Rose, ma'am," Nathan said obediently, attempting to conceal his enthusiasm.

"Very well," she smiled proudly. "Come now, let's see you off."

Nathan picked up the bag and they began downstairs. His thoughts suddenly turned to Emma, wondering when, if ever, he would be allowed to visit her, to secretly meet around the corner of the building, to finish the kiss they had missed.

With most of the children gawking at the vehicle, Miss Rose escorted Nathan toward it. He hadn't seen the chance to escape her and go to Emma to say goodbye, but he waved toward her and the others with the hand that was not holding the reddening cloth to his nose, while Sara and Floyd looked on with obvious jealousy at his apparent good fortune.

"Like you mean it, son," reprimanded Clifton as Nathan weakly offered a timid handshake. "First impressions are all you get in this world, young man," he ordered, "now take a firm grip and look up here." He pointed the index and middle fingers of his left hand at his own small, but friendly brown eyes.

Albert Clifton was a short and stout man of forty-seven years, with matted black hair parted neatly down the middle and thick, bushy eyebrows. He had grown up in Maine, the son and grandson of a shipbuilding family originally from the northeast of England. His chubby face suited his convivial demeanor, but under his soft exterior lay a shrewd and intelligent civil engineer. He had made his way west to California after the earthquake, commissioned to design replacements for many of the structures which had been destroyed by the quake.

Clifton returned his derby hat to his head and walked toward the front of the vehicle to crank its engine to life. He cupped the crank-arm which protruded from the front of the vehicle with both hands, being careful to place his thumbs underneath it with the rest of his fingers; a precaution to avoid having them snapped backward from their joints if the engine kicked back during cranking.

"Good luck, Nathan," said Miss Rose loudly, above the noise of the six-cylinder engine. "Listen carefully to Mr. Clifton and you'll do well in life."

"Yes, ma'am... Miss Rose."

"Oh, and Nathan," she added, "remember your prayers." She presented him the Bible that Nathan had attempted to abandon under his bed.

"Yes, Miss Rose," he obliged as he reluctantly accepted it.

With a tip of his hat and the loud goodbyes of the children, Mr. Clifton put the shiny black vehicle into gear and began motoring away from the orphanage.

"Now I don't know what sort of shenanigans you were getting up to at that place," he said, contemptfully referring to Nathan's bloodied nose, "but there'll be no horsing around under my watch."

"Yes, sir." Nathan's head was circling in excitement as he examined the beauty of the automobile. Its glossy black exterior was contrasted by two heavily-padded, red bucket seats and the sleek white tires with spokes that glimmered against the temperate Spring day. The automobile could seat as many as six adults comfortably, with a retractable roof and the latest technology in axle suspension.

Once Nathan was satisfied that he had perused all of the features of the automobile, his gaze shifted westward toward the orphanage - his home for almost as long as he could recall, nearly his whole world of memories, and his lovely Emma.

"She's a beauty, ain't she?" he laughed. "We'll be back in San Jose in no time."

Nathan suddenly panicked, his head filling with dread at the comment. "San Jose? --How far is that?" he pleaded over the roar of the motor.

"About fifty miles give or take, but this beauty'll make it just fine, just fine indeed," replied Clifton as he tapped the dashboard with a laugh. "Play your cards right and you'll have one of your own some day," he added brightly.

Nathan's heart sank in his chest. He sat in silence for the remainder of the hour-long journey. As Nathan sat pitifully and endured Mr. Clifton's stories of business endeavors and negotiations, which seemed endless, he was lost in his own thoughts of wondering how much worse his life could possibly become.

Their pairing was no fluke, for although he had the tendency to ally himself with miscreants such as Slug, Nathan's innate capacity for understanding mathematics handily surpassed that of the other children. Clifton, a confirmed bachelor, became intent on cementing his legacy by bequeathing his knowledge to a young apprentice and Nathan fit the role.

"...Because there's two things I know for sure, son..." Clifton proclaimed loudly and he continued to ramble, "Ya can't teach stupid, and ya can't reason with crazy." He proceeded to laugh heartily at his own sense of humor. Nathan feigned a grin toward Clifton and returned to his distant gaze and self-pity.

*

Emma's stare was intense as she purposefully scraped a sharp stone into the gray bricks the next day. She was angrily retracing the shape of the heart outline she had been scraping diligently into the wall since recess had begun. The night before had been a mostly sleepless one, with Sara consoling Emma until exhaustion outmatched her sympathetic whispers from the bunk above.

The pleasant sunshine of late June had seemingly sensed Emma's sadness and had transitioned abruptly, willfully encouraging her tears by blowing whisps of dense fog eastward across the rolling hills of the peninsula to blanket the orphanage in a somber, gray jacket of mist.

"Young *lady*," chided one of the young staff toward Emma when she discovered her. Startled, Emma dropped the stone and gasped in consternation. "Come with me this instant!" She grabbed Emma by the arm and yanked her little frame around the corner and toward Miss Rose's office.

Emma sat in silent apathy in one of the two simple chairs facing Miss Rose's desk, staring downward, inwardly wishing her teddy bear were there to provide her with something, anything with which to release some of the anger that welled inside her. She suddenly missed her parents and began vividly recalling the early mornings she had crept downstairs to visit Monsieur Dubois to enjoy his company and delicious treats.

The simplicity of what she viewed as her disappearing youth flooded into her head copiously, a reflex to combat her despondently obvious heartbreak. She began to cry unabashedly as Miss Rose's footsteps could be heard to enter the room.

Miss Rose began reprimanding Emma to her back as she entered the room, explaining the nuances of her errors and how she would have to pay for her mistakes. She walked directly to the bureau and snatched the yardstick, which now had splotches of dried blood in various places along its length.

When she arrived at her desk and gazed toward Emma however, she paused, noticing the demure girl was no longer listening to her beration. "Emma, what is it," she stated dryly. "Do you still miss your parents after all this time?" she chuckled. "--Well, I'm afraid they are long gone young lady... And that is *no* excuse for--"

"Why did you send him *away*," she exploded angrily at Miss Rose's face.

"Excuse me?!" Miss Rose moved closer to Emma, confounded at the sheer audacity of the petite child to interrupt her. "How *dare* you interrupt me when I am speaking, you are *entirely* out of line!" She raised the yardstick high above her head, preparing to deliver its full force to Emma's bare arm.

Emma was heaving as she sobbed. "I... I *love* him and you sent him *away*," she screamed, then inhaled in a series of stuttered breaths. "You sent him *away*!" she repeated in a fit of tears.

Miss Rose stared intensely at the sobbing child for several moments, finally connecting the young girl's emotions with the events of the previous day. It became clear that Emma was upset for a completely different reason than the loss of her parents. Miss Rose's thoughts trailed off momentarily. As her mind began recalling her youth and a similar feeling of loss, the yardstick began falling slowly to her side. She recollected everything about the young man with whom she had shared her first intimacy, her eyes closing briefly at the thought of his face.

"Oh, ...dear Emma... No, sweet child," said Miss Rose as she morphed into an empathetic state. She knelt gently toward Emma and placed her free hand on Emma's forearm as she placed the bloodied weapon to the ground. "Nathan--," Emma's crying paused upon hearing his name, her head shooting upward with a hopeful glance. "--is a wonderful boy.

He'll surely come back to find you, Emma, when he is ready. But for now he must become a man on his own... My dear child, you are entirely too youthful to be strained to such a degree," she consoled softly. She began to return her piety and professionalism as she collected herself. "I'm aware that this may exceed your emotions today, but please trust me when I say that you can find joy in your heart that is grander that any boy," she smiled, placating her own emotional baggage with piety. "The word of God will show you more happiness than anything, my dear, if you remain focused on faith."

Emma became deaf to her words upon sensing Miss Rose's digression toward religion and away from Nathan. She eventually became calm and was granted her freedom from the clutches of Miss Rose with a warning. Before she fell asleep that night, Emma resolved to bury any emotions toward Nathan. From that night forward, she dismissed any thoughts of emotion that crept into her mind toward the boy who had nearly connected her lips with his.

XIV

"Every man has a sane spot somewhere."
   - R L Stevenson

*   *   *

Within a year of each other in 1865, Bummer and Lazarus were both killed. Lazarus had been poisoned on some meat that had been tainted with rat poison. Bummer was supposedly kicked by a drunk and had died a lingering death. Both were given Royal ceremonies, but Lazarus was clearly the more popular of the two. San Franciscans put up a $50 reward for the capture of Lazarus' poisoner, but no one was arrested. *The Daily Evening Bulletin* featured a long obituary entitled "Lament for Lazarus" in which they praised the virtues of both dogs and recounted their various adventures together. And after Bummer died, a eulogy appeared in *The Californian* on November 11, 1865:

The old vagrant 'Bummer' is really dead at last; and although he was always more respected than his obsequious vassal, the dog 'Lazarus,' his exit has not made half as much stir in the newspaper world as signalised the departure of the latter. I think it is because he died a natural death: died with friends around him to smooth his pillow and wipe the death-damps from his brow, and receive his last words of love and resignation; because he died full of years, and honor, and disease, and fleas. He was permitted to die a natural death, as I have said, but poor Lazarus 'died with his boots on' - which is to say, he lost his life by violence; he gave up the ghost mysteriously, at dead of night, with none to cheer his last moments or soothe his dying pains. So the murdered dog was canonized in the newspapers, his shortcomings excused and his virtues heralded to the world; but his superior, parting with his life in the fullness of time, and in the due course of nature, sinks as quietly as might the mangiest cur among us. Well, let him go. In earlier days he was courted and caressed; but latterly he has lost his comeliness - his dignity had given place to a want of self-respect, which allowed him to practice mean deceptions to regain for a moment that sympathy and notice which had become necessary to his very existence, and it was evident to all that the dog had had his day; his great popularity was gone forever. In fact, Bummer should have died sooner: there was a time when his death would have left a lasting legacy of fame to his name. Now, however, he will be forgotten in a few days. Bummer's skin is to be stuffed and placed with that of Lazarus.

—Mark Twain

Norton again retreated to the confines of his dingy little room for several weeks in ponderance, affected deeply by the loss of his cohorts. When he had voiced his frustration aloud, a series of thumps resonated through the wall of the adjacent room. "Quiet down!" the muffled voice had yelled through the thin wall. He had replied by repeatedly swinging his sturdy cane against the wall in a violent frenzy until a substantial amount plaster had fallen to the floor.

Again he emerged after several weeks to greet his royal subjects, arduously attending to his Royal duties and the humble citizens of his Empire. Politics returned to his focus as he issued regular decrees, chastising members of both parties for their incompetencies until his level of frustration warranted Imperial action.

PROCAMATION

Norton I., *Dei Gratia*, Emperor of the United States and Protector of Mexico, being desirous of allaying the dissensions of party strife now existing within our realm, do hereby dissolve and abolish the Democratic and Republican parties, and also do hereby decree disfranchisement and imprisonment, for not more than ten nor less than five years, to all persons leading to

any violation of this imperial decree.
Norton I. Given at San Francisco, Cal. this
12ᵗʰ day of August, A.D. 1869.

San Francisco Herald
Friday, August 13, 1869

He took great pride in the city of San
Francisco as one of its earliest settlers. He was
concerned that because the Central Pacific railroad
tracks ended there, that Oakland would usurp San
Francisco as the largest and most prominent city in
the West. He therefore gifted the island that lay
between the two, known then as Goat Island and later
as Yerba Buena Island, to Oakland as an act of good
will. Later in the month, he effectually collected
on his generosity when he issued another royal
decree:

PROCLAMATION

WHEREAS, it is our pleasure to acquiesce in
all means of civilization and population:
NOW, THEREFORE, we, Norton I, Dei Gratia
Emperor of the United States and Protector
of Mexico, do order and direct first, that
Oakland shall be the coast termination of
the Central Pacific Railroad; secondly, that
a suspension bridge be constructed from the
improvements lately ordered by our royal

decree at Oakland Point to Yerba Buena, from thence to the mountain range of Sacilleto, and from thence to the Farallones, to be of sufficient strength and size for a railroad; and thirdly, the Central Pacific Railroad Company are charged with the carrying out of this work, for purposes that will hereafter appear. Whereof fail not under pain of death. Given under our hand this 18th day of August, A.D. 1869.

He may have held a prestigious title, but his lifestyle was anything but aristocratic. The Freemason society to which he had belonged had offered to pay his rent and the Eureka Lodge indefinitely in exchange for his endorsement toward causes they supported. His political influence was palpable, a harsh word toward His Majesty could literally ruin a campaign. The society's treasury ran dry however, in 1865, and Norton was forced to become creative. He had designed a device which he claimed would automatically shift tracks on a railroad. The bank was unimpressed, but in Norton fashion, he declared them bankrupt due to owing him (them) money. The strategy somehow worked, likely due to its ludicrous nature, and the bank forgave him his debt.

PROCLAMATION

WHEREAS, the First National Bank refused to honor a small check of $100, to pay the value of a model for a Railway Switch invented by us, thereby endangering our private personal interest to a large estate:
AND, WHEREAS, it is publicly notorious that one or two of the Directors have large amounts in trust belonging to our personal estate;
NOW, THEREFORE, we, Norton I, Emperor of the United States and Protector of Mexico, do hereby decree the confiscation to the State of all interest of said Bank as security for any losses we may sustain by reason of their acts.

October 1869

His Majesty experienced a stroke of genius in late 1869, when he realized that his dominion should print its own currency. He quickly designed a series of bond notes, which he had printed in denominations ranging between fifty cents and ten dollars, to be paid in full plus four percent interest in 1880.

He planned to issue yet another series of bonds in 1880 which would subsequently mature in 1890 and likely would have perpetuated his ponzy scheme into the twentieth century had he lived long enough to do so. The notes were identical in size to the widely circulated US Dollar, and not surprisingly were accepted throughout most establishments in San Francisco as currency at face value.

PROCLAMATION

We, Norton I, by Grace of God Emperor of the United States of America and Protector of Mexico, being aware of the deplorable conditions affecting finances and desiring above all to alleviate suffering and afford to all our people a sound and safe security for their savings, have caused to be issued Treasury Certificates which are secured by all property of the Empire, and will be paid out of my private fortune if necessary, and which I decree shall be accepted everywhere as of the same value as gold coin or currency of the Realm. In the name of God, Amen.

November 1869

Once only was he arrested. In 1867, a newly-appointed, young and zealous deputy apprehended Norton and took him before the Commissioner of Lunacy after he had made a public speech, decrying as usual the state of politics in America.

The next day, when he was brought before the proper authorities, he was promptly discharged with an apology. The verdict was, 'that he had shed no blood; robbed no one; and despoiled no country; which is more than can be said of his fellows in that line." There were returned to him the key of the palace and the imperial funds amounting to $4.75 lawful money. For these, the Emperor regally gave his royal receipt and returned to business as usual.

His hair was now an unkempt mess of curls, his moustache and a thick goatee of graying hair below it had grown long and full. One of his admiring loyal subjects had gifted His Majesty a beaver-skin top hat decorated with a peacock feather and a rosette after the Civil War had ended, which he now adorned pridefully in place of the tattered Army hat he had worn for nearly a decade.

He frequently ran into his neighbor Samuel Clemens, who had changed his name to Mark Twain while living in Nevada just prior to moving west to San Francisco in 1864. Exchanges between the two intelligent eccentrics were generally brief, sometimes consisting of as little as one utterance from each. And Twain, along with any theatrical performance that dared open, would always reserve a balcony seat for the Emperor at his lectures. On one occasion, Norton had commented to Twain on the weather:

"Bloody cold, eh mate?" said Norton. "Can you recall any a Winter coldah than thess?"

"Yeah,... Last Summer," was all Twain had said.

His Imperial Majesty just grinned and stalked off with his usual dignity.

*

Emperor Norton continued to issue proclamations on a regular basis throughout his reign, motivated by both his own discontentment of the evils of the American government, whose existence he adamantly opposed but eventually obliged, and those of his royal subjects. But the issue regarding Oakland's rising prominence, which posed a threat to San Francisco's status as the beacon of the West, was consistently of great concern to His Majesty.

PROCLAMATION

The following is decreed and ordered to be carried into execution as soon as convenient:

I.   That a suspension bridge be built from Oakland Point to Goat Island, and then to Telegraph Hill; provided such bridge can be built without injury to the navigable waters of the Bay of San Francisco.

II.   That the Central Pacific Railroad Company be granted franchises to lay down tracks and run cars from Telegraph Hill and along the city front to Mission Bay.

III. That all deeds by the Washington Government since the establishment of our Empire are hereby decreed null and void unless our Imperial signature is first obtained thereto.

March 1872

During a journey to Oakland with the intent to convince representatives there to follow his instructions toward constructing a conduit between the cities, he noticed that many of the railcars of the Central Pacific Railroad Company were scrawled with the word FRISCO. Appalled by this, and believing it an insult to his great City, he issued fair warning:

PROCLAMATION

Whoever after due and proper warning shall be heard to utter the abominable word "Frisco," which has no linguistic or other warrant, shall be deemed guilty of a High Misdemeanor, and shall pay into the Imperial Treasury as penalty the sum of twenty-five dollars.

1872

When word returned a few weeks later that the inscriptions had not immediately been removed nor painted over, Norton's patience grew thin. But being the regal diplomat that he was, he tempered his words toward his sister city across San Francisco Bay and proposed again a measure that would effectually concentrate the power and prowess of the two cities.

PROCLAMATION

WHEREAS, we issued our decree ordering the citizens of San Francisco and Oakland to appropriate funds for the survey of a suspension bridge from Oakland Point via Goat Island; also for a tunnel; and to ascertain which is the best project; and whereas the said citizens have hitherto neglected to notice our said decree; and whereas we are determined our authority shall be fully respected; now, therefore, we do hereby command the arrest by the army of both the Boards of City Fathers if they persist in neglecting our decrees.

Given under our royal hand and seal at San Francisco, this 17th day of September, 1872.

Since the earliest days of his reign, newspapers and telegram operators had played practical jokes on the Emperor, urgently exchanging the proclamations he brought to them for hasty publication with falsified telegrams from politicians and royalty abroad.

One of the earliest was purportedly from Jefferson Davis, who had telegraphed to inquire if it were true that Norton was in sympathy with Lincoln accompanied by the request that $500 be sent, as Davis had but one pair of trousers, and even that was worn out. Another telegram was from

Lincoln. The then sitting President had thanked the Emperor for his support, explaining that he had a good story to tell Norton, but at present was engaged in settling accounts with a seedy individual named Davis.

If not for the timely visit of a certain regal man, Norton would have surely surmised their counterfeit nature much sooner. In 1876, Dom Pedro II, the Emperor of Brazil, visited San Francisco and asked to meet the Emperor of the United States. A messenger was dispatched jokingly to the smarmy Eureka Lodge and hours later Norton met Emperor Pedro at a royal suite at the newly opened Palace Hotel.

With an interpretor at his side, Emperor Pedro and Emperor Norton conversed for over an hour, divulging their opinions on a broad range of subjects. Dom Pedro gifted Norton an ornate cane, its elephant-molded handle cast of solid gold. In return, Norton issued Dom Pedro a silver key to the city of San Francisco and a promise to visit the Emperor at his beckoned call, if ever Brazil needed his assistance. It is unknown whether Dom Pedro II ever realized that the United States did not officially have an Emperor.

In the final hoax played upon Emperor Norton before his momentary lucidity ended the charade, Norton was induced to believe that, by marriage with Queen Victoria of Britain, he could bind closer the ties of the two great nations. As he read the telegram, he realized that the verbiage was dissimilar from the way a British Royal would scribe or dictate a royal letter to such a degree, that he very judiciously denounced this and previous claims, imposing new regulations toward the accepted validity of any and all communications.

PROCLAMATION

WHEREAS, there is every now and then a street report that the Emperor has received a telegram, or that he has done so and so, and on investigation found to be without foundation or fact;

WHEREAS, we are anxious that there should be no deception, and also that no imposter should make use of our authority;

KNOW, THEREFORE, all whom it may concern that no act is legal unless it has our imperial signature.

The Evening Bulletin, 1872

He unrelentingly pushed for recognition of his Empire and its Empirical status, both by admonishing government and by seeking support from organized groups such as the churches and synagogues he regularly attended.

PROCLAMATION

WHEREAS, there are great commotions in different quarters of the terrestrial globe, arising from discussing the question, "The Purification of the Bible--its True and False Lights," and fears are entertained that a war may break out at some remote point and spread all over the world, carrying in its winding course death, pestilence, famine, devastation and ruin;

WHEREAS such a state of affairs is to be deplored by all liberal-minded Christians, who oppose bigotry, charlatanism, and humbuggery, and who follow the golden maxim of the lamented Lincoln, "With malice toward none--with charity for all";

AND WHEREAS, Religion is like a beautiful garden, wherein the False Lights may be compared to the poppies, which fall to the ground, decay and are no more, the True Lights...bloom in everlasting etherealism, blessing forever the Creator and the Christian world by their Love and Truth;

NOW, THEREFORE, we, Norton I [etc.], do hereby command that all communities select delegates to a Bible Convention, to be held in the City of San Francisco, State of California, U.S.A., on the second day of January, 1873, for the purpose of eliminating all doubtful passages contained in the present printed edition of the Bible, and that measures be [adopted] towards the obliteration of all religious sects and the establishment of an Universal Religion.

1872

Logically, he was attracted to royalty. Lithographs of Queen Victoria of England, Queen Emma of the Sandwich Islands (Hawai'i), Empress Carlotta of Mexico, and Empress Eugenie, the wife of Napoleon the III graced his squalid walls. The Emperor of Brazil had once visited him in person and bequeathed him a walking cane of solid gold, oblivious to the possibility that Norton was not Royalty.

Among his final proclamations was to the effect that the Emperor contemplated marriage, but to avoid arousing jealousy among the fairer sex, he played no favorites and they were to decide for themselves which one of them should be Empress. In truth, he had grown tired of living in conditions of squalor at the disheveled Eureka Lodge and had pushed forth the notion in order that he be given more suitable accommodations:

PROCLAMATION

Whereas, it is our intention to take an Empress, and in consideration of the visits by the Royalty abroad, we, Norton I, Dei Gratia Emperor of the United States and Protector of Mexico, do hereby command the builders of the Palace Hotel to fit up a portion of their building for our Imperial Residence, as becoming the dignity of a great and hopeful nation.

1875

On a crisp evening in January 1880, the old man made his way toward his destination, a balcony seat reserved for him, and a lecture entitled, "Decay of the Art of Lying." But the old man would fail to arrive at his destination. As he paused after only a few blocks to take another swig from his flask, his heart suddenly jolted.

His eyes now flaring, he intentionally dropped the flask and clutched his chest, struggling to balance himself with his cane, managing to do so only long enough to collapse against a street lamp and slide toward the earth with a THUNK! He reached into his breastcoat and handed a young boy the one item he valued most.

The following day, the *San Francisco Chronicle* published the man's obituary on its front page:

PROCLAMATION

Le Roi est Mort

On the reeking pavement, in the darkness of
a moonless night under the dripping rain...,
Norton I, by the grace of God, Emperor of
the United States and Protector of Mexico,
departed this life".

January 18, 1880

Initial funeral arrangements included a
pauper's coffin of simple redwood. However, members
of the Pacific Club established a funeral fund that
paid for a handsome rosewood casket and arranged a
suitably dignified farewell. Norton's funeral was a
solemn, mournful and large affair. Respects were
paid, as it was reported, "...by all classes from
capitalists to the pauper, the clergyman to the
pickpocket, well-dressed ladies and those whose garb
and bearing hinted of the social outcast."

Some accounts report that as many as 30,000
people lined the streets to pay homage, and that the
funeral cortege was nearly two miles long. He was
buried at the Masonic Cemetery, at the expense of
the City of San Francisco, and his funeral
attendance remains the largest in San Francisco to
date. A tribute to his life, Dr. George Chismore
dedicated a poem:

NORTON IMPERATOR

"No more through the crowded streets he goes,
With his shambling gait and shabby clothes,
And his furtive glance and whiskered nose--
       Immersed in cares of state.
The serpent twisted upon his staff
Is not less careless of idle chaff,
The mocking speech or the scornful laugh,
       Than be who bore it late.
His nerveless grasp has released the helm,
But ere the Lethean flood shall whelm
The last faint trace of his fancied realm,
       Let us contrast his fate
With other rulers and other reigns,
Of royal birth or scheming brains,
And see if his crazy life contains
       So much to deprecate.
No traitorous friends, or vigilant foes,
Rippled the stream of his calm repose;
No fear of exile before him 'rose,
       Whose empire was his pate;
No soldiers died to uphold his fame;
He found no pleasure in woman's shame;
For wasted wealth no well-earned blame
       Turned subjects' love to hate.
No long and weary struggle with pain;
One sudden throe in his clouded brain
Closed forever his bloodless reign,
       With every man his friend.
For Death alone did he abdicate.
What Emperor, Prince or potentate,
Can long avoid a similar fate
       Or win a better end!"

                *   *   *

XV

* * *

Hey," said Sara, nudging Emma while they sat at a cafe in North Beach, "isn't that Nathan?"

Nearly six years had passed, but Emma's heart began racing as if she was meeting him around the side of the orphanage the day they had almost kissed. She and Sara had recently completed high school and were studying nursing as interns at the University of San Francisco Medical Center, USFMC.

"Oh my, it *is* him, *look at him*," exclaimed Emma, her hand suddenly covering her mouth in awe. Nathan had grown from a boy into a man in the six years that had passed. He wore a sleek brown suit, polished shoes, and one of the newly popular straw boater's hats that every man seemed to be wearing that year. He had recently reached the age of twenty-one and was working toward his civil engineering degree from San Jose State University.

"Nathan?!" yelled Sara. He was across the street looking at the War headlines on the paper he had just purchased from the paperboy. His gaze arched and looked around. "Nathan!" she repeated.

Nathan finally spotted the girls seated at the cafe across the street, Sara waving furiously while Emma squirmed uncomfortably in her chair. He squinted at them in confusion, then looked both ways for traffic and smoothly walked across the street with the newspaper neatly tucked under his arm.

"Emma?" he guessed at the sight of her flowing auburn hair. "Sara? --Wow! What are you-- How, how are you?" he finished awkwardly. "Geez, look at you both! I guess we're all grown up," he laughed.

"Look at yourself," said Sara flirtatiously.

He focused his gaze to the young lady at his left. "Hello, Emma."

"... Hello, Nathan," she said nervously. The re-emergence of the feelings she had suppressed for six years had flooded back into her head like a tsunami, but she fought them as best she could by acting coy and aloof.

"Gosh, how about this, huh? I thought you two would be long gone by now, how long has it been, five years?"

"Six," chided Emma dryly, quickly regaining her confidence.

Sara spoke up in Emma's stead. "What, so you're a bigshot now? Couldn't swing by to say hello?"

"No, no," he said cheerfully. "It's not like that at all... I was taken down to San Jose, didn't they tell you? I tried to visit, but, well...

Mr. Clifton has this great business and I--" He sensed that he was blabbering and altered his discourse. "Say, Emma... Are you, um, perhaps free for dinner this evening?" he asked meekly.

Emma was taken aback momentarily and looked over at Sara for direction. "Oh," she said as she began to blush. "Um, why yes, Nathan, that would be lovely."

"How rude of me, Sara," Nathan added, "would you both like to join me this evening?"

"No, no," Sara replied quickly as she shook her head, "I'd just be in the way." She smiled fakely at Nathan and peered over at Emma.

Nathan clapped his hands together and turned toward Emma again. "Swell... Say, eight-ish at the Tadich Grille? Um, or I can collect you? Where are you stayi--"

"--The Tadich?" Sara interrupted jealously. "Sounds like a certain someone is doing quite well for himself."

"Yes, well... I've had good fortune these past few--"

"--Eight o'clock sounds fine," interrupted Emma. "I'll meet you there."

"Very well, then. Eight o'clock it is... Ladies." Nathan tipped the brim of his hat graciously toward them and returned across the street, dismayed by his luck and suddenly becoming nervous. Emma had crept into his mind from time to

time over the years, but seeing her now sent a
shockwave through his spine. It was as if he was
meant to run into her at that particular place and
time, when everything was going his way.

*

The Tadich Grille in downtown San Francisco had
been around since the Gold Rush and continued to
cater to the elites of the city. Even sixty years
later, it offered an ambiance resembling that of the
Old World. Classic stained-glass lamps with red
bulbs surrounded by velveteen furniture, a massive
mahogany bar with rivoted and plush barstools, and
bartenders who seemed as if they had been under its
employ for decades.

Nathan stood outside against the wall, smoking
cigarettes in succession and hoping Emma wouldn't
stand him up. He doubted himself every few minutes
or so, beginning to pace back and forth across the
establishment's frontage, looking up from his shoes
nervously from time to time to see whether Emma
would be in sight. Seven forty-five and then Eight
o'clock arrived quickly on the face of his
wristwatch. A cool sweat came over him at twenty
minutes past, realizing that his ego's recollection
of his suave invitation was being betrayed by a
lesser reality. *Why would she come*, he thought to
himself. *I never even tried to visit...*

Just as he began contemplating leaving, she appeared. The streets were bustling with the sounds of musicians playing ragtime piano and horns piping festively through open windows of the many saloons and restaurants that lined this boisterous part of town. Pedestrians were scattering about, some more inebriated than others.

But there she appeared, standing out like a cherry on an ice cream sundae. Her auburn hair, now long and flowing with neatly curled bangs, was clipped back by a large dragonfly barrette that sparkled against the fog-swept streetlights as her hips trounced toward him with pre-determined confidence. She wore a heavy red coat with large wooden buttons over a gray dress to her knees which allowed half her regular stride and wide-heeled strapless shoes.

Nathan discarded his cigarette without moving his stare. The moment at the orphanage became an instant ago and he was mesmerized. He swiftly straightened his appearance, matting his hair and clothing as she approached while playing his best act to conceal his excitement at her arrival.

"A Whiskey Sour and... What would you like, Emma?

"Oh, a Tom Collins please."

"Miss, you sure you're old enough to be served," asked the bartender. "I wouldn't ask, but I smell bacon if ya catch my drift..."

"Oh, yes sir," Emma replied, "I turned eighteen a few months back."

The bartender nodded and began fixing their drinks. The crowd was noisy, but Nathan and Emma managed to yell short questions and compliments toward each other and began laughing as the alcohol crept into their systems, increasingly enjoying their reunion. They tasted each other's dishes when they arrived at their dimly lit table and shared a bottle of Bordeaux. Emma was clearly impressed and Nathan was on a cloud.

"And what about this war, huh?" said Nathan. "Amazing. I thought we were clear from it... And Floyd? All those miles away?"

Floyd had joined the Army and had been one of the first to be deployed to Europe after Russian submarines had destroyed several US vessels in the North Atlantic, forcing a reluctant President - Woodrow Wilson - to enter the United States into what he had hoped would be 'a war to end all wars.'

"Miss Rose directed Floyd toward the military because of his infatuation with those silly airplanes," said Emma of the recent invention.

"You'd never get me up in one of those things. Apparently he's stationed in Rome right now, but too bad he can't enjoy it," she added. "Miss Rose said-"

"--Oh, *good God*," interrupted Nathan. "How is that *wicked* woman?" Did she ever show you her beating stick?"

Emma's thoughts returned to the awful day that she had confronted the Headmaster of the orphanage. Her gaze shifted downward in discomfort at the thought.

"Oh, Emma, my apologies," he retracted. "I didn't mean to stir up--"

"--No," Emma said as she looked up and managed a smile, "it's alright, Nathan. She meant well I suppose, but... I feel sorry for her," she said, allowing her empathy to subside. "After all, she helped to enroll Sara and I into the nursing program... So I guess she wasn't *so* bad, right?"

Nathan refrained from sharing his traumatic experiences with Miss Rose. "Well that's just swell, Emma. Hey, my boss has me workin' on some projects down in San Jose next week," he said as he changed the subject, "but I'd love to bring them up and show them to you sometime."

"Oh, Nathan, that would be wonderful, but I'm in school an awful lot until the end of the month. Three weeks more and I'm officially a Nurse!" she beamed.

"That's great!" They toasted their glasses in celebration, allowing their past to drift away. "Well it's no problem, I can take the train up here next weekend or anytime and visit... That is, um, if there isn't... I mean--"

"--That sounds lovely," Emma interrupted.

"I just broke it off with a boy recently if you

must know," she admitted bashfully.

Nathan smiled. "Shall I walk you home?"

"Yes, that would be delightful," she said playfully.

They finished their wine in silent adoration of each other as they enjoyed the ambient atmosphere of the sounds that filled the busy restaurant. Nathan paid the bill in crisp five dollar bills when it arrived and courteously assisted Emma into her jacket, and the couple made their way outside into the chilly evening.

"That was simply wonderful, Nathan," said Emma as she tucked her hair into her knitted cap. "You're quite the gentleman."

Seeing this as his opening, Nathan placed his arm around Emma's side and pulled her toward him. He gazed at her intensely as he planted a kiss firmly on her lips without pause. Their connected energy caused both to lose themselves in each other for a moment, forgetting themselves in a sea of lust. As they slowly released, gazing at each other in a daze, Emma blushed and took Nathan's hand in hers, struggling to keep her feet on the ground.

He hired a taxicab to deliver them to Emma's campus in Cole Valley a few miles away, the driver grinning at the obvious energy emanating from the rear seat. They sat in silence, holding hands and imagining their futures together. At the door to her dormitory, they kissed again, sealing their connection. Emma slowly entered after the door was opened, blowing Nathan a kiss as she disappeared.

*

"It was magnificent, Sara... He's *so* sweet... And *so romantic*," she added as she hugged herself and swiveled her torso. "He kissed me once below the streetlamp, and then--"

Emma paused, sensing that something was wrong. "Sara, what is it?" She sat down next to Sara on her bed. "--Oh, Sara, don't worry... You'll find someone soon, I promise," she consoled.

"No, Emma, that's not it," Sara deflected seriously. "It's quite far from that... Millions of miles from that, actually." She looked up at her dearest friend. "They're sending us to France, Emma."

"What?" Emma stood abruptly. "Who, the school?"

"No, Emma, the Red Cross."

"To France? Why?"

"We leave Thursday morning, so you should start packing your--"

"This Thursday?! Sara, that's in three days! What about Na--, What about school?!" As the words left her mouth Emma's world was flipping upside down in front of her.

"Emma, please, you're hurting my ears... Remember when those ladies came into our classroom and asked for future volunteers of America?"

"Yes, but that was *future* volunteers Sara, not *three days from now* volunteers," Emma retorted. "Okay... Let's be rational about this," she said as she began pacing rapidly. "I mean... I guess it would be exciting to see Paris, right? ...And we'll be together," she said nervously as she paced. "...And think of the food, Sara--"

"--Emma we're not being sent to France to shop and meet boys," Sara interrupted, "this is a *war!*"

The girls stared at each other in terror until Sara collected her thoughts and spoke. "We're only being sent because the other nurses were killed by *bombs,* Emma... *Killed.* We're not going on a *goddamn vacation!*"

Noticing Emma's discomfort, Sara softened her tone and attempted to explain the information she had been given. "We're being sent to someplace called Brest, wherever that is, and we'll--"

"Breast?" interrupted Emma with a tearful snort. "Are you pulling my leg, Sara! That's not funn--"

"--*Dammit*, Emma, Brest! Brest!... *B-R-E-S-T.* It's a real place in France!"

Emma thought for a moment as she continued pacing between the beds of the small room. "Are all the girls going?"

"Seven of us from school and loads more apparently, from all over the country. Miss Cline said that our names were near the top of the list because we're, um... because we don't have any family," Sara explained. "She said the real nurses would help us with the final lessons when we arrive." Sara suddenly burst into tears. "Emma, I'm scared..."

Emma had only witnessed Sara cry once, and on that occasion she had broken two of her fingers when a window had slammed down onto them. She calmed herself and sat next to Sara again, attempting to be the stronger of the two, but quickly embraced Sara as they both became overwhelmed with emotion.

Nathan had disappeared momentarily from her mind for the past few hours, but crept back into it again as she struggled to fall asleep. She panicked when she realized she had no way to inform him of her departure. She began regretting the outfit she had bought for the date, as it had fully depleted her savings and had even forced her to borrow money from Sara's. Worse yet, she wouldn't receive her stipend for another week. And with that thought, she wondered whether she would receive anything at all now that she was being shipped overseas.

Regardless of her lack of money, she had no address with which to contact Nathan. *What was the name of the man he mentioned,* she thought to herself... *Clifford? Kaufman, was it?* The name escaped her. Emma's hopes of seeing Nathan again before her departure   eventually resolved to its impossibility, her thoughts giving way to the enjoyable evening they had shared to lift her spirits.

The next day when the girls arrived at class, their teacher handed them each a diploma, specially printed and signed by the dean. They were officially nurses and for a brief moment their heads filled with pride, the bittersweet reality of their pending departure to foreign lands taking its place. Their teacher dismissed them from her care, hugging each with a tear in her eyes and wishing them safety.

As Emma and Sara began packing their things, they began to discuss their journey to the unknown land of France. They wondered how far they were from France, what it would be like to ride a train, to see new places, where Brest was, and what their responsibilities would be.

A few days later, Emma and Sara boarded the ferry headed for Oakland with their luggage, proudly wearing the American Red Cross uniforms that had been furnished to them. The dress was made of gray cotton with a wide white collar and white cuffs and the Red Cross brassard on its left sleeve. Accompanying the dress was a folded white hat, also with the Red Cross logo, and tall leather boots that laced up through tens of eyelets.

*   *   *

XVI

*   *   *

Nathan thought of Emma constantly throughout the week following their encounter, reminiscing every detail of every moment with her. From his first glimpse at the cafe, to the stunning, auburn-haired figure approaching him on the street later in the evening, he realized what true beauty could be. He retraced their conversation at dinner and their first - and second - kisses. He became distracted in school and in the evenings at Mr. Clifton's office, to the degree that Mr. Clifton remarked of being able to see a red arrow sticking out of Nathan's back.

The following Friday at exactly five o'clock, Nathan jumped up from his desk at Mr. Clifton's company, grabbed his jacket and hat, and double-checked to make sure the locket he planned to gift to Emma was on his person, and made haste to the train station in San Jose. The ride was agonizingly long as his head swirled with uncertainty, but eventually he calmed himself and settled into reading the newpaper he had bought at the station.

REAL DOGS OF WAR, RED CROSS AIDS,
ON WAY TO BATTLEFIELDS STREWN WITH WOUNDED

The article went on to say that hundreds of surgeons and nurses from throughout the United States were being deployed to the battlefields. It warned of an increase in drug prices due to the demand for morphine and other war-time remedies. Nathan thought of his childhood friend Floyd, wondering where he was and the horrors he must be enduring, of those dead or wounded, and how the War would unfold.

He arrived in San Francisco around seven in the evening and hired a taxicab to drive him to Emma's dormitory in Cole Valley, stopping briefly at a florist to purchase a bouquet of fresh flowers for his new sweetheart. It was another beautiful Spring day, which only heightened Nathan's buoyant mood. He arrived at the campus and scurried toward her dormitory with long, purposeful strides. At the formidable arched wooden doors, he knocked loudly. Moments later a young lady opened the door to greet him. He removed his hat and smiled broadly at her.

"Good evening, I'm here to see Emma Haley."

"Oh," said the girl, "I'm afraid gentlemen are not permitted inside."

"Of course, Miss, I understand that. But if you

would be so kind as to alert her of my presence," he asked politely.

"Very well, please wait here."

"Thank you kindly," he grinned smugly.

She closed and locked the door, as instructed by the dean during her orientation. Several minutes later, she returned and unlocked the door. Nathan cleared his throat in nervous anticipation, eager to lay eyes on his Emma after the long week of anticipation.

"Oh, I'm very sorry, sir," she said, "Emma is no longer here."

"Pardon me?" Nathan asked with bewilderment. "You mean she's out for the evening?"

"Um, not exactly," she lamented. "She's part of the group that was sent over."

Irritated, Nathan became less polite. "Young lady, I don't follow what you are trying to say. Sent over *where* exactly?"

"Well to the War of course," she said. "Several of the girls--"

"To the *War*? What do you mean, to the War!" Nathan was confounded.

"I'm real sorry, Mister," she added sheepishly, "They left a few days ago..."

Nathan was beside himself with devastation, his world had been shattered in an instant. He stood staring at the girl for a while, digesting the information. "I see," he finally said under his breath. He thanked the young lady and turned away, a flurry of different emotions sweeping over him. He departed the school and wandered aimlessly through the evening and into the night. He found himself downtown near the Tadich and proceeded to imbibe excessively, becoming boisterous when the barman cut him off and eventually being forcibly removed.

He stumbled a few blocks toward the embarcadero and sat at the water's edge, sad and deeply concerned for Emma. As if adding insult to injury, a fresh dollop from a seagull splattered his forehead the moment he removed his cap. He hardly reacted, blankly staring forward at the island that dotted the bay and the hills beyond Oakland behind them.

The wind blew a chill beyond his already cooled mood and the squawks of the gulls flying overhead made the intermittent moon among the clouds fittingly ominous. When he awoke late the next morning and collected himself, he made his way to the main offices of the school to attempt to learn more about the details of Emma's deployment.

"Well how the heck should I contact her?"

"Sir, please calm down... As I said, we have no way of knowing which outpost she'll be serving until next week when we receive the manifest," said the woman.

"Golly, tight ship you run here," he quipped sarcastically. "Apologies," he added a moment later. "I'm just upset is all."

"I understand young man, these are troubling times," the woman consoled. "If you'd like to leave a letter, we can place it in the post with the rest when we have more information on her whereabouts."

"Yes, that's a fine idea, thank you," he said.

Nathan borrowed a writing tablet and fountain pen from the woman and took a seat on the bench in the lobby. He stared at the ceiling for several minutes before pouring his thoughts.

San Francisco, CA September 16, 1917

Dear Emma,

I've just been informed that you have been
deployed to France. At first I was upset that
you did not contact me, but now I realize you
have no means to do so. I'm very distraught
as I pen this, as your school seems to know
nothing of your whereabouts thus far.
Oh Emma, how I had wished to gaze upon your
sweet face this evening and the next, and the
next after that. The anticipation to see your
lovely face was my constant distraction, and
now I feel the pain of our distance yet again
as you are far from my grasp. I hope that you
enjoyed our evening together as much as I.
You cast a spell upon my mind... My dear
Emma, please be safe and know that my
thoughts are with you and Sara. I anxiously
await your reply and miss you dearly.

Yours Truly and Sincerely,

Nathan

Clifton Engineering Consultants, Inc.
1003 W. Main Street, San Jose, CA, USA

*

Prior to the completion of the Transcontinental Railroad in 1869, the journey across America took several months, often proving perilous by the hazards of nature and the elements. With its completion, more and more Americans were traveling into and settling the vast lands of the mid and western states in relative comfort and safety.

Now, in mid-1917, the journey from San Francisco to New York City could be completed in as little as five days, depending of course on the number of stops and class of travel. With the timely importance of their arrival in France, the Red Cross was subsidized by the Federal Government to see that all of their travel needs were met expediently. Emma, Sara, and the rest of the hundreds of American surgeons, nurses, and volunteers were well-accommodated and arrived in just four and a half days, stopping briefly in Chicago to pick up more recruits and soldiers.

Emma and Sara were easily distracted from the dangers of their destination by the newness of travel. Neither had ever even been over the Bay to Oakland, let alone ridden a train across the entire country. They marveled at the natural beauty and diversity of the landscape through the Sierra Nevadas, the Rocky Mountains, and the great plains leading to Illinois. They slept soundly with rocking buzz of the grand machine and enjoyed the journey immensely. When they arrived in New York, they were immediately taken to the *Saratoga* to embark for the sea voyage to France.

The *Saratoga* had had transported the first wave of Red Cross volunteers in 1915 and had returned with over two thousand injured men. The ship was previously a steamer for the Ward Line on the New York to Havana route, and considered the fastest steamship in coastal trade. She was over four hundred feet in length and could carry over twelve hundred passengers. She was hurriedly outfitted for troop transport and medical duties, outfitted with state-of-the-art operating rooms and X-ray labs, and became part of the first group of the American Red Cross convoy to France.

"My goodness," gasped Sara, "look at the *size* of it!"

"Yes, it's quite unbelievable," said Emma with less enthusiasm. Her thoughts were a few steps ahead of Sara's; of arriving in a foreign land and testing her newly acquired knowledge, of tending to badly injured men with fear in their eyes. The journey had already overwhelmed their senses to a strange point of calmness, where their minds were acute to everything around them more readily than ever before.

"Emma, please," said Sara. "Try to enjoy things while we can, hmm?"

Emma realized that Sara was right. There was no immediate danger and here they were, about to embark onto a massive ocean vessel toward a new land and a good cause. She did her best to perk up and ignore the negative thoughts that swarmed in her head. Emma managed a smile and grabbed Sara's arm, laughing as they skipped toward the ramp.

As the convoy of Red Cross ships made their week-long voyage across the Atlantic toward Brest, submarines intercepted their positions and began firing torpedoes. The two ships that accompanied the *Saratoga* narrowly avoided being hit and the convoy dispersed. They regrouped the next day but were forced to re-route to Saint-Nazaire, a few hundred kilometers south of their original location. Once they arrived, passengers were quickly placed on trains toward various destinations.

Emma and Sara were sent to the southern border of France, atop a hill near the beautiful coastal city of Marseilles. The previous Red Cross encampment had been further east near the border of Italy until a bomb killed half of the already wounded soldiers and several nurses and medics. Emma and Sara arrived safely at nearly midnight after the long ride and were immediately shown to their quarters.

Sara awoke to the abruptness of the voice.

"*Incoming wounded! Incoming!*" yelled one of the nurses before rushing away to assist with the wounded. She nudged Emma firmly as she moved from her bed and began getting dressed. Emma was completely disoriented, only realizing her new surroundings once she noticed the speed and intensity of Sara's movements. She jolted upright and began looking around at the chaos that ensued.

The dozens of cots in the large canvas tent were swarmed with nurses who were agitating like disturbed hens in a coup. She quickly stood and put on her dress, laced up her tall leather boots, adorned her white cap, and made her way outside of the large tent with Sara and the others.

The sun was just above the horizon and she momentarily noticed the beautiful dichotomy of scenery in the background. Toward her south at the water were neatly placed homes and buildings, painted in white with red-tiled roofs, the square steeples of several churches only adding to its splendor. Further in the distance atop a hill appeared an old stone castle with four rooks at its corners and the whitewash of the sea's waves was gently crashing upon its deserted shore.

Sara grabbed Emma's arm, jolting her out of her daydream and into the moment, a reality for which nothing could have prepared her. Sara brought her along begrudgingly, joining the others who were running toward the medical tent.

As they approached the tent with the large red cross emblem sewn into it, several trucks were being unloaded. Those who could walk or limp were assisted by one nurse, while others who were more gravely injured were hoisted on gurneys by two or three men toward the intensive care portion of the tent. Instinctively, Sara and Emma ran to the aid of two unaccompanied men who were limping, one of which bandaged over a significant portion of his face and head.

Upon entering, the sporatically lit tent felt and smelled as if they had entered the bowels of hell. Four rows of twenty beds lined the tent and the few that were vacant were filling up quickly. Sara escorted the wounded man to a desk, where a receptionist sat disillusioned and bereft of emotion.

"Name and hometown," the woman asked flatly.

"Corporal Randy Thompson... San Francisco, California."

"Randy?!" exclaimed Sara.

"Yes, that's right," he replied calmly.

"Oh my goodness, Randy," she said, "It's --It's me! Sara, from home!"

His gaze turned from the woman behind the desk as he looked Sara up and down with his unbandaged eye. "Well I'll be a son of a gun! What are--"

"--Miss, please," interrupted the woman,

"you'll have time for that later. I need to admit this young man and have him attended to."

"Oh, yes of course," said Sara accordingly.

The woman asked him several questions and then directed Sara to accompany him to a bench where several of the lesser-wounded men were sitting idly. "What happened?" she asked.

Randy explained the calamity of the day's events; that they were on a routine scouting mission and were attacked by surprise upon exiting their trenches through a heath by mortars and gunfire.

"I don't know how I'm still alive, honestly," he laughed half-heartedly. He shook his head in a daze and looked up to the darkened canopy.

"Well you are, so thank your lucky stars," Sara consoled. "Looks as if your friends aren't so lucky..."

"Hell," he said flatly, "has no place for me."

His upward stare was confusing to Sara, whose eyes grew more and more dilated from the depth of his words and the sheer quantity of bloodied faces in her peripheral. Her head darted in every direction for sanctuary, finding only more disfigurement, the sounds of agony caustically overwhelming her senses. She aimlessly dabbed the unharmed side of Randy's face until he graciously moved her wrist to its other side. She was in a dream state while awake, her subconscious feeding her brain melodies of sincerity to combat her inability to cope with things.

"So why did you stop visiting the orphanage? Did you move?" Sara asked without thinking.

"Oh. Um," he momentarily relished in the diversion. "Well I was out there one day on the lawn, showing Floyd some stuff we picked out of this house, and that bully Slug layed into me somethin' fierce," he laughed. "Bet I could whoop him now, though," he added boldly, his face becoming contorted as it struggled against the bandages.

"Floyd was there too...in the field, I mean. But I think he took a bullet, not sure if he made it."

Emma arrived at the bench next to Sara with her wounded soldier and helped him sit. As they began tending their wounds, Sara mentioned that Floyd might be among the wounded. Emma had been reluctant to send a letter to Nathan because neither of the girls could remember his surname. She hurriedly finished bandaging her patient and ran to the receptionist, who pointed to Floyd's bed at the far corner of the tent. She made her way through the dozens of medics and came to Floyd's bed.

"Floyd? Oh my goodness," she gasped and covered her mouth. "It's me, Emma Haley...from, from home!"

The entire left half of Floyd's face had been mangled by shrapnel and he had been shot in the right shoulder and leg. An attending surgeon was working to remove the bullet in his shoulder.

"Emma," he murmured through the half of his mouth and lips that still functioned, "It hurts ...real...bad."

"Oh, no. Floyd, sweety. You hang in there, be strong, okay? The surgeon will fix you up right as rain, I promise," she said with a forced grin. Floyd's good eye fluttered, trying to stay open against the morphine. Sensing she had little time, she continued to talk to him, telling a quick story of better times at the orphanage, when Floyd had hit Slug with a pitch and was chased around the field. As he struggled to grin, she seized the opportunity and selfishly asked Floyd about Nathan's name. He struggled to find the answer in his shell-shocked brain, his eye moving to the left and right as he stared toward the ceiling.

"--Pur... Purcell," he finally whispered.

Of course, Emma thought to herself, *how could I forget.* She consoled Floyd for the next few moments until another nurse stole her away toward other patients. As she was reluctantly guided away, she looked back at Floyd with grave concern. His head fell to the side and his eye fluttered closed. Moments later, Floyd took his final breath.

Emma had already revised her original letter to Nathan several times as the journey had unfolded, but the events of that day warranted starting a completely different one. She discarded the old letter and added Nathan's surname to the envelope before beginning a new letter. It was marked for delivery to Nathan Purcell, care of Mr. Clifford, San Jose, California, USA. Still a longshot, she was more confident that he might receive it now that she had Nathan's full name.

Marseille, France   September 28, 1917

Dear Nathan,

You must be angered and concerned all at once. My deepest apologies for being unable to inform you of my sudden departure, but I promise you that it was equally surprising to Sara and me. Rest assured that we are safe for the moment and somewhat comfortable, although I would much rather be with you sweet Nathan. We are stationed on the south coast of France in a place called Marseilles, which sounded like mar-say when the conductor said it. The other nurses have been wonderfully helpful and already our knowledge has grown by leaps and bounds.

How I delighted in your company when we met last. It seems so long ago already, and such a contrast to where I find myself this evening. I very much hoped we could meet again, but was suddenly thrust into this awful war. On the bright side, they pulled us out of schooling and awarded us both nursing degrees early. I meant to send this letter sooner, but I could not recall your surname until today. I also cannot recall the name of your employer, for which I feel like a dunce, but will try nonetheless. I hope with all my heart that you receive this letter, sweet Nathan.

Yours Truly,

Emma

XVII

*   *   *

Nathan was becoming irritated. "Well when was it sent?"

"Young man, please lower your voice," said the woman at the University. Nathan lowered his head in agreement. "It was mailed Thursday of last week."

His head jolted up again. "Last Thur--" He paused to lower his voice. "Ma'am, I gave you that letter nearly three weeks ago."

"Yes, you did," she retorted condescendingly, "and I mailed it as you wished. I only received word last week. The girls were originally intended to arrive in Brest but landed instead in a place called..." She looked at the letter she had received. "Saint-Nazaire. The next day I mailed all of the letters."

Nathan calmed himself and ran some calculations in his head. *About ten days for Emma to arrive in France. Another few weeks or so for word to return to California.* "I see," he said. "Well here is my card, would you be so kind as to ring me if you receive anything? ...And my sincere apologies for my outburst, Ma'am."

"That's quite alright, Mr. Purcell. I will ring you if I receive anything in your name."

"Much obliged." He tipped his hat and exited.

In the US, the post office maintained possession of each letter from the mailbox to its final destination. The method of addressing letters with towns, states, and street numbers was well understood by the public. But international mail and Army mail was a different matter entirely.

A letter sent by the mother of an American soldier in France, who was in the 5th Division of Company 'L', could easily be lost, as there may have been as many as seven Companies or Batteries 'L' in the 5th Division. Or perhaps it was the 5th Regiment, or the 5th Brigade, or any of the other hundred or so '5ths' in France. Then there existed the likeliness that the man may have become wounded, sick, or had been transferred out of Company 'L'.

Further confusion was a result of censorship regulations whereby no soldier in France was permitted to divulge his location nor permitted to utilize a French post office. Although the Red Cross was slightly less censored, sending and receiving a letter frequently took several months.

Nathan's letter first arrived in Chicago where, along with thousands of other letters, it was received by one of many new and temporary Post

Office employees, who likely had a rather hazy idea of the military. The employee took a chance by putting the letter into one of the many mail sacks marked 'Red Cross' and the letter continued its journey. The Post Office in Chicago delivered it to a pier in New York, where the Army Quartermaster Corps placed it aboard an Army or Navy transport ship, which then delivered it to Saint-Nazaire, France.

The Army Transportation Department then unloaded it onto an Army Motor Transport Corps (M.T.C.) truck and delivered it to the Post Office department to be sorted and marked with a destination. Once the Post Office marked Nathan's letter, it was returned to the M.T.C. for delivery to the French railway to be shipped as ordinary freight.

Once it arrived in Marseilles, the French railway delivered it to another M.T.C. who in turn delivered it to the Marseilles Post Office, where it was marked for delivery to Emma's Red Cross unit, returned to the M.T.C., and finally delivered to the camp.

As the weeks passed, Emma and Sara adjusted to the blood and gore they witnessed on a daily basis. Emma had changed drastically. Her shy and demure demeanor had all but vanished, usurped by the wisdom gained from facing the fragile faces of life and death on a daily basis. She had wept at Floyd's death, but had since learned to detach herself emotionally from the constant sight of men who were wounded.

Her mind often wandered to Nathan during her rounds as a sort of coping mechanism to allow her to withdraw from her immediate surroundings. On the first day that she had been given leave since her arrival, she had walked all the way through Marseilles and up the hill to the castle she had seen upon first arriving. As she walked, she suddenly realized that she hadn't thought of Nathan for a few days, which upset her, but her anger subsided as she began calculating the possibility of if and when Nathan may have received her letter.

Let's see, we left San Francisco on September fourteenth and arrived here on the twenty-eighth. I mailed it the next day, so he would have received it around the tenth. Therefore-- She began thinking the words and dramatic inflections in her favorite detective's voice. *--if he in fact received it and isn't sore at me, he would have written back by the twelfth and I would receive his letter around... the twenty-fifth.*

She made her way up the hill on a narrow stone-lined foot path toward the gigantic wooden rivoted doors of the castle.

--Today is October twenty-seventh. She sighed to herself. *He mustn't have received it... or he's upset with me.* As she approached the foot of the

castle, she had a sudden epiphany. *Oh my God, Emma, how could you be so stupid!* She turned and rushed to make her way back down the path and through the streets of Marseilles to a cafe, where she managed to surround the few French phrases she knew with intensely acted charades in order to borrow a pen and writing paper.

Marseille, France October 27, 1917

Dear Nathan,
   By now you must be very sore at me, that is if you consider me at all. I sent a letter when first we arrived, but at that time I could neither recall your surname nor the employer you mentioned, and therefore must assume you did not receive it. To assume otherwise would simply crush my feelings. I'm unsure whether you have attempted to write to me, but if you can find it in your heart to forgive me and do indeed receive this letter through my school, please contact me. I would very much like to hear from you.

Yours Sincerely,

Emma

"Oh my stars and stripes," said Sara in disbelief, "of course he would visit the school and expect a letter there. Why didn't we think of that sooner?"

Emma shrugged and tilted her head to the side, as if to imply that they weren't the sharpest tools in the shed. Sara giggled, "I guess we're no Einsteins, huh..."

"You can say that again," she agreed.

Emma's letter to Nathan eventually arrived at the University on December twefth, nearly three months after she had been deployed to France. Nathan had diligently visited the office of the University every weekend since her departure, but lately had grown pre-occupied with schooling in San Jose and had skipped the passing two weekends. The woman at the University had attempted to call Nathan when Emma's letter arrived, but was forced to leave a message with Mr. Clifton's assistant.

Clifton's assistant had placed the message on his messy desk, where it sat amidst a stack of papers through the weekend and the following week. The next Friday was Christmas eve and Mr. Clifton had decided to finally sort through his affairs of the year. When he found the note, he called the dormitory at Nathan's University. Several minutes later, Nathan picked up the receiver.

"Hello?"

"Hello, Nathan," said Mr. Clifton in his usual jovial tone. "I wanted to wish you a Merry Christmas."

"And to you, sir," Nathan replied.

"I have a very special gift for you this year. A rare opportunity indeed," he said.

"Oh, Mr. Clifton, you don't have to--"

"I insist, Nathan. After all, your sketches were instrumental in landing the Langsey deal. You've worked hard and been a great deal of help these past years. You're like a son to me, Nathan, and you deserve something special such as this," he continued. Nathan held the receiver, uncomfortable with the accolades. "As you know, there's a war on, yes?"

"Yes of course, sir."

"I have connections with certain people as you are aware and... Well let me be frank with you, son. I have recommended you to the Army Corps of Engineers and they have accepted. You will be designing and supervising the construction of essential thoroughfares, bridges, and the like, Nathan... This is a huge opportunity, son.

"But, sir I'm not sure I--"

"I realize you may feel overwhelmed at this opportunity," said Clifton, "but I have every confidence in your ability, son. Just stick to the details, don't let them try to cut corners for the sake of cost! Understand?"

"Yes, sir," Nathan replied flatly.

"I'm sure you'll do fine, son, just fine. Now, I'll need you to head over first thing Monday morning and familiarize yourself with the schematics. I have your tickets and itinerary, along with some spending money, you depart next Wednesday."

"--Yes, sir," said Nathan obediently, "I'll be there at eight o'clock sharp, Mr. Clifton."

"That would be fine. Very well, Nathan have a-- Oh! ...I nearly forgot," he chuckled. "I thought you might like to know that a woman called from that University up in San Francisco you were on about, and--"

"From the University?" Nathan's heart began to race. What did she say? Is there a letter?"

"Let me see here," Clifton exhaled slowly as he audibly fumbled for the note. "It says: From the offices of the UCSF Medical Center. Please inform Mr. Purcell that we have received a letter from a Miss Emma Ha--"

The phone went dead. Nathan had dropped it and had one sleeve of his jacket pulled onto his arm before Clifton had even sensed the silence at the other end of the line. Nathan dashed out the door and ran several blocks to the train station. When he reached the city an hour later, he nearly knocked over a woman as he lunged toward the nearest taxicab.

"UCSF Medical, step on it!" he urged the driver, handing him a five dollar bill to emphasize his haste. The driver sat up and adjusted his brimmed hat, accelerating and swerving through the other cars up Lombard toward Van Ness Avenue, causing several pedestrians to take notice and nearly clipping the side of a trolleycar. Nathan paid and ran at full speed up the walkway to the offices of the University. "Keep it," he yelled as he ran from the cab.

"Oh, hello Mr. Purcell," greeted the woman behind the desk at the University.

"You have a letter for me?" he asked impatiently.

"Yes, I believe so," The woman was upended by Nathan's maniacal urgency. She turned to the desk behind her and retrieved the letter. As soon as it was within reach, Nathan snatched it from her grasp and began violently tearing it open. "It arrived a few weeks ago... I called your office and left word, did you not--"

"--Thank you," interrupted Nathan with a beaming smile. He immediately turned and darted toward the nearest bench in the room, sat quickly, and began reading the letter. He read it at least twenty times before remembering to breathe. When he approached the woman again, she instinctively handed him a pen and paper. Noticing his awkward manner, he calmed himself slightly and thanked her sincerely and with a direct gaze. He returned to the bench and constructed a new letter, trying to calm the pace of his heart, which was still beating out of his chest.

UCSF Medical, December 24, 1917

Dearest Emma,

Merry Christmas! How it joys me to hear from you! I began to think the worst when I did not receive a reply to the letter I sent. I was told that you were in a place called Saint-Nazaire, but clearly you have been re-stationed. There is so much I want to say to you, sweet Emma. The evening we spent together sweeps me into a world of daydreams each and every time I recall it. How I mourned your departure each day and night, wondering if you are safe in that forsaken place.

I have heard incredible news today, my dear Emma. I have just been recruited into the Army Corps of Engineers! In my haste, I forgot to inquire regarding where I will be deployed, but anywhere that is closer to you would be fine Emma, just fine! How I miss you now more than ever, I wish the War would end soon... On the eve of the new year I will look up at the night sky and hope that we are gazing at the same bright star, wishing the same wish. I worry for you every day my sweet, wishing we were together.

The city is buzzing with confidence for the American efforts and some people are saying that the War could end in a few months. Gosh, I hope so Emma. I hope to see you soon my dear, I will write to you as soon as I arrive. I don't know what I would do if something happened to you. Please be safe and assure me that you are well and that you forgive me for not reaching your letter more quickly. On an aside, I find it rather amusing that you could not recall my full name, seeing as it was yelled so frequently in reprimand by our teachers.

Yours Truly and Sincerely,

Nathan

*   *   *

XVIII

*   *   *

With his bags packed, Nathan thanked Mr. Clifton and boarded the train. Tracks diverged from the original Transcontinental railroad to most parts of northern California by the turn of the century, allowing Nathan to board in San Jose rather than having to make the journey up to San Francisco and over to Oakland via ferry.

Although he was extremely grateful for Mr. Clifton's generosity, the Second Class tickets offered a bumpy and uncomfortable ride in crowded cars with no access to certain dining and leisure cars enjoyed by Second and First class travelers. As he stared at the locket from time to time during the trip, he envisioned the couple living out their lives, their futures, their unborn children. He began daydreaming about saving enough money to purchase a ring and wondering where and how he would propose to her if he could manage to summon the courage.

In his lifetime, Nathan had traveled as far north as Sacramento and as far south as Monterey. But much like Emma and Sara, he had rarely been outside the Bay area and had never crossed the border of California. But aside from being seasick through the entire sea voyage, his journey was very similar to theirs; save for the fact that his ship was not attacked by submarines.

January 10, 1918

Dearest Emma,

I have arrived safely after a tumultuous journey, the details of which I will share when we are together, which I very much hope will be soon. I have been stationed in the north of France, but would risk severe reprimand by disclosing the exact location to you, as it is strictly forbidden. I was able to dispatch this letter to a new friend who agreed to post it from Belgium when he arrives. I pray it reaches you. If it does, please reply with only my name and Company 'C' of the US-ACE in France.

I have immediately been assigned several large projects and may be shifting locations my dear, but will attempt to write you as often as possible. I feel I am hardly qualified for such projects, but Mr. Clifton has apparently embellished my qualifications and my commanding officer has not questioned my abilities. I hope his trust in me is warranted. I beg you do not ask me to elaborate on my work precious Emma, I would much rather speak from my heart of your beautiful voice, your supple lips, and matters of a lighter nature.

The newspapers I read during my journey say that President Wilson believes we should see peace within a few short months and that the Turkish Army's exit from the Central Powers has great effect on our likely success.

I happened upon our old schoolmate Slug a few weeks prior to my departure. We shared some libations and he told me of his fascinating story. He was returning to work to collect his jacket (forgetful as always), when a former high school teammate asked him to fill in at third base due to an injured player. He jumped at the chance. In the eleventh inning of the game, a scout in the bleachers watched as Slug hit a game-winning double and signed him to a professional contract right there and then! Can you believe his luck?

He began laughing when he told me that his signing bonus had been a spaghetti dinner. Well, apparently he did so well the following year that he was picked up the professional Detroit team! He's earning nearly as much as the President, Emma!

Anyway, I informed him of the latest regarding you and Sara. He sends his best wishes to you both and thoughts for your safe return. Apparently underneath his rough exterior he has become quite the gentleman, if you can fathom that... I suppose success has that affect on us all. Missing you as always my dear Emma. Please be safe and give my best to Sara.

Yours Sweetly,

N.P.

***

Marseilles, France March 2, 1918

Dear N,

I am beside myself with happiness as I
write, barely able to hold the pen in my hand!
I have received two of your letters this week,
are there more? Oh sweetheart, of course you
are forgiven. There is nothing to forgive!
Yes, I am safe, as is Sara. I think we've aged
twenty years from all of the devastation. It's
dreadful, simply dreadful! I suppose we may
look back upon it with some semblance of
understanding when it is all said and done,
but I would trade anything to erase the
horrors we have witnessed.

Oh my goodness, 'Slug' and 'Gentleman' in
the same sentence? I laugh with Sara as I
write this, she is shaking her head in
disbelief! Well good on him, please pass our
best wishes to him if you rendezvous again.

It seems the world has gone bonkers, my dear
~~Nathan~~ N. One moment we are tending to the
wounded, disfigured, and dying, the next we
are listeing to a Ragtime band of colored men
from New Orleans. It's utter chaos! And to see
that your letter was posted nearly three
months ago makes me realize that I must
divulge some news that I would have preferred
to share in person.

With regards to your aside, I have some
unfortunate news my dear. When we first
arrived, a unit of soldiers were brought in
from Italy. Among them were Randy and Floyd.
Randy suffered severe injury to his face and
neck from shrapnel, but has since mended and
was sent home last month with honors.

You might look him up and see that he
adjusts upon his return. But as for Floyd...
I'm sorry to share bad news darling, but Floyd
passed on a few moments after I was by his
bedside. He was badly injured and I knew not
what else to say to him as I stood in shock

watching him agonize in his final moments.

I suppose he would be glad to know that we were able to make contact due to him telling me your surname, but Sara and I cried for several days at his loss. We made sure to include you in our blessings at his burial, but have not attended another and have no plans to visit that depressing place anymore. I'm certain you would have been proud of his bravery. I know he was a good friend and we will all miss him dearly.

Yours Truly,

Emma

* * *

June 5, 1918

My dear Emma,

I was very saddened to hear of Floyd's passing. He was a dear friend and surely he would be proud to know that he assisted our communication. I attended services at a nearby chapel yesterday to pay respect to him and the others.

My apologies for not contacting you sooner my dear. I had scarcely finished reading your letter when I was informed we must evacuate. Fighting has been quite heavy here as of late, the Germans are pushing forward and the local Red Cross unit is flooded with wounded. I'm told that we may be evacuated for a little while, but I will write you as soon as I am able. I hope you are safe my dear, I miss you more than ever.

Yours Truly,

N.

* * *

Nathan's company was indeed moved further inland as the Central powers pushed their lines back toward Paris. They had developed a long-range artillery gun which became known as the Paris Gun. It was a super-heavy howitzer weighing over 250 tons, with a barrel tube which reached nearly 100 feet into the air and which was able to shell Paris from 75 miles away, allowing the perception of incoming German troops.

Allied troops were brought toward the front lines just north of Paris at the height of the German efforts, successfully pushing the lines back toward Belgium over the course of several months. By the time Allied powers had regained control of the north of France, Nathan and the others had been relocated several times. In September, he was finally repositioned in Cambrai and two of the seven letters Emma had sent him were finally delivered.

* * *

September 14, 1918

Emma my dearest,

How I wanted to contact you sooner my sweet
girl. I narrowly escaped the shrapnel of a
bombardment by the Germans, but rest assured I
am alright and in one piece. We recently
regained the line and have nearly completed
construction of a top secret project near the
border... I'm sorry I cannot provide more
details as I am very proud of this
accomplishment and have been promoted in rank
to Sergeant First Class! Oh Emma, how I miss
you. Please tell me you are safe and that you
miss me too.

Yours Truly,

N.

***

As the British, French and American armies
advanced, the alliance between the Central Powers
began to collapse. Turkey signed an armistice at the
end of October, Austria-Hungary followed on November
3. Germany began to crumble from within. On November
9 the Kaiser abdicated, slipping across the border
into exile in the Netherlands as a German Republic
was declared and peace feelers were extended to the
Allies. On the morning of November 11 an armistice
was signed in a railroad car parked in a French
forest near the front lines. The Great War had
ended.

***

Marseilles, France November 11, 1918

Dearest Nathan,

Oh my sweet Nathan, can you believe it? The War has finally ended! It is so nice to be able to write your name! Nathan, Nathan, Nathan! Sara and I are so relieved! I'm sure you will receive this letter long after the papers print the news, but I feel the need to share my joy today.

Neither of us have discussed our plans for when we return to San Francisco, but for now we have decided to visit Paris to join in the celebration! We've always wanted to go and this seems possibly the only chance we will have. Are you able to rendezvous with us there? Please say yes, it would simply crush me to hear otherwise.

We are told Paris was only lightly bombarded from afar and we're told the celebrations are simply divine. I'm afraid I must keep this letter brief as we must prepare for the journey, my dear, but know that you are at the foremost of my mind and heart. Please come to Paris when you receive this if you are able my dear.

Sealed with a kiss,

Emma

***

Cambrai, France   November 11, 1918

Dearest Emma,

How I am rejoicing today upon learning of
the end of the War! How I regret not being
able to alert you to my position all this
time, sweet Emma. It was forbidden by our
commanding officer, surely you understand.

Oh Emma, to hold and kiss you at this moment
would fulfill my soul in a way like no other.
I have some very exciting news my sweet! I
have been given leave and will be arriving in
Marseilles in a few days! I cannot wait to
hold you with all of my love. See you very
soon my dear.

                              With Love,

                                 Nathan

              *   *   *

XIX

*   *   *

As Nathan set off on his way to rendezvous with Emma, there were hundreds of uniformed military personnel embarking onto trains toward Paris and the west coast of France toward America. He made his way by bus to the train station and purchased a ticket to Marseilles via Lyon. Meanwhile, Emma and Sara had completed their tour of duty.

There was a palpable sense of accomplishment on everyone's faces and they caroused for a few days and nights before heading back to camp to sort out their belongings. While Nathan was aboard a train headed to Lyon, Emma and Sara boarded the train in Marseilles, oblivious to Nathan's pending arrival.

They had been able to receive wire with a portion of their stipend from the Wells Fargo & Co. bank in San Francisco. It was a meager amount, but enough for them to stay at a decent hotel and see the sites. They were excited to put the events of the war behind them as quickly as possible.

Nathan's couchette car consisted of four bunk
beds, two on either side, with narrow but
comfortably cushioned benches at their sides and two
windows, which could be opened slightly at the
bottom by crank. Most passengers debarked in Paris
to head further west to the coast, leaving but one
cabin-mate for the remainder of his journey.

Nathan discovered immediately that the civilian
man spoke not a word of English, electing to bury
his head in an assortment of French newspapers to
deter any possible conversation. When his nerves
began to flutter from the thought of seeing Emma,
Nathan decided to make his way up to the dining car
for a drink. A few people sat idly, scattered evenly
and alone throughout the car, but otherwise it was
bereft of activity and conversation.

He ordered an early dinner, *poulle con pommes
frites* – chicken with french fries, wondering when
he received it why Americans referred to the fried
potato strips as such when the French did not. He
thanked the barista and returned to his couchette
car. The Frenchman peered above a corner of his
newspaper only briefly when Nathan returned, shaking
his head slightly in disgust at the inconsiderate
American who apparently knew nothing of French
manners.

Half way through his meal, the train arrived in
Lyon. He gazed across the dark tracks to another
train sitting idly, boarding passengers to head the

opposite direction. He could see several couchette cars filled with military men in his immediate peripheral, but when he leaned forward to see more, his gaze intensified. Four women were chatting actively and laughing freely in a dimly lit couchette car only ten meters away.

He could see the Red Cross brassard on the left arm of one of them, and just as he noticed it, the woman next to her leaned forward, laughing heartily... *Emma?* he thought to himself. *It can't be... Surely she knows I'm arriving today.* He continued to stare intensely, watching the movement of the red-haired woman's lips and her body language like a hawk studying its prey, searching for matching idiosynchrasies. He began retracing the timeline of his letter and calculating the possibilities. He closed his eyes and shook his head forcefully, placing his meal next to him on the bench and gazing back again.

Oh my Lord. "Emma!" he yelled as he began banging the glass of the window, waving both arms frantically. He cranked one window and then the other, but it made no difference; the window of her other train was shut. He stood and continued his tirade, banging frantically and yelling to her.

The Frenchman sat in utter bewilderment of the maniac, uncomfortably sliding as far to the edge of his bench as possible. Sunndely Nathan's train jerked into motion and began moving south along the tracks, picking up speed quickly as it exited the station.

He banged relentlessly with both fists now, rattling the window's foundation and causing his car-mate to stand in frightened dismay. Nathan reeled around toward the car door and knocked the man backward against the bunk behind him, rushing out the door as if ablaze.

As he ran the full length of the car and nearly passed through the threshold into the next car, when he remembered his valuables, the ring in particular, which he had since stowed safely within his luggage. He pounded once with both fists heavily against the partition door in frustration and ran back toward his car. The Frenchman, who was holding the back of his head and peering down the hallway, recoiled quickly into a safe corner of the car as Nathan burst back into it and fumbled atop his bunk for his baggage.

"Apologies," he managed to utter as he repeated his flurried exit. But it was too late, the train had reached a point of inertia that made obvious that fact that its next stop would be far into the distance. Nathan came to his senses and this realization as he approached a conductor and looked out the window at the rapidly passing French landscape of hills and vineyards.

"Is everything alright, sir?" asked the conductor calmly.

"Yes, um, oui," huffed Nathan. He swirled his head in disgust and straightened his posture, swallowing several times. "...Just needed some air."

He inhaled and exhaled deeply, trying to catch his breath.

"Ah oui, mais you ah okay?" he asked again, "You look, em, disturb-ed."

"No, no...very certain. Everything is fine, thank you," he countered quickly. "When is the next stop?"

"Za next stop is Valence, monsieur. Sirty minutes or so."

"Merci," said Nathan as he grinned sheepishly and turned back yet again toward his couchette car, dreading the glare he would soon receive from the unsuspecting Frenchman whom he had bowled over moments earlier. As expected, the man had abandoned his reading to glare angrily at Nathan for the remainder of their uncomfortable time together with his hand rubbing the back of his bruised head.

At the next stop, Nathan quickly debarked and made his way across to the other platform. He purchased a ticket to Brest via Paris on the *Limité* line for twice what he had paid for the ticket to Marseilles, for he had no idea which destination was Emma's. As scheduled, he would arrive twenty-five minutes before her train in Paris, if that was indeed where she was headed.

But if not, he would arrive in Brest forty minutes after her with slim chance of tracking her. Boarding the train heading north was like waking from a coma. The energy was palpable, with overcrowded hallways and patriotic American songs radiating throughout the train cars above the sound of the heavy rain that fell throughout the journey. When he finally found his couchette car, it was filled with overjoyed men in military uniforms. They were only slightly younger than Nathan, but he felt out of place all the same.

He jostled his way through the ten soldiers who were standing and sitting in seemingly every part of the cabin, sitting finally next to the window with his shoulders folded inward, straddling his suitcase. A bottle of cognac was offered by the soldier seated next to him and he begrudgingly obliged, taking a small sip. The soldier grimaced and gestured in disapproval, so Nathan obliged him again, this time realizing that he might as well join them as it would be several hours before the train reached Paris. By the time his train arrived, Nathan had taken several large swigs of the brandy and was utterly blotto. He only realized that he needed to debark when someone asked him where he was headed.

"...I'm going to Paristh to find my girl Emma!" he slurred loudly above the singing. With his announcement, they all cheered - *To Emma* - in unison and took generous swigs of cognac.

"Well you better get to it, bud," said a soldier from Kentucky.

Nathan attempted to shake off his inebrity as he fumbled with his suitcase toward the cabin door. He waved drunkenly to the men and made his way to the exit, smiling and oblivious now to the complexity of the task that lay ahead of him. He debarked the train and stumbled to the first vacant bench he could find, the adrenaline quickly fading as he swayed his upper body and murmured the end of the tune that was being sung as he departed the soldiers.

Twenty minutes later, Emma and Sara said goodbye to their new friends and stepped off of the train and onto the platform. A porter hoisted their luggage down the steps and tipped his hat in refusal when Sara offered him some coins.

They wrapped their scarves tightly to their necks against the chill of the evening and excitedly continued their conversation about the sites they planned to visit, until Sara suddenly interrupted Emma to point out a man who slumped over his luggage at a nearby bench. Their instinctive nursing habits kicked in and they approached the man. Sara tapped and then jostled his shoulder until his head drunkenly lifted. He was grinning, drooling, and his eyes were still closed in a peaceful world which seemed far, far away.

"Nathan?!" exclaimed Emma. Nathan's grin widened within his dreamy state, his eyes still closed. "Nathan!" She tapped his cheek softly several times with her gloved hand and he began to awaken. Disoriented, he struggled to focus for several moments. "Nathan, How? What in God's name are you doing here? I only sent the letter yesterday!" She looked at Sara in confusion.

His head swirled at the comment, suddenly replaying his priorities in his head... He had to find Emma, he saw her on the train and, he met...soldiers. He drank...he... "Emma?" he slurred as she came into slight focus.

"Oh my goodness, Nathan," she whispered instensely. "I can't believe it... What in the world are you doing in Paris?"

"I, I sent you a letter," he mumbled. "I saw you...on the train." He pointed toward the vacant tracks.

"Come now, Nathan," said Sara, "let's get you somewhere dry." They helped him to his feet and walked to the street behind the station to hail a taxicab. They checked in at their hotel a few minutes later, a small but sufficiently adorned place on the outskirts of the city. Seeing that Nathan was entirely beyond resurrection from his exhausted inebriation, they seated him in the armoir in the room, covered him with a blanket, and settled in for the night.

Nathan awoke earlier than the girls, just as the sun arose, and was again discombobulated with his surroundings. He had remembered seeing her, but spent several minutes attempting to place the pieces together in a way that made sense. He exited the room and walked down the hallway to the restroom of the cheap hotel and splashed water on his face several times.

Noticing his messy appearance, he straightened his regimental uniform and jacket and wetted his hair to flatten it into a more tidy state. When he returned to the room, he realized that he had no key. He knocked timidly at first, hardly making a sound. He thought of venturing outside to pass some time, but opted against it, as the girls might mistake his disappearance for a permanent departure. He knocked solidly and waited. Several moments passed before Emma came to the door.

"Emma, it's me, Nathan," he said softly. She opened the door and threw her arms around him. The two stood in the doorway in silent embrace for several moments. When she finally released her grip, Emma took Nathan's hand and led him into the room. Sara eventually awakened and the group slowly collected themselves, dressed for the chilly and wet weather, and ventured into the streets of Paris. They found a lively outdoor cafe a few blocks from the hotel and enjoyed fresh fruit and pastries with champagne to celebrate their reunion.

"How is it possible that you received my letter so quickly?" asked Emma. "I assumed it would take weeks or months to reach you. What if you hadn't seen me on the train?"

"I guess my heart was doing most of the thinking," he said lovingly.

"Maybe I should leave you two alone," said Sara sarcastically. Emma and Nathan chuckled and apologized.

*

As day turned to evening and a chilly mist blanketed the city, the trio returned to the hotel to book another room for Nathan and then headed out for dinner at a quaint restaurant. They ate like royalty, Nathan finally having a place to spend his small, yet ample purse, gifted from Mr. Clifton a year earlier. Later in the evening, they went out on the town.

Although parts of Paris had been bombarded and damaged in the conflict, much of the city had already been rebuilt and eerily seemed at times as if nothing had occurred at all. They again dined at the restaurant overlooking the Seine and then went out dancing. The music was lively, similar to what Emma and Sara had been exposed to when the traveling New Orleans band had paid a visit to their camp in Marseilles, but the dancing was altogether foreign.

"It's a new step, called the *Foxtrot*," said Nathan loudly against the sounds of the horns in the band. "I saw them doing it at a club in San Francisco before I came over...just follow my lead." He took both her hands in his, raising them to shoulder level. Then he began following the fast-paced beat with quick steps, kicking back one of his heels on alternate beats. Emma stared at his feet and giggled, attempting to mimic his erratic movements in her head before mustering the courage to let loose and go with it. Within moments, she was smiling and laughing as the pair fell into the frenzied choreography of the latest fad in music and dancing.

Sara had been asked to dance by an American sailor and had picked up the steps just as quickly as Emma. The girls beamed at each other, finally beginning to allow the present to pervade their minds over the constant thoughts of the recent past. After the dance, the two couples exited the club and walked along the promenade against the streetlamps and the chilly but dry midnight air.

The sailor tugged slightly at Sara's side and, as the couple allowed Nathan and Emma to advance, turned her toward him and kissed her gently. She paused only seconds and reciprocated, the two lost in their own world as Emma turned to notice. She nudged Nathan and he stopped.

Here goes, he thought to himself.

"Emma," he said softly. Emma remained distracted by Sara and her new beau, but slowly turned her head toward Nathan.

"Yes, Nathan."

Gazing purposefully into her eyes, he began, "When I lost you the first time we were very young and--" He cleared the nerves from his throat and began again...

"When I learned that you had been sent over... here, it was as if I had lost you forever. Not a day has passed that I haven't thought of you and worried about your safety and missed you.

"Oh Nathan, I--" Emma consoled.

"Please, Emma," he interrupted. "...I want us to always be together. I, I love you, Emma. I think I always have."

Emma watched as Nathan's gaze withdrew from hers, withdrawing his hand from his coat pocket. She had tears in her eyes. The war, the years at school, and the confusion of it all swirled in her head like the first day she had arrived into the chaos of it all. But she was sure of this, this was easy.

"I've wanted to give you this for so many years, Emma... I look at it every day and think of you," he said, gazing into her eyes. "I never want to be without you again... Ever. I know it's not a ring, but for now..." He slowly bent his leg and knelt on the moist cobblestone that lined the promenade. "For now, Emma, I just want to know that I will not lose you again. Will you be my wife, Emma?"

"Nathan," she said emphatically, "Of course I will, my dear. And it's lovely," she said as she accepted his gift. For the first time in Emma's life, she felt confident, complete, and loved. He stood and the couple embraced for a very long while.

*   *   *

XX

*   *   *

Oh, Nathan, it's beautiful!" said Sara when the two couples arrived at the hotel bar. Emma opened the locket to look inside, her hand immediately covering her mouth as she and Sara began to giggle. "Na—than!!" she laughed, "Is this a joke?"

"Oh, nuts!" Nathan laughed as he smacked his own forehead. "I meant to take those out, Emma... I'm sorry. I, um, I didn't have any photographs of us, so--"

"Oh," she sighed in relief, "I thought you were playing a joke on me, silly goose," she said whimsically. "Well, let's remedy that shall we?"

"What do you mean?" asked Nathan.

"We passed a photography studio down the street. Let's go and have our photographs taken tomorrow," she beamed.

"Jack has invited me to visit the Louvre museum," said Sara with a glimmer in her eye. The couples agreed to meet the next evening for dinner at a nearby restaurant which was owned by Jack's Uncle. Jack was the Americanized version of his name. Jacques was the son of French immigrants. After the war had ended, he decided to explore his roots and had been staying with his Uncle in Paris.

The next day, as they walked through the misty streets to have their photographs taken, Nathan told Emma the story of how he came to possess the locket, how he had wanted to give it to her at the orphanage and again at the University.

"That's very sweet, my dear, but I'm glad things ended up this way," she said. When they arrived at the studio, they had two photographs taken of themselves together - so that they could each keep one handy - and two more individually, to be placed into Emma's engagement gift.

"Zey will be ready tomorroh," the photographer had said. Nathan paid the man and they spent the day walking the streets of Paris.

*

"*Oh my goodness,*" gasped Emma. The next morning as the foursome were walking, Emma glimpsed a man who bore an uncanny resemblance to someone she thought she recognized.

"What is it, Emma?" asked Sara. Emma did not reply. She shuffle-stepped quickly to the window to peer more closely and then entered the store. A portly, dark-haired man was looking downward into his display case, taking inventory of his baked goods. Emma approached the counter timidly and cleared her throat. The man met her gaze.

"Bon jour, monsieur. Je voudrais un croissant, s'il vous plait," she said with a sly grin, purposefully replacing the correct pronunciation, **cwa**ssant, with **cra**ssant as a hint. The man simply looked at her contemptfully for a moment and began to open the door to the display case. *Stupide Americans*, he muttered to himself.

As the man crouched down to collect the croissant and Emma's expression flattened in disappointment, another man emerged through the curtains from the kitchen, gazing downward at his hands as he fervently patted away the flour from them against his apron. The man looked up briefly but quickly returned his gaze to his apron. Suddenly his head shot upward. "--Emma?" he asked cautiously. Her gaze lazily met his. "Mon Dieu... Emma?!"

"Monsieur Dubois?" It had been nearly a baker's dozen years since Dubois had saved the young girl from the grips of death in the Spring of '06 and, although his hair had become more gray than black, it was definitely her old friend and neighbor. He waddled gleefully around the counter as quickly as he could manage and the two embraced in a swaying hug for several moments, Emma buried against his flour-caked apron. "I never thought I would see you again... You, you never visited me and so... When did you return to France?"

Dubois' grasp of the English language had never been above par, but after thirteen years back in France, it had all but vanished. "Emma, yes. You big! So big now! Yes, I come back apres le quake. Mon Deiu, you come work in za war, n'est pas?"

Emma stammered through the little French she could remember. *"Yes, I am big. I work with Red Cross. We visit Paris now,"* she said shyly as she fluttered her arm into the air.

"Oh, please. No pay," he insisted, turning to his younger brother and scolding him for charging Emma, briefly explaining their history to him.

Emma brought Dubois outside to meet her new fiancee and the others. They stood awkwardly for a few moments as communication became more difficult and soon were wishing each other well and parted company. They made their way back to the photography studio and collected their photographs, meeting Sara and Jack for dinner that evening. Sara described the wonderful paintings and sculptures, bragging about Jack's extensive knowledge of the finer things in life.

The hour grew late and the group retired to their rooms, Jack inviting Sara out again the following day for a leisurely ride on the Seine river. She had grown exhausted by the long day of walking through the museum and slept soundly on the other small bed in the room, so Emma sat up, illuminated the lamp next to her bed, and picked up the locket to take a closer look. She noticed the inscription on the back of the locket:

PE-SA 1848

To my love

Then she unclasped and opened the locket, giggling again as she gazed at the photographs of the dogs. *Bummer and Lazarus*, she whispered to herself. *What odd names for such lovely dogs.* She reached into her hair and withdrew one of the bobby pins that held it in place. She inserted one of its small edges into the partition at the edge of the glass on the left and pried open the cover.

Immediately she noticed that the photograph of the dog named Bummer had been oddly cut into a square shape rather than fitted professionally, and that it had been placed atop another photograph. She used the pin to pry Bummer's photograph away from the man whose visage lay beneath it. *Oh dear, the fashion those days,* she thought to herself as she giggled softly again. She decided to pry up the other side to glimpse at this oddly dressed fellow's better half. *So pretty, I wonder if they had children,* she thought to herself.

Looking at the couple side-by-side, her parents entered her thoughts. *They would have loved this...*

I wish they could see me now... She missed them dearly, but had stayed strong, only crying on the first Christmas without them. She then reached over to a drawer and withdrew a small pair of scissors from the sewing kit in the drawer next to her bed, placing it next to the photographs of her and Nathan at her side.

She carefully pried up the photo of the stately gentleman, traced the photograph of Nathan with the scissors as she carefully cut his photograph to match its dimensions, and precisely slotted it into the left side of the locket. She did the same for her photograph and removed the one of the pretty woman, but as she did, something struck her as odd. There was an inscription behind the woman's photograph. Emma squinted to read it:

> phantsi   umthi   ishumi
> iziteps   empuma
> sobonana   my   dear

What on earth?, she whispered to herself, *fancy umthi ishmay izi--* *What on earth??* She scanned forward, *--my dear?* She stared at the two words for a while. Then she tried rearranging the letters of the others, realizing it might be a glyph. *Pants? Ph-faints? Ants? Maybe it's just a few letters for each?* she began thinking. She spent another half hour trying to solve its riddle, but to no avail.

When she noticed her clock and the late hour, she decided to give up trying for the night. The next day, she showed Sara and told the story of how Nathan had *procured* the locket when they were at the orphanage.

"But it says in plain English, *my dear*, Sara," Emma pleaded. It must be a code of some sort.

"Well maybe Nathan knows what it means," suggested Sara.

That morning, Nathan and the girls met at Mr. Dubois' patisserie while Jack went to visit some relatives to the south of Paris.

"So you never discovered an inscription in all those years?" asked Emma incredulously. Nathan looked at her curiously and shrugged. Emma removed the locket from her neck. "Here," she said. She unclasped and opened the locket and then took a pin from her hair and pried open the faceplate on the right side. She carefully removed the photograph of herself and handed the locket to Nathan. "See? Just there in the middle."

Nathan brought the locket closer to attempt to read the inscription, a quizzical look growing upon his face as he read. "Is it Latin?"

"Perhaps," she said. "But the last two words appear to be in English... *-my dear-*," she pointed.

"Oh yes, I see," said Nathan. "Well maybe your friend's Uncle knows of a jeweler," he said to Sara.

"That's an excellent idea, Nathan," said Sara.

XXI

*   *   *

Bon jour," the small bespectacled man said as the bell on the door jingled. He was bald on the top of his head, with peppered hair and a large moustache. His shirt was striped in navy blue and the hair on his forearms was extraordinarily long and fluffy.

"*Hello, sir,*" said Jack in fluent French, "*I wonder if you would be so kind as to take a look at this locket for us?*"

"Yes of course," said the man. "*Interesting... Where did you obtain it?*"

"Where did you buy it?" Jack asked Nathan.

"Oh, it was a gift. I mean, um, San Francisco... California," his words stumbled.

"*I see,*" said the jeweler as he examined its exterior. He turned it over and then unclasped and opened it, looking closely at the inscription when he discovered it.

"*Interesting,*" he said softly.

"Ask him if it's Latin, Jack," said Sara.

"*Noh Latin,*" said the jeweler, understanding Sara's question on his own. Jack explained the confusing existence of the English words "my dear," leading them to believe it was created by someone who spoke English.

"*Ah yes,*" added the jeweler. He then asked Jack, "*How do you say Afrique du Sur in English?*"

"South Africa," Jack replied.

"*Yes, as I suspected... You would have to go to South Africa to learn the meaning...or send a telegraph. Very expensive,*" he said, shaking his hand as if it was heavy.

"South Africa?" exclaimed Emma in astonishment from Jack's translation. "Why South Africa?"

Jack translated as the jeweler explained. "*Do you see these letters here?*" The jeweler turned over the locket to show them.

"Those are the initials of the people who owned it, right?" Emma guessed through Jack's translation of the question.

"*No, Madame, these are for the place where the item was fabricated,*" the jeweler explained. "*This one here was made in Firenze, Italy. See here? FZ-IT,*" Jack translated as the man pointed to a timepiece nearby with similar markings. "*Let me see...*"

The man turned to an atlas. He opened and turned several pages until he reached one of southern Africa. The atlas had several markings designating the minerals which were mined at each. "*Is it similar pronunciation in English,*" the man asked Jack as he pointed to a spot on the map.

"*Yes, it's identical,*" he replied.

"Couldn't it stand for South America?" Sara asked through Jack's translation.

"*No, Miss,*" the man shook his head, "*the initials are of the city and country, never the entire continent. And besides, those words inscribed look nothing like Spanish as far as I can tell.*"

It is a fine piece," he added. "*If you would like to sell it, I could offer you a fair price, Madam,*" he added.

"No merci," said Emma after Jack translated the question.

"This is so exciting," said Emma once the group exited the jewelry store.

"Emma, what's going through that head of yours," asked Sara seriously.

"Nothing," she said suspiciously. "--but it would be interesting to get to the bottom of it, right?"

Nathan stopped walking and looked at her, allowing Sara and Jack to continue walking ahead. "You're joking, right? I mean, that's nearly as far away as San Francisco," he laughed. Sara and Jack noticed they had paused and waited a short distance in front of them.

"Besides," Nathan added, "I already sent word to Mr. Clifton that I'd be returning within the month, darling."

"But what if it's a fortune! Oh, it's going to eat me up inside if we just leave it alone, sweetheart... Can we at least try to find out what the inscription means?"

"Ya know," interrupted Jack from a distance, "a buddy of mine was talkin' the other day about how the Navy's been shipping some POWs around... Let me see if any are headed that way, maybe you can tag along."

He noticed the perturbed look on Nathan's face as he finished his sentence and shrugged apologetically.

"Oh Nathan, *pleeease*," Emma pleaded.

"Alright Emma, but let's not get ahead of ourselves..."

*

When Britain declared war on Germany in August 1914, the Union of South Africa was immediately involved as a member of the British Empire. Prime Minister Botha promised full support, assuring Britain that the Union would defend itself. The Union would invade German Southwest Africa (Namibia) at the request of the British.

By 1917, troops had been dispatched to East Africa, Palestine, Libya, and Egypt.

More than 12,000 South Africans died in the war – over 8,000 whites and 4,000 blacks. South Africans also served in British army, navy and airforce units and as advisers to the Allied forces. Prisoners of war who had been held in France were now being swapped with their Allied counterparts held in Africa.

Jack transcribed the words in the locket onto a piece of paper and made a call to his friend at the Port of La Havre, forty minutes north of Paris. Jack's friend, Frederick Sullerton, or 'Sully' as he preferred to be called, then approached a group of black African POWs who were being readied for return. They were thin and frail from months of minimal food rations, but cautiously optimistic that they would soon arrive home safely.

"Listen up," he yelled to the forty or so men being held in the fenced encampment. "Anyone of y'all from South Africa step forward." The men looked at each other but none moved. "It's okay," Sully assured, "just need somethin' translated is all."

"But... We're all from South Africa," one of the men said apprehensively.

"Oh, shit... Um, anyone from *Port Eliz-beth*, South Africa, step forward."

Three of the men reluctantly stepped forward. "What you want? Da war is ovah, when we go home?" one said contemptfully. The others began nodding with stern faces.

"Well, I'll tell you what. If y'all can tell me what this says, I'll see what I can do. Deal?" asked Sully.

"We don't read nothin', Mista," said another with equal contempt.

"Alright," said Sully as he cleared his throat. "Uhh, let's see here... Fancy, um-thee, ishu-mee, izzy--teps, a puma, sobo... sobonana--" *What the hell*, he sighed to himself in embarrassment as the men began laughing. His Carolina drawl combined with his mispronunciation added to the amusement of those who had heard familiar words. - *Sobonana* had sounded like subba-banana, for example.

"Dis not Zulu, Mista," one of them said through his laughter, "--but similah Zulu... Sound like dis say undah, ten...um, new day, but I no know what mean izitep, Mista."

"Hang on, now," he said as he took out his pen and began writing. "What was that again? --Which words mean what, fella?"

"Ah. Yes, okay," the young man smiled, still amused. As Sully repeated each word one by one, the young man began to emphasize the translation with gesticulation and charades.

"*Phantsi*, yes... So-- *Phansti* mean undah, yes, undah." He crouched and pushed his raised palms forward several times. "*Umthi* mean tree, um--" He pointed to the group of trees in the distance. "*Ishumi* mean ten." He held up his hands and began counting. "*Empuma* mean, um--" He conversed with his cohorts briefly. "--new sun come." he looked at the sky and then behind himself and raised one hand slowly from near the ground. Then he stood and smiled in satisfaction with his translation.

"Oh, I see... And what about this one?" she asked, pointing, "Soba...so-bananas?"

"Ah," the men burst into laughter again. "*Sobonana* mean bye-bye next time...yes." Several men began waving and repeating *sobonana* while chuckling and smiling broadly, happy for the distraction from monotony. Sully thanked the young man and called Jack later in the day.

Jack rushed back to join the others after Sully called him at his Uncle's restaurant with news. He shared the translation with the group:

> phansti - *under*
> umthi -   *tree*
> ishumi - *ten*
> iziteps - *?*
> empuma - *new sun*
> sobonana - *goodbye, next time*

"Interesting, huh," said Jack. "Sure sounds like a treasure map to me..."

"Under-tree-ten-blank-new-sun. Goodbye, next time, my dear," repeated Sara. New sun, that seems like it could be sunrise... Could it be Under-Tree-Ten-Blank-East?"

"Ooh, that's excellent, Sara," exclaimed Emma, "Oh my, this is so exciting."

"And maybe 'Until next time my dear' could be 'Until we meet again,' as if they've been forced apart?"

"Yes! This man must have been arrested or something and gave it to her," said Sara, "but she never found the clue!"

Nathan sat listening quietly with a combination of patience and reticence as he listend and watched Emma becoming increasingly enthralled by the locket. He wondered what they would be doing instead had he only exchanged the locket for a simple ring, or simply pawned it to pay for school.

The girls continued their fervent banter. "Oh, right...and maybe the Iziteps one is feet," suggested Emma. "Under tree ten feet east... Or ten yards?... Steps? *Izitep* sounds a lot like step, right darling?"

"I don't think it works that way, sweetheart," chided Nathan.

"No, she's right," said Sara. "Makes sense that there would be some sort of action in between the other words."

"Ohh, I wonder what it's like in South Africa," Sara added.

"Oh, I bet it's just beautiful," said Emma.

"Just because something in one language sounds like something in another, you can't simply *assume* they're the same," said Nathan in a condescending tone.

"Oh Nathan, you're being a wet towel," Emma chastised. "Don't you think it's fascinating, darling? Where's your sense of adventure," she laughed playfully toward Sara.

Nathan was becoming infuriated at what he percieved as a mocking nature in her public humiliation of him. His gaze grew intense as he could not sit idly any longer. "Okay, Emma," he said sharply, "Let's look at this realistically, shall we?" He was sitting up straight in his seat, his hands and fingers rigidly chopping the air as he spoke.

Emma's eyes widened. She hadn't seen this side of Nathan. "Darling, please--"

"--Let's suppose Jack's friend, Sully was it?" Jack nodded in cautious compliance. "Let's suppose Sully could actually arrange for our transport. How would we return to France? Huh? Or America for that matter Emma?" he admonished. "We're already half the damn way around the world!"

Emma gazed at him with wide eyes. "I--"

"--And how would we even know where to *look*, Emma," he continued emphatically. "We hardly know what the damn thing *says* and you want to risk our lives and spend money on a whim?? I've spent the past year at war--"

"Nathan,"

"--hopped blindly onto a train,"

"Nathan!"

"--and proposed to you...*without a ring* I might add--"

"*Nathan!*" Emma yelled above his rant. Nathan cut off his words abruptly and attempted to compose himself with swift, jerking adjustments in his chair.

"We're going to go for a stroll," said Sara flatly as she reached for Jack's arm. Emma nodded and returned her gaze to Nathan, who's head was now reddened and drooping forward in embarrassment.

"My apologies, darling," he said finally. "It all seems a bit *ludicrous* is all." He brushed his bangs to the side and reclined forcefully into his chair.

"Nathan, darling," Emma said sweetly as she placed her hand on his arm, "we don't have to go anywhere. I just-- I thought it would be a fun adventure is all."

"I know, sweetheart," sighed Nathan.

"We were just getting caught up in the fun of it, my dear, *of course* we don't have to go," she added.

"Well, it's just that I'm trying to be *pragmatic* about things, Emma. I had hoped we would return to some semblance of normalcy after this atrocious *war*," he said in disgust.

"You're right, dear. Let's agree to have a good time in Paris and we can leave this silly nonsense alone, okay? Nathan?" His eyes lifted to meet hers and they connected with a kiss.

*

Later that evening the couples met and laughed at Nathan's awkward outburst. Sara imitated Nathan – *And I ran and ran and jumped onto the speeding train... I just had to find my Emma!*

Emma finally calmed her laughter enough to come to his defense. "Well I'm glad he did," said Emma pridefully. "He's my smart, wonderful man and we have all the treasure we need right here."

"Aww, that's so...so boring," laughed Sara as the booze flowed easily.

"Hey," joked Nathan, "you go track it down then, down in *fantasy*-land, if your so keen."

Sara laughed. "No thanks, I quite like it here," she said as she kissed Jack. "The jungle would play havok on my hair anyway..."

"It's so sad, though," digressed Emma.

"What is, darling," asked Nathan.

"The poor man was never able to give it to his wife... Maybe the tribal people were chasing him!" She crouched like a tiger.

"Then why not just inscribe it in English," suggested Jack.

"Oh, good point," Emma agreed. "So... Perhaps he wrote it in jibberish to hide it from English-speakers."

"...and he knew the jibberish people wouldn't find it," continued Sara.

"Yes, but his wife understood it," added Emma. "That makes sense, right? And she came to America, where no whites would understand it."

"Yes, and years later Randy found it in the rubble and gave it to me," Nathan lied. "And I--" he said playfully as he tapped Emma's nose, "--gave it to you."

"Wait. But if she went to San Francisco, what would the hint refer to," asked Sara. "Did he know she was there? Or was he there all along?"

"Oh, geez, you're right. What a quandary," said Emma. The girls began volleying ideas as the men listened with amusement.

"No wait," exclaimed Sara. "The jeweler said that it was made there in South Africa, remember?"

"Oh, of course," said Emma.

"Okay, so what about the dogs? Maybe the person who put the dog photographs on top of the man and woman knew about it and dug it up already."

"I don't think so, Sara. If he was lazy enough to leave them there, he probably didn't see it, right?"

"Yes, I suppose that makes sense."

"...So somewhere in South Africa is a tree," Emma continued in her serious detective's voice, "and from said tree, one would walk ten steps east and find treasure!" The group laughed collectively.

"Come darling, the hour is getting late," said Nathan.

The couples retired to their rooms for the night. Nathan fell forward onto the bed and almost instantly into a deep sleep, exhausted by the rush of adrenaline and subsequent libations.

Emma stood at the mirror of the bureau fixing her hair. She removed the locket from her neck, placing it in her toiletry bag. As she did, she glanced again at the old photographs of the couple, admiring the beauty of the woman's face. She picked up the photograph again and gazed in wonder.

Who **are** *you,* she thought to herself in her inebrity. As she gazed into the mirror, comparing herself to the woman, she attempted to kick remove one of her heeled shoes with the other. She lost her balance and fell heavily to the carpet of the hotel room floor, dropping the photographs of the couple. *Dammit*, she whispered loudly. Nathan snorted at the interruption, but quickly rolled onto his side and resumed his steady rhythm.

Emma sighed, realizing her exhaustion. *Oh well*, she sighed, *I guess we'll never know.* She clumsily removed her other shoe and collected the photographs. When she stood and placed them on the bureau, a faint squiggle reflected from the back of one of the photographs. She brought it toward her hazy focus and squinted. *More light*, she thought in a lazy, inebriated inflection.

She placed the photograph under the lamp on the bureau. Alongside the faint and curving discrepancy was a series of blank indentations. As if instinctively, she picked up the lipstick cylinder and sloppily slid the lever upward with her thumb to expose the tip. She dabbed a finger on it and smeared a small amount across the back of the photograph.

Oh my goodness... Oh my goodness, she thought to herself. *N,* she peered behind herself at her sleeping husband as her finger continued moving across the back of the photograph. *...O, N, T-O-N...*

Nonton, she whispered excitedly. *Oh my goodness...* She squinted closer. *Norton!*

...Oh my goodness!

*   *   *

XXII

*   *   *

Minutes passed in an agonizing crawl as Emma twitched anxiously beside Nathan, her mind vacillating wildly between waking her slumbering future husband and allowing her newest discovery to fade away.

Her impatience finally erupted. "Nathan, wake up. Wake up!" She shook him until his crossed blue eyes glazed through the long bangs which draped clumsily over them. Nathan darted up as she shook him, bewildered.

"Huh? Wha-?" he said in a slurred panic.

"Oh Sweety," she said softly, "you were having a nightmare, you poor thing."

Nathan cleared his throat and brushed back his bangs in a confused state. "Was I?"

"Oh, Nathan, you were so frightened, I didn't know what to do--"

"What time is it," he interrupted.

"--You scared me Nathan," Emma snuggled coyly.

"I did? Oh, I'm sorry darling," he said.

"Yes sweety, you were floundering around like a fish out of water," she pouted lovingly. Emma cupped the back of his head gently and pulled it toward hers while arousing him with her free hand. As Nathan began to reciprocate, she sat up abruptly and illuminated the lamp next to the bed. Nathan covered his squinting eyes.

"Emma, what gives... Geez, turn out the--"

"--Sweety, *look* what I *found*." Emma showed Nathan the back of the gentleman's photograph.

"See?"

"Yes, dear," he said blindly as he began kissing her neck. She quickly pushed him away.

"*Look*," she insisted.

"I know, darling" he lied. Nathan was still half-asleep as he continued his unrequited groping. "Well these things happen, sweetheart... We'll buy you a new one--"

She pushed him away forcefully and flung her leg over to straddle his stomach, shaking the lipstick-smeared clue in his face. "Norton," she said soberly. "Norton. Port Elizabeth. South Africa." Her voice was intense, one he didn't recognize at all.

"Darling," he sighed, "it's the middle of the night."

"You said we don't know where to look, Nathan," she said sternly. "Well we know where to look now. Norton. Port Elizabeth. South Africa, Nathan."

"Emma, please," he moved her off of his body and rubbed the sleep from his eyes. "We discussed this, sweetheart."

"No, Nathan. *You* discussed it."

"Emma, that photograph is ancient," he said.

She grunted in frustration at his ignorance. "Fine, I'll go with Sara!" She scooched her way toward the foot of the bed, hopping off its edge and stomping toward the door, hoping her antics would speed her arrival at Port Elizabeth.

Nathan raised his arms and dropped them to the bed, trying desperately to make sense of the woman he loved.

"The ink must have dissolved, but look! It says Norton, clear as day," said Emma, now only slightly drunk.

"Did you show Nathan?"

Emma nodded.

"Well? What did he say?"

"It doesn't matter, Sara, this gives us the *name!* We have to wake up Jack and ask him when Sully is leaving," she whispered loudly in desperation.

"Jesus, Emma," Sara said sleepily, "it's the middle of the--"

"Jack?" Emma pushed Sara out of the way and barged past her and into the room where Jack lay dead asleep. "*Jack, wake up,*" she demanded as she leaned and began nudging him. "*Jack!*"

Sara reacted swiftly, pushing Emma away from the bed and causing her to fall. "Emma, stop!" Emma ignored her as she quickly crawled toward the bed and lunged toward Jack. "*Jack, wake up!*"

Jack had awakened and now mimicked the confused expression Nathan had displayed minutes earlier.

"*Emma, calm down,*" yelled Sara. She pushed Emma, who again fell awkwardly to the floor. She sat up defiantly, but stayed put.

"But we have the name, we have to go," she pleaded in frustration.

"What name?" asked Jack in a daze. "What's going on, Sara?"

"Emma found a name on the back of one of the photographs from the locket," Sara explained flatly.

Emma nodded. "Norton," she said as she now sat calmly next to the bed. "It was there the whole time, we just couldn't see it," she explained as she offered the photograph to Jack.

"Norton," repeated Jack as he read it. "What time is it?"

Sara looked toward the alarm clock behind her. "Four thirty," she said.

"What did Nathan say?" he asked.

"Don't worry about him, when is your friend leaving?"

Jack thought for a moment. "Pack your things," he suddenly ordered as he jumped into action, quickly gathering his clothes and dressing.

Emma stood up with alacrity and bounded out of the room.

"Wha-? Where are you going," asked Sara as Jack reached the door.

"To get my Uncle's car," he said, "I'll be back in twenty minutes, meet me outside."

*

"Emma, have you lost your *mind*," croaked Nathan as he watched Emma's quick movements. "It's the middle of the night!"

"Get dressed, Nathan," she demanded.

"I-- Emma, what's gotten into you?"

"He leaves today, we have to meet Jack outside," she explained as she shoved clothes into a suitcase. "Come *on*, Nathan. Get up!"

Nathan began to speak but stopped himself, sighing heavily in defeat instead. He looked at her and begrudgingly flung the covers away. Shortly thereafter they exited the front of the hotel. Jack arrived a few minutes later in a 1913 Unic, the automobile his Uncle had used as a taxicab before saving enough money to open his restaurant. It was similar in shape and design to Mr. Clifton's Model T, but had a retractable top and electric starting device rather than a crank.

"When I spoke to him, he said they were shipping out on the tenth," said Jack as they drove through the darkness. "I didn't think it mattered after...after the argument yesterday, so I didn't bring it up." The bumpiness of the road contrasted the calm countryside of northern France as they motored toward the Naval base at La Havre.

"Well, I guess we're in luck then," said Nathan with as much civility as he could manage.

"You know what, Nathan," said Sara, "you can kiss a goat's behind--"

Nathan's demeanor froze into shock at her comment.

"--You have a girl who loves you and a wide open adventure, but you're too scared to enjoy it, just like when we were young."

"Sara please," interrupted Emma. "Please don't do this," she pleaded.

"Wake up, Nathan," Sara scolded before she turned forward in the front seat and clasped Jack's hand.

The couples sat in distant silence for several minutes before Nathan spoke. "You're right," Nathan said solely Sara slowly turned her head toward him as Emma lifted her sleepy head from his shoulder. "I don't know what I'm afraid of," he continued. "Ever since the, the quake... I've just wanted things to be normal. I always envied you and the others, you seemed so...unaffected, and I... I just wanted to forget... But I just can't seem to."

"Oh, Nathan," Emma consoled, "we all want to forget."

"I cried every night for a month when I arrived," admitted Sara.

"*You?* But you were so *strong*," Emma insisted. "You made it okay for me to be, happy...to sort of, start over."

"Yeah, I thought you were cool as a cucumber," added Nathan. "Nothing seemed to bother you, not even Miss Rose."

"Well," said Sara with a grin, "not everything is what it seems. The only reason Miss Rose was nice to me was because I acted tough. I never cried the time she whipped me with that damn ruler--" She chuckled at the thought of being free from it, "--but at night, I cried like a baby every night."

With their fears on the table, the three began sharing stories and laughing together, reminiscing the good and bad until they arrived in La Havre. As the sun began to rise, a few guards approached the slowing vehicle. Jack had stopped just long enough during the journey for everyone to change into their regimentals and Red Cross uniforms respectively. The guards let them through, pointing toward the furthest pier where they thought Sully would be embarking.

"Sully," yelled Jack as he closed the car's door. "Sully!"

He turned in surprise and squinted toward the silhouettes approaching. "Jack?"

"Yeah, it's me." They shook hands heartily. "These are the folks I told you about."

"Ohh," he said in a long descending note... "Well, jeepers, quite a looker you found, huh?" He nudged Jack as he gazed at Sara.

"Hey," Jack kidded with him. "Hands off, she's taken."

"Gosh, I wish you'da told me you were comin'..."

"Well, yeah, I figured you'd be surprised," said Jack.

"Thing is, we got a handful more POWs yesterday, so I'm not sure there's any open bunks is all," said Sully.

Nathan was quietly pleased at the direction of the conversation, while Emma bobbed up and down against the morning chill.

"We won't be a bother, we promise," said Emma, "Right Nathan, honey?"

"Huh? Oh, right darling, no trouble at all," said Nathan.

"Well, I suppose we'll find a place for ya, seein' as your doing all the grunt work," he laughed.

"Grunt work?" asked Emma in confusion.

"Well yeah, findin' whatever's *under tree ten banana* or whatnot," he laughed again. "...Better you than me," he added.

"Will you, um, excuse us for a moment please, Sully?" asked Jack. He led Emma and Nathan several yards away. In the distance, men were being unloaded from a military truck and led in a closely watched line toward the pier.

"What is he talking about, Jack," asked Emma suspiciously.

"Well, it's like this, see," Jack began. "I sort of offered him a share of the loot... For the ride and all," he said defensively.

"A *share*. What do you mean, a *share*, Jack," quipped Emma. Nathan stood in reticence, again becoming pleased with the direction of the conversation.

"Well I had to offer him *something*, Emma," Jack explained. "He could be courtmarshalled, ya know--"

"Jack, what sort of deal did you make with this man," she accused.

"Emma, it's complicated," he said flatly. "Trust me, it'll be fine."

"Oh, well please explain it so that I...we can understand," she said with her hands on her hips. Nathan stood at her side like a potted plant.

"Look, he wasn't gonna even help with the clue if I didn't agree to give him two free meals at my

Uncle's place... That's just how Navy men are, Emma," he explained. "When he got the translation, he said he wanted half of whatever--"

"*Half!*" barked Emma. She sighed heavily in disapproval.

"--But," he tried to calm her, "I talked him down to twenty-five percent," he explained.

Emma looked at Nathan for support, to which he scratched the back of his head. Sully called to Jack, gesturing toward the docks as a signal that they were ready to depart.

"When exactly were you planning on telling us this, Jack," Emma asked.

"Look, after I got the clue from him you two had your little... spat. I just didn't think it mattered on account of you weren't gonna go anyway," he explained. "And then I was just focused on getting you here, which I did," he reminded, "and then you were busy talking about Miss Rose and some guy named Slug and, well, I just didn't find the right spot to interrupt, Emma," he said apologetically.

"Well," said Emma in resolve, "I guess it is quite a long way, right darling?" she said. "I suppose we shouldn't be greedy." Nathan simply nodded obediently as Sara walked toward the group.

"They're leaving. Are you going or what?" Sara asked impatiently.

"Come dear, our treasure awaits," Emma said excitedly.

The couples said their goodbyes and walked quickly toward the dock to meet Sully.

"Wait, isn't this the ramp, Mr. Sully?" asked Emma as they walked the length of the hundred-fifty foot vessel.

Sully stopped and turned. He laughed, "No Ma'am, we're not takin' that jalopy. It was a passenger-liner with one smokestack and two masts, similar but smaller than the ship that had brought her, and separately Nathan, to France. As they neared the bow of the ship, another much smaller vessel came into view. Nathan had seen enough and his patience had worn thin. He was tired, hungover, and at the end of his rope.

"Wait," he said as he stopped and grabbed Emma's elbow. "Emma, this has become ridiculous. Look at that thing," he said as he pointed to the sixty-foot motorboat. "Emma, South Africa?" he asked. "I can't be cooped up in that, that *thing* for weeks and weeks! And, and we don't know a *thing* about Africa... Not to mention where the damned treasure is...or who the hell this Norton person--"

"Nathan," Emma interrupted as she gently placed a finger against his lips. "Listen to me. It'll be fine, I promise," she consoled. "We'll figure it out together, okay? ...Okay, darling?"

Nathan stood in silent irritation for several moments.

"I get seasick, Emma," he said flatly.

Emma laughed, "Oh Nathan, we all get seasick from time to time, darling. Come now my brave man," she said as she pecked his lips, "let's just enjoy the moment." She stared at him and fluttered her eyelids.

Nathan sighed in resolve. "Your right. I don't need to be anywhere but by your side, my dear. Besides, if we find the treasure, we can do whatever we want, right?" he said, attempting to persuade himself more than anything.

"You mean *when* we find it," smiled Emma.

"But what if we don't, sweetheart," countered Nathan. "I mean, how the hell would we get home?"

"You comin' or what," yelled Sully.

Nathan looked into Emma's eyes. He couldn't resist her and he knew it. His better judgement was incapacitated and enthralled by her venomous beauty. Moments later they boarded. Emma grinned with excitement as Nathan shook Sully's hand. "I must warn you," said Nathan, "I have a bit of a weak stomach."

"Well just head astern if you feel bad," instructed Sully, "it's only a few days out."

"A few days?" asked Nathan incredulously. "I thought it was several weeks," he added.

Sully laughed, "No sir, This baby'll hit thirty-two knotts in open water, we'll be in Cape Town in five days."

"Oh, I see," said Nathan brightly toward Emma, delighted at the good news.

"You see, darling," said Emma, "things are already looking up."

"Wait, did you say Cape Town?" asked Nathan.

"Yep, that's where these fellas are headed," replied Sully.

"How far is that from Port Elizabeth," asked Emma as the ship began too move.

"Gosh, I don't rightly know, Miss Emma," he said, "but we'll have time to look at the charts when we get movin'."

Sully began barking orders at the other officers and enlisted men as the boat picked up speed. As they made their way below deck, they saw a dozen or so POWs cordoned behind a metal gate on the starboard side. They sat on several of the lower bunks, talking quietly among themselves as an enlisted man stood guard.

Sully joined them below shortly after and led them through the corridor toward the large room at the bow of the boat, the three balancing themselves with their hands against the heavy rocking motion. They passed a small kitchen and lavatory, several bunks, and arrived in what appeared to be the stateroom.

"This is where you'll sleep," he said as he pointed to a long padded bench along the wall. "If I knew you were comin', I'd have, well--"

"It's fine, right darling," said Emma.

Nathan was pale and turning a bit green. He was doing his best to maintain his composure, but Sully sensed time was running out.

"This way, buddy," he ordered Nathan, "follow me." He led Nathan to the lavatory door and cranked the wheel to open it. Nathan entered and headed straight for the toilet, kneeling and vomiting in relief. He would spend the next three days of the trip in the cramped five by five foot room, occasionally being visited by Emma with water or food.

Emma felt bad for not fully comprehending the magnitude of Nathan's warning, assuring him she was grateful that he was willing to follow her on what she realized was a wild goose chase. "Oh Nathan, I promise it will be worth it. I promise," she continued convincingly. Nathan would simply nod in silence, retching everything he attempted to ingest and pleading that Emma leave the room almost immediately after she would arrive so that he could react to his body's displeased reactions to the turbulence of the speeding boat.

She spent her time planning and calculating using the maps and protractor Sully had taught her. She measured the distance from Cape Town to Port

Elizabeth, four hundred miles. Without telling Nathan, she convinced Sully to make the additional journey to Port Elizabeth in exchange for an additional twenty-five percent and with two conditions: One- They had but one day to find it, otherwise Sully's tardy return would become questionable by his Commander. Two- Forty dollars up front for additional fuel and rations, which would be considered collateral, refundable upon returning to Sully with half the treasure.

As Nathan curled his miserable body under a bundle of blankets, Emma sneakily extracted fourteen dollars worth of French Francs from his wallet and twenty dollars more from a compartment she discovered in his bag. A good thing, considering she had a mere twelve dollars to her name. This meant that between them, Emma and Nathan would have six dollars with which to eat, sleep, and travel.

When he finally began feeling better, Emma convincingly told him the Sully had agreed to take them to Port Elizabeth after dropping off the POWs in Cape Town. Nathan was not thrilled, suggesting that they travel by land instead. Emma refused, saying that without knowing the land, or whatever languages were spoken along the way, the safer bet was to take Sully up on his generous offer.

After dropping off the POWs in Cape Town, Sully began heading east toward Port Elizabeth. But within a few hours, the other enlisted men had begun questioning their direction, threatening to report Sully upon return to France. Sully explained the conundrum to Emma as Nathan had returned to being ill and took up residence in the lavatory once again.

"*What*," she exclaimed. "That's ridiculous! That would leave us with twenty percent," she angrily explained to Sully. The three other men had insisted on ten percent of whatever Emma and Nathan found after Sully had bargained with them.

"I'm sorry, Emma," he pleaded, "but I'll be courtmarshalled if they speak a word of this to anyone... Ten percent fer each is pretty darn reasonable if you ask me. Otherwise I'll have to turn around immediately."

Emma looked toward the three men scornfully. "Very well," she finally uttered. *Greedy bastards,* she thought to herself.

*   *   *

XXIII

*　　*　　*

Early afternoon approached that Saturday when they arrived in Port Elizabeth. Nathan was visibly relieved to be on terra firma and the color had returned to his face. It was a busy port, but most vessels were small fishing boats and mid-sized cargo boats, no larger than the one on which they made the journey. They scurried quickly off of the boat and began up the dock, listening the Sully's warnings

"One day," he warned. "We leave at noon tomorrow...not a minute after," he added.

A long row of neatly-fitted stone and brick merchant shops and cargo storage buildings lined the boardwalk at the front of Algoa Bay. They were all painted white and had red-tiled roofs, also reminiscent of the older piers in San Francisco. Beautiful hills and dunes with sparse trees speckled the landscape in every distance and the steeples of churches could be seen to the east behind the boardwalk buildings toward downtown.

The population was reminiscent of San Francisco's, aside from the majority being black-skinned. Chinese, British, Spanish, and many others comprised the burgeoning port in the hundreds, buying and selling their spices, furs, and textiles.

Coincidentally, Port Elizabeth endured a bubonic plague outbreak during nearly the same years as San Francisco, but negative sentiment was directed toward the squalid conditions of the blacks, whose housing locations had already been segregated and were now being forced to abide by the newly-imposed restrictions placed upon inter-town travel.

"No," said Emma as she pushed Nathan's arm down as he attempted to hail a taxi. "It's, um, better if we walk, darling... We might miss a clue if we hire a taxicab." Nathan shrugged slightly in agreement and suddenly withdrew his wallet. Sully had insisted that they leave their luggage on board as collateral and they had obliged. But now Nathan was secretly worried about the money he had stashed in one of his bags. He opened his wallet and discovered it was empty.

"Emma," he said as he stopped abruptly. "That bastard robbed me!"

"What?" she asked in dismay.

"I've been robbed, dammit," he insisted as he showed her the empty leather wallet.

"Oh dear, um," Emma began to blush uncomfortably. "Nathan, I have a confession to make."

"Oh? And what would that be," he sneered, already irritated by the numerous surprises which seemed endless as of late.

She nervously explained the bargain she had struck with Sully and the subsequent blackmail of the rest of the crew. To this, Nathan threw his bag several feet in disgust. "You did *what*," he yelled as he began to pace. "Emma, that's absurd! How do you expect us to eat?! And for that matter, where will we sleep! Jesus Christ, Emma, what were you thinking!"

"Darling, pl--"

"No, Emma, I've had enough *darlings* and *sweethearts* for the time being."

"*Here*," she said as she thrusted the six dollars from her purse toward him. "This should be enough, Nathan. Please try to calm down," she insisted. Nathan looked at the money and took it from her hand.

"Six dollars," he said flatly. "Emma, this is worth half as much in Pounds Sterling, are you aware of that? This will scarcely buy us a meal, let alone a room. Goddammit!" He paced more furiously, finally walking away from her and toward the edge of the cobblestone road to gaze blankly at the hills in the distance.

"I'm sorry, Nathan," Emma said softly. "Please. Nathan, please forgive me," she pleaded to his back. He stood defiantly with his arms crossed, considering everything...

He had spent the past five days being miserably ill, mostly curled in a ball on the floor of a boat. His fiancée had managed to hoodwink him into following a vague clue toward uncertain treasure. A man he hardly knew had already given away a fourth of said treasure. And now an even lesser-known stranger had left him with the clothes on his back and six dollars, not to mention the looming possibility that he was rifling through Nathan's bags at that very moment. Nathan turned slowly after a long pause.

"I love you, Emma," he said with nearly no emotion, "so I will forgive you."

"Oh, Na--"

"*However*," he continued. "When we get through this... *If we get through this*, you must promise me that we can go home and begin a normal life, with *no more shenanigans*."

"I promise, swee... I promise," she said with all sincerity. She stood close to him, hoping he would embrace her, but he did not. He moved around her to collect his small bag and began walking east toward the main square. Emma followed closely behind him, carefully, silently, until she saw something curious.

She spoke meekly. "Is that a jeweler?" A placard picturing what appeared to be three golden balls dangling from a curved rod hung above the door.

"No, but it's a start," said Nathan flatly. He walked purposefully toward the door of the pawn shoppe and they entered. A variety of brass instruments, lamps, and figurines were displayed in the window and Emma caught herself before commenting excitedly.

*

"It was made hyah, of thett I am cehtain," said the diminutive pawnbroker in a thick accent. "Fine piece," he added.

"How would we find the jeweler who made it," asked Nathan.

"Well, thet's easy. Only one hyah thet long ago was Fishah's," he said. "His son runs the pless now, but he clohses at two on Sata-dees. You had best hurry if you want to catch him."

"Where?" Emma asked frantically, breaking her silence.

"Oh, it's quite nyah, ectually. But best to hire a taxi."

"What if we were to walk," asked Emma.

"Oh, I see," said the man as he looked at Nathan's stubble. "Em, it's at the end of fohdeen,

but quite fah to walk...and he's closed tomohrrow,"
he said. Emma looked at Nathan in confusion. "Down
to the wateh, tuhn lift, and straight to the end,"
he explained.

"Um, sorry, could you write that down please,"
Nathan asked.

"Eh? Oh," he said, "cehtainly." *Fischer's -
Pier 14.*

"Oh," Emma laughed. "Thank you so very much,"
she said with a smile. They darted out the door and
back down to the promenade. Looking east, they saw
the distance. *That's at least two miles,* Nathan
thought to himself.

It was warm... Very warm. Summertime in the
southern hemisphere, an oddity that neither of them
had remembered to anticipate. Their clothes stuck
heavily to their bodies and neither had bathed
properly since the previous week. "Give me the
locket," said Nathan.

Emma looked at him scornfully for a moment, but
then understood. She removed the necklace and placed
it in his hand. He said nothing, simply wanting to
get to the end of this silly charade. He dropped his
bag and began running, awkwardly at first but then
at a steady clip.

Emma watched him for several minutes as his
figure became smaller. Most onlookers stopped to
watch him too, confused by his haste, looking toward
Emma's direction for the fire from which he ran.

They saw none. Emma eventually took their small bags and found a seat in the shade.

When Nathan finally arrived, a man was turning the key to the front of the building. "Wait," he gasped.

The man stood upright suddenly and turned around to see the drenched lunatic who was hunched over with his hands on his knees, gasping for air. He was a short, pudgy man, whose stature reminded Nathan of Clifton. But this man was older and had a larger nose and darker skin... And, Nathan could already surmise, was slightly less jovial by nature.

"Please," Nathan managed as he outstretched a hand toward the man. The man began to stutter step away in fear. "Just a moment, *please*," he begged.

"I'll cawl the police, young min," he warned, "if you mean me hahm."

"No, no," Nathan pleaded, beginning to catch his breath. He withdrew the moistened necklace from his pocket. "Just... Please, can you tell me if you...your father made this?" He breathed heavily and brushed his bangs back as his straightened his stance.

The old man squinted toward the piece curiously for several moments until Nathan timidly walked toward him, presenting the necklace as he did. The man reached for his handkerchief and gazed at Nathan suspiciously as he took the locket. He turned it over, noticing the inscription on the back. He gazed at Nathan curiously. He then unclasped and opened the locket, seeing the photographs of Emma and Nathan, who looked much less frightening through the glass frame.

"Wheh did you find thess, young min," he asked as he continued to examine the piece.

"It was a... San Francisco," he said.

"America," said the man in a curious voice.

"There was a photograph of a man with the name *Norton*. We're... My wife, um, fiancée and I are trying to find something," he said. "You see there's an inscription...under the photograph on the right...just there," he pointed. The man looked up as if asking for permission. Nathan nodded. "We've had most of it translated, except for one word," he explained.

The man used one of his smallest keys to pry the glass open and removed the photograph. He squinted toward it, mouthing the words. "Thess looks like Xhosa," he said.

"It says something about east of a tree, but we're missing the rest."

Without another word, the man turned, unlocked the door behind him, and entered. Nathan timidly followed the man into his store and watched as he went into the back room. Several minutes passed before the man re-emerged carrying a large and very old book. He used the same handkerchief to dust the old book before unclasping and opening it. He fixed his spectacles and ran a finger down the page.

"I hev a prohposition foh you, young min," said the man as he removed his glasses. Nathan lifted his head to meet the man's gaze, unsure what to expect. "I will tell you whett the inscrihption means. I will tell you wheh this Nohton lived... I will even tek you thyah. But I am a business man, Misteh--"

"--Purcell," said Nathan as he offered his hand, "Nathaniel Purcell."

"Elliot Fischer," replied the man as they shook hands briefly.

"What, um, did you have in mind, Mr. Fischer," asked Nathan.

"Ten pehrcent is stendahd, I believe, Mista Puhrcell," said Fischer.

"*Ten per--*," Nathan calmed his voice and thought for several moments. Sully was owed fifty percent and his crew another thirty. Ten more would leave he and Emma just ten percent of whatever they found. He stood in silence for several moments. *Better than nothing*, he finally thought to himself... *And he'll take us right to it.*

"Very well, Mr. Fischer," agreed Nathan, "but you must agree to bring us back to the docks afterward."

"Agreed," said Fischer, managing a grin.

"Oh, just one moh thing," said the man before he disappeared into the back room.

"What's that," asked Nathan.

"I will need to keep hold of this foh colletral," he said flatly.

Emma will murder me... "Very well," said Nathan reluctantly. The words had parted his mouth before he could process the thought further.

*

"*What*," Emma whispered loudly as Mr. Fischer's old car struggled across the bumpy dirt road. Nathan had explained that along with his generosity, Mr. Fischer was also a business man and would be expecting ten percent of whatever they hoped to find.

"Look, he explained the inscription and he knows where Norton lived," explained Nathan. "We'll still keep over half, Emma," he rationalized, "and we've been driving for miles. How else were we to get there?"

Emma's exterior feigned agreement, but inside she was terrified. Fifty percent to Sully, thirty more to the crew, and another ten now promised to this man. Sully would surely use Jack to hold Sara for ransom if they didn't find something. Plus there would be no easy explanation for the disappearance of Nathan's regimentals and Emma's Red Cross uniform, which Sully had insisted on holding. She leaned toward Nathan's ear and began whispering. "I have a plan," she whispered. Nathan nodded.

"We'll take half of whatever we find and drop it in the mail," she added.

"But they'll check our bags," Nathan whispered. Emma cocked her head to the side, as if to imply that Nathan was a few sandwiches shy of a picnic. "Ohh," whispered Nathan, realizing there were *other* hiding places.

Several miles and nearly a half hour later, Fischer turned the car up a long tree-lined road. A Spanish-styled villa stood at the end of the road, with several other smaller buildings dotting the landscape of the hills behind it. They had climbed a few hundred feet of elevation and the view was spectacular.

Emma and Nathan briefly shared a romantic moment, forgiving each other for their outbursts and becoming excited at the prospect of growing nearer to their fortune. Mr. Fischer had pointed out several dilapidated structures, explaining the history of the settlement of Algoa Bay by Norton and a few thousand others almost exactly a century earlier. He then explained the translation of the inscription.

"Undeh a tree, you will face due east," he said as he pointed behind them. "From theh, you will wahlk ten paces and deeg."

"But how will we dig without tools?"

Fischer smiled. "Dun't worry, Miss Emma, evrahbody hyah has a spehd..."

XXIV

*   *   *

Although Apartheid in South Africa would not officially rear its ugly head for several decades, tensions between whites and non-whites were palpable as early as the turn of the century. In 1908, the all-white government began the process to establish South Africa's independence from Britain, allowing non-whites to vote but forbidding them from holding office.

A few years later, the South Africa Act took away all political rights of black Africans in three of the country's four states and in 1913, the Native Lands Act gave merely seven percent of the country's land to black Africans, who made up eighty percent of the population. Blacks were prohibited from owning land outside their region and were allowed to enter white land only if they were working for whites.

Less than twenty percent of black Africans were literate when Emma and Nathan arrived, and the few who were educated at missionary schools had already begun attempting to organize to resist white rule and gain political power, but to no avail. Wages for blacks were a fraction of those of their white counterparts and their jobs were increasingly taken away and given to whites without explanation or recompense.

As Mr. Fischer's vehicle approached the villa, several children of various ages were kicking a ball back and forth and a very old man sat rocking in the shade on the deck under the eave. Through the door next to the old man, a woman wearing an apron was stirring a large pot of liquid and she instantly became alarmed when she noticed the car come to a halt. She frantically ran outside and beckoned the children inside with a frightened look on her face.

"*Dis my lend,*" the old man yelled in a raspy croak when the motor quit. He had begun waving his ornately-decorated cane at them.

"It's Misteh Fisheh and some frrinds, Toku," yelled Fischer toward the man.

The old man lowered the cane when he sensed the familiarity of the voice, gazing toward them intensely as he leaned forward.

"Fishah?" he repeated, searching his memory for the connection to the name among eighty years of others he had known. The woman returned to the doorway quickly and asked the old man something. "*It's okay. Just old friends,*" he assured her softly in the Xhosa dialect.

She nodded, offering a shy grin and placing the shotgun she had held behind her back to the side of the doorway. "Would you lek some tea, just made it," she asked uncomfortably.

"Oh, that would be lovely, dyah," said Fischer. The others nodded and the thin woman went inside to the kitchen.

"Diamond man, haha," said the old man as he scratched his short gray beard. He had done business with Fischer's father many years earlier, selling him diamonds for a very reasonable price with the man's promise that he would not report Toku to mining officials.

"Yes," said Fischer. "How ah you, young min," he asked toward the woman as she returned with a tray. The woman instinctively began translating the conversation.

"Ah, hahaha. *Alive as evah,*" replied the old man in Xhosa. "*Toku have eighty yeahs last week.*"

"My friends found an old photograph," said Fischer as the group approached the porch. The woman translated again as Fischer climbed the steps and handed it to him.

"Oh, haha... Missa Noto," he remembered.

"Yes, Mistah Nohton," repeated Fischer. He signaled to Nathan for the necklace. "We found an inscrihption and were hoping you might help us," he said. He handed the locket to the woman. "This was his lehnd, yes?"

Toku sat up curiously as the woman translated the inscription. He asked the thin woman something in dialect. "He ask wheh you find dis?"

"America," said Emma excitedly. "San Francisco," she added.

"Ah, San Francisco," said the old man as he reclined and began rocking again. He had a brief conversation with the woman and she fetched him a bowl of food.

She translated when she returned. "He tell me, tell you he don't know what you look foh, but okay to look at trees," she said as she vaguely pointed to a row of trees nearby. Nathan and Emma quickly set down their teacups in anxious anticipation.

"Would you heppen to hev a spehd handy, Miss," asked Fischer.

"A spehd," she asked with a confused look.

"Oh, yes, um," Fischer acted as if he was digging.

"Oh," she smiled shyly. "Yes, a spehd. Up in the hut," she said. She walked down the steps and to her left, the trio following closely behind her. She pointed up the hill in the distance to a small, crooked wooden shack. "In dyah a spehd," she said.

"Thank you," said Emma. She looked eagerly at Nathan and Mr. Fischer.

"*Thank you*," Fischer said in Xhosa. The woman nodded with a smile and returned to the porch.

"Sobonana," said Toku with his hand raised.

As they began to walk around the side of the villa toward the hill, a broad smile came across the old man's face.

*

Mr. Fischer waved them onward, explaining that he was expected somewhere and would return to collect them later in the evening. But as Emma reached for the locket in his hand, Fischer's expression changed and he glared at Nathan.

"More collateral," Nathan explained to Emma as he shrugged.

"But Nathan," she pouted.

"Don't fret, Miss Emma," consoled Fischer, placing the locket in his vest pocket and patting it several times. "You'll get it beck." He turned and walked toward his car.

The property was a beautiful landscape of rolling yellowish-green hills, but there were at least fifty trees speckling the three-acre property, giving the young couple pause as they made their way up the overgrown path. A simple white fence traced the perimeter of the elevated estate. A few brown horses and a small flock of sheep grazed busily near the far edge of the western-most fence, a small cemetery of crosses defiantly leaning as the constant wind swept the long grass surrounding them. Beyond, the hillside dropped sharply toward the ocean below and a steamship could be seen nearing the port.

When they arrived at the structure, it became clear that nobody had been anywhere near it in years. They hastily removed the debris and fallen branches from in front of the door and noticed a rusted padlock, which was unlocked but rusted beyond mobility. Nathan kicked its casing several time and removed it from the heavily rusted chain. The couple entered the shack. It had clearly been scavenged, but how many years prior remained a mystery. Several random items lay strewn around the room and a rake fell to the floor as Nathan shouldered the door ajar and ducked inside.

The sun had crept over the hillside and now shown in through the pane-less window facing southwest toward the villa and the sea beyond it. As they scanned the room for a shovel, Emma noticed an empty crate of whiskey laying on its side and large shards of dust-covered glass strewn around its opening. Nathan located a shovel and large steel pickaxe on the floor behind the door. As Nathan recoiled in fright from the critters which reacted to his movement of the tools, Emma assessed the room.

"Someone must have lived here, look," she said, pointing to a stack of termite-infested logs near a large iron pot.

Nathan fumbled with the heavy and rusty

equipment. "We don't have much time, darling," he said flatly.

"Right, sorry sweetheart," she replied as she picked something up from the dirt-covered planks of the floor.

"We must look for the trees with--

"--*Oh my goodness*," Emma interrupted. She had unfolded and was reading a piece of parchment. "Listen to this..."

Nathan had recoiled from Emma's sudden outburst, bumping into the door and dropping all of the tools he had gathered onto the ground.

Dearest Julia,

Tis with a heavy heart and a head swimming in spirits that I scribe this. You have always stood by my side as a good woman, strong and beautiful. Our lives have been blessed with health, children, and wealth my dear. As I scribe, an illness grows in me and fear that I shan't see the morn of fortnight next. How I've strained against the conceal of my feverish condition from you and the children my love, but alas it is my lot to protect you all from the hardships of life. This small token of our lives together marks our anniversary, my sweet. Place it around your neck and keep me with your thoughts always, look within if hard times beset you and the children. Love of my life, you are dearest to me as none other. Be well my dear Julia and see our children through this time and beyond.

Your most humbled husband,
James

"*Nathan*," Emma gasped as her mouth dropped open in awe. "This is the letter. *Oh my goodness*," she beamed in exhilarated satisfaction, her big, green eyes becoming saucers. "Do you know what this *means*?" she asked emphatically.

"I, um--"

"It means we are standing at the *exact* place where Mr. Norton wrote this." Her face was fixed in an expression of ecstasy.

"Darling," Nathan said sternly as he moved slowly toward her, "if we do not gather the tools and select the correct tree before the sun sets--" He paused and covered his eyes and forehead, suddenly overwhelmed. "--Emma, we're a million miles from home...in a goddamn shack in the middle of nowhere...with *six fucking dollars* to our names," he said. He paced around in a circle and then began collecting the tools. "I'm sorry, dear... Can we just find the damned tree, please."

Emma realized her excitement was misplaced. "Of course, Nathan, of course." She set down the note on the nearby table and quickly moved behind Nathan, picking up the heavy spade with a determined look on her face. Nathan wiped his sweated brow and sighed. They moved silently for the ensuing minutes, transporting a few tools into a clearing a few feet from the doorway outside.

The sheep had moved to the sunnier areas and fresh grass of the southern part of the enclosure, continuing to graze and inspect their surroundings as they chewed. Several noticed the bipeds in the distance, but merely as scenery in their larger order of routine. Surrounding the shack were three medium-sized trees and two large ones, the branches of one of the latter having been cleared away from the door half an hour earlier by Nathan.

Emma diligently studied the trees and looked up at the sky, attempting to use the sun's position as a compass. Nathan began scraping the tools against one another to dislodge the heavy rust and dust that coated them. It was nearing Four o'clock according to Nathan's wristwatch, which translated to nearly Five o'clock where they stood - meaning the sun would set within an hour.

The wind had grown stronger as the sun had moved further west over the ocean and the sweat which had soaked Nathan's only shirt had dried to form an ugly brown pattern to compliment his matted hair and stubbled chin.

"How about this one?" asked Emma as she stood next to the nearest tree.

"I don't think so, darling," said Nathan.

"Oh? And why is that Mister Smartypants," asked Emma.

Nathan stopped scraping the metal tools against each other momentarily. "How old is the locket?"

Emma was never very good at math. "A hundred years?" she guessed quickly, admiring the tree's canopy as she leaned back against it.

"Try again," said Nathan as he resumed preparing the pickaxe.

"Um, Eighty years?"

"Closer," replied Nathan. "It's 1918...and locket was made in 1848. So that's seventy years," he said with a grin.

"Meaning the tree is pretty old, huh." Emma's gaze wandered again to the animals grazing on the cliff.

"Indeed, my sweet," he said. "That tree is probably around twenty years old." He stopped scraping briefly to gesture to the acacia tree under which Emma stood. "A tree that has lived for eighty years or more is what we're seeking. So, you see," he began speaking in a W.C. Fields voice – which caused Emma to smile and pay attention – "it can only be one of four trees, see." He pointed to three massive trees in the distance near the grazers and thumbed behind him to indicate the fourth.

A Baobab tree could live for three hundred years or more and could reach a height of nearly ninety feet, its trunk growing to thirty feet or more in diameter. With its bushy branches covering its massive trunk, it had the appearance of a gigantic broccoli crown when its leaves were full.

Emma walked away from the tree and moved toward the baobab next to the shack. Its trunk was nearly ten feet in diameter and was abutting the wall of the shack. Emma gazed upward in awe as she walked around its circumference.

"*Nathan*," she said suddenly from the other side, "come quick!"

He dropped the tools and stood up, jogging around to the other side of the large tree. "Look," Emma pointed. Nearly ten feet off the ground was the bulbous protrusion of the shape of a heart. Emma moved away further to examine the disfigurement. "Nathan, this must be it," she declared, "there are words..."

Emma began jumping around wildly and prancing in circles while Nathan stared intensely at the markings.

Unbelievable, he thought to himself. It had been over seventy years since the sapling had ballooned to its enormous size, expanding and healing the wound that was carved into its bark so many years before. As he stepped back from the tree to study it, a faint figure appeared in his peripheral.

In his heightened state of awareness, he merely shifted his eyes toward the figure. To his south down the hill, Toku held a cane and slowly scratched his short white beard as he watched them, then turned and slowly disappeared behind the front of the villa.

"Sweety, Emma," he said, "this way... This way is east." He pointed toward the sloping hills beyond the nearby fence, toward the descending landscape and scantily-built structures of the impoverished black-African slums they had passed a few hours earlier with Fischer. Daylight began to fade, the sheep and horses becoming silhouettes as their features diminished.

Emma ran toward where Nathan stood and excitedly placed her heels at the edge of the tree's trunk, pacing forward with exaggerated strides, counting aloud as she did. "One, Two, Three..." When she had taken her tenth step, she was nearly at the foot of the border fence and proudly turned to face Nathan in triumph.

"Here," she said smirkishly as she pointed to her feet.

"Emma, um--"

"Nathan, this is the spot," she declared. "Ten paces east from the tree... That's the special tree and this is ten paces," she said.

The tree's trunk had grown to ten feet in diameter, wider than the small structure in which they had just entered. He calculated in his head that seventy or so years prior, the trunk would have been smaller, meaning the distance of the treasure from the tree would have been much closer. But how much smaller? How much closer? With the sun fading quickly, he walked to the middle of the tree's northern side and faced east.

"It's likely twice as big now, darling," he said, allowing her to process the information. Emma simply stood in place with her hands at her hips, not wanting to desert her spot. He stepped forward about a yard and assessed his position. A fourth of the tree's diameter reached further east than where he stood. He began pacing eastward with generous strides, mimicking Emma's audible count. When he had stepped ten paces, he paused, side stepped to his right twice, and stomped on the spot in which he believed the treasure to be.

Emma stood facing him nearly six feet away, a disagreeable look on her face. He heeled the foot-long grass until the dirt below became visible. "Here," he said flatly. He ran around the tree and collected the tool, hacking vigorously at the earth when he returned.

*

Nathan was frustrated, exhausted, fed up. He had dug two gaping holes in the ground, one at the spot he had arrived, the other - to her utter enjoyment - on Emma's spot. Each hole measured nearly three feet in depth and about two feet in diameter. He dripping in sweat as the sun began its descent. He noticed Emma nearing the animals in the far distance, lost in her own carefree world.

What the heck, he thought as he sat at the edge of the second hole and became lost in the sheer beauty of the tree. As he rested, his thoughts turned to the events that had led to this moment; of the war, of his life in San Jose, to his stupidity in agreeing to get on the blasted boat.

He became irritated... The ugly grass, his ugly smell, the ugly greed of Scully. The fat baker Dubois, the loss of his parents, his yelling at Emma, his scuffed and bleeding arms, his exhausted- *Wait a second...*

"Emma!" He stood abruptly and waved wildly for her to return. "Emma!" Her darkened silhouette came into focus moments later as she ran toward him. The skyline began to grow orange as the sun was being swallowed in its haze.

"Honey, look, it's a butterfly," Emma said playfully, in profound contrast to what he had been thinking.

"Yes, dear, that's lovely... I think I may have an idea," he said as he held her shoulders. "I want you to stand here," he said as he positioned her at the same spot from which he had started. "Good, now walk normally ten paces..."

"But, you already--"

"Yes," he interrupted her, "but I assumed Norton was my size."

"Well how do you know he wasn't?"

"I had to duck to get in the shack, remember?"

"Ahh," Emma sighed in understanding. She gazed at him as she cautiously began tiptoeing forward. On the tenth pace she stopped and moments later moved out of the way as Nathan spasmed into a fit of digging, throwing his frustrations into forceful blows, the sweat dripping steadily from his brow. His heart began beating audibly. Thunk, thunk, thunk, *twenty-five to Sully*, thunk, thunk, thunk, *twenty to Fischer*, thunk, thunk, thunk, Better. Be. *Here*. As he thought the word his pickaxe struck audibly.

He gazed briefly at Emma and dropped to his knees, digging furiously with his hands. Emma knelt too and the pair fervently clawed at the dirt like dogs on a sandy beach, gazing excitedly at each other as the surface of wooden slats became visible. Nathan stood and cautioned Emma away before he began scraping away the dirt at the sides of the box.

It was smaller than they had imagined it would be, rectangular and only a foot or so in length and half that in depth. He dropped the pickaxe and quickly freed the box with both hands, pulling it out of the ground. It was also much lighter than he had imagined it would be. He squinted closer to try to read something, but dusk had given way to twilight. He pulled his Army lighter from his pocket, opened its cover, and struck the flint-wheel, but the wind rendered the struggling flame useless.

"In the room, the shack," Emma said intensely as she pointed. "I saw a candle!"

They rushed around the tree and into the shack, where Emma crouched and felt around in the darkness. Her hands then fumbled across the smaller items on the messy table along the front wall.

"*Here*," she exclaimed as she lifted the candle by its curled brass holder and placed it near Nathan. Through the window, Nathan noticed the headlights of what he assumed was Mr. Fischer's vehicle as it made its way up the long dirt road toward the villa. Emma brushed away the excessive layer of dust which covered the candle's flint as Nathan struck the flint-wheel of his lighter again and held it to the candle.

"Imperial Shoes & Boots," Emma read a moment later.

"San Francisco's Finest," read Nathan. "...What in the world?"

They looked at each other in bewilderment.

"Well *open* it, Nathan," said Emma impatiently.

Nathan pounded the sides of the box's lid and began sliding the cover through the reluctantly jammed slats which held it, fitfully yanking at it when his fingers were able to fit into the opening. He began sweating again, pulling the lid while pushing the other end, finally managing to move it nearly the entire way. He stopped and reached inside, grabbing a handful of the contents.

"*Hot damn! We're rich,*" he exclaimed as he shook the paper bills in Emma's face and let out a raucous laugh.

"*Oh my goodness, Nathan! Oh my goodness,*" gasped Emma, joining him as he jumped up and down in circles wildly. They danced and celebrated for several seconds before Emma noticed something odd.

"Nathan?" she asked as he continued to dance. "Nathan!" Her inflection was serious and Nathan's dance and smile began to slow and fade. "Is this African money?" she asked as she grabbed his hand to examine it. Nathan realized he hadn't looked.

*   *   *

XXV

"Everybody understands Mickey Mouse.
Few understand Herman Hesse.
Only a handful understood Albert Einstein.
And nobody understood Emperor Norton."

-Discordian Society.

*　　*　　*

Well it must be," said Nathan. "We're in Africa, after all." They moved toward the candlelight and placed a stack of bills beside it.

"Oh my goodness," gasped Emma. "My father once told me a story about a crazy man who thought he was the Emperor." She went to the door and reached into her bag. "These must have been his parents," she said as she looked at their photographs. "...and the dogs..." Her thoughts trailed off as she tried to make sense of things.

Nathan was pacing again, his hand rubbing vigorously at his forehead in frustration. As he walked past the window of the shack, a flicker of light caught his attention. "Oh no," he said.

Fischer was approaching with a lantern. "What do we tell him?"

Emma looked out the door and quickly stood and walked over to the box. As she organized the bills neatly, she replaced them in the box.

"The truth." She winked at Nathan, who cocked one eyebrow in confusion. They blew out the candle and brought the box and their bags to the clearing in front of the shack. Nathan was clumsily kicking the dirt back into the three holes when Fischer arrived.

"Well hello thyah," he said. "Any luck?"

"Oh, Mr. Fischer, it's *amazing*," she beamed. "Look!"

She picked up the box and walked to meet him as Nathan brought the tools into the shack and closed the door upon exit. They were covered in dirt and sweat. Emma's usually kempt hair was an array of tangles and her fingernails and hands were indistinguishable from those of a vagrant. Fischer lowered his spectacles and peered into the box, then picked up one of the bills.

"Isn't it *amazing*?" said Emma, "There must be thousands!"

Fischer inspected both sides of the bill excitedly, the back of which was blank. He adjusted his glasses and placed the bill next to the lantern to read it:

> No. _____   United States
>
> ## The Imperial Government of Norton I
>
> *Promise to pay the holder hereof, the sum of* **Ten**
> **Dollars** *in the year 1880, with interest at 5 per cent,*
> *per annum, from date, the principal and interest to be*
> *convertible, at the option of the holder, at maturity,*
> *into 20 years 5 per cent, Bonds, or payable in Gold*
> *Coin.*
>
> *Given under our Royal hand and seal*
> *this _____ day of _____ 18*
>
> *Norton I, Emperor*

"Um, yes, quite amazing," Fischer said in a quizzical tone. "I'm afrehd I've nevah seen notes lehk these," he admitted.

"You haven't?" asked Emma. "Well I suppose you wouldn't have, would you," she said coyly, "being so far away and all."

He looked up at her curiously as Nathan had collected the bags and joined them. "Incredible, isn't it," he said, overhearing Emma's comments. "I bet there's at least five thousand in there!"

Fischer looked at them both and his eyes became wide. "Thet much, eh?" he said in a pleased tone. "Well let's be off then and find some propeh lighting, yes? I'll bring you beck to yoh hotel and we can settle things thyah," he said jovially. Fischer placed the note into the box and began walking down the long hill to the villa.

Emma and Nathan looked at each other uncertainly and shrugged, hoping the strategy would work. "Oh, we haven't exactly, um, reserved a room yet," said Emma.

"Oh?" said Fischer from several paces in front of her. "Well you'll not find a room at thess hour... No matteh, you'll be my guists. It's the least I can do, eh? You'll be quite comfohtable I assure you."

"Oh, um, well--"

"That would be lovely," Emma said above Nathan's murmur.

The group descended the hill, Emma and Nathan conjuring a discussion of all the wonderful things they were going to enjoy with the treasure.

When they arrived at Fischer's small cottage home, he furnished them with towels and gave Emma a dress which had belonged to his late wife and found a shirt that his son had left behind before moving to England. They sat at the small table in the kitchen and counted the notes while Mr. Fischer tended to a stew he had begun prior to picking them up at Toku's villa.

"I have four-hundred ninety," said Emma when she had finished counting her stack.

"And I have... That makes five hundred exactly," said Nathan as he counted the last note. "So that makes nine-hundred ninety, at ten dollars each... Nine-thousand nine-hundred and ninety!"

His voice was shrill and excited as Fischer's back was turned, but as he said it, Nathan's eyes rolled toward Emma in jest, causing her to laugh. She masked her sudden outburst by coughing repeatedly and excused herself to the restroom. "We must have dropped one, darling," he said loudly as Emma tried to control her laughter.

"And you say these Nortons are good cuhrency, eh?" asked Fischer as he turned to look over his shoulder.

"Oh, yes," said Nathan confidently. "I believe the exchange is nearly equal to the Pound Sterling," he added.

"Excellent," said Fischer. "Then you won't mind accompanying me to the benk next Monday, yah?"

"Oh--" said Nathan. Sully would be at the docks the next day at noon. *Not a minute later...* "--Yes, of course," said Nathan.

"Excellent," said Fischer.

When Emma composed herself and returned to the kitchen, they all enjoyed a pleasant meal and some local wine to celebrate. The conversation shifted briefly to the war, their lives, and the beauty of Port Elizabeth. After dinner, Mr. Fischer reclined in a chair on the porch while Emma and Nathan settled in for the night.

"Do you think he bought it?" whispered Emma.

"I don't know," replied Nathan, "but he wants us to go to the bank with him on Monday."

KYLE A. TURK   346

Emma sat up quickly and turned to him. "Nathan, *Monday*? We have to leave *tomorrow*."

"I know, I know... Don't worry, we'll tell him we want to sightsee tomorrow at the docks and slip away."

"But what about the *locket*, Nathan?"

He had forgotten. "Right, um..."

"I've got it," said Emma after a few moments. Minutes later, they fell asleep, exhausted from the events of the day.

The next morning, Fischer was reading the newspaper and enjoying his toast and tea as Emma approached.

"Here's your share, Mr. Fischer," she said with a smile. "Two thousand."

"Oh, delightful," he said. "I trust you slept well?"

"Yes, yes, and thank you again for your hospitality, and for helping," she replied pleasantly. Emma placed the box on the coffee table and outstretched her free hand, teasing the man with the stack of notes in the other. Fischer gazed at her curiously. "The necklace, please, Mr. Fischer."

"Oh, yes, I see," he said reluctantly. "Yes, very well..."

Fischer set down his tea and made his way to the kitchen. After some clanking sounds, he returned, placing the locket in Emma's hand.

"Thank you for watching it," she said. "Surely it would've been badly soiled in all that mess," she added with a giggle. Emma handed the stack of notes to Fischer.

"Indeed. But if it tuhns out thet the benk will not exchange these, em, Nohtons, Miss Emma," he warned, "I will expect the necklace retuhned to me."

"Of course, of course." Emma smiled. "Darling, are you ready?" she asked to Nathan in the other room.

"Yes, dear," he replied.

"Mr. Fischer, would you mind... Could you perhaps be so kind as to drive us into town?" asked Emma. "We'd like to walk around and get to know the place and find a suitable hotel."

"Cehrtainly, Miss Emma," said Fischer. In the daylight, Fischer proudly pointed to buildings of interest as he motored along, waving frequently to friends he passed as they made their way toward the docks. When they arrived at the main square, he pointed to a hotel, saying that the owner was a very pleasant one. "Meet me hyah tomorrow at ten, the benk is just up the way," he said.

"Ten o'clock. Yes sir, Mr. Fischer," said Nathan.

"Thank you again, we'll see you tomorrow," assured Emma. As they walked through the square and cut through a small alleyway to the docks, they sighed in relief.

"You think Sully will buy it?" asked Nathan.

"Practice makes perfect, darling," she said slyly with a wink.

The couple wandered through the shoppes along the dock, parting with the few dollars they had when they finally found a shopkeeper who would accept them. A few hours passed and they made their way along the pier to the dock where Sully would be waiting. As they approached, his expression became lively, noticing the wooden box tucked under Nathan's arm.

"*Now*," whispered Emma.

From thirty feet away, Nathan extracted a handful of Nortons and waved them vigorously in the air. Sully offered two thumbs up in return and was smiling broadly. Convinced he had bought it, Nathan returned the notes and closed the lid, which moved more readily but still refused to open more than half way.

"Well, well, well, look what the cat dragged in," he joked when they arrived. Nathan was dreading the return voyage and had already convinced himself that he would set up camp in the lavatory. Sully helped them aboard and ordered his men to ship off. He eagerly led them into the stateroom and began wringing his hands in excited anticipation. Nathan stalled and began recounting their adventure, attempting to buy time as the boat motored further from shore.

Sully grew impatient quickly. "Well let's see it, already," he said.

"You do the honors," said Nathan.

In a somewhat maniacal act of glory, Sully decided to open the lid of the box and haphazardly dump the contents of the box onto the table. As he noticed the unfamiliarity of them, his smile flattened. He flung the box against the hull, smashing it into several pieces.

"What in tarnation is this?" he barked.

"Wait, no! I can explain, Sully," pleaded Nathan.

As Nathan explained that they were an old bond certificate used after the Civil War due to counterfeiting, Emma noticed a small piece of paper next to the broken box. She picked it up and unfolded it:

Eureka Lodge - San Francisco - August, 1872

Dear Toku,
Please keep these safe for me. Good lad.
Sobonana,

Norton I - Emperor of the United States
- Protector of Mexico.

*

"Well hello thyah young min," said the jeweler, "Is Mistah Nohton about?"

"Doctah, dem go doctah," replied the young Xhosa boy. He was just ten years of age, but was instructed to care for the villa by Mrs. Norton while they rushed Mr. Norton to the nearest doctor.

"Ah, I see. Well, then," said the man in a chipper tone, "would you please be so kind as to ensuhre Mistah Norton receives this upon his return?"

"Yes, yes. I give Missa Noto," smiled the boy, feeling a sense of responsibility. The man gratefully handed him a small box and a receipt. "Sobonana," the boy said cheerfully as the man returned to his wagon. He watched to ensure the man's car was a safe distance before closing the screen door and retreating into the large and spacious room of the villa.

Fifteen years later, the grown boy began buying the diamonds that his tribal people had smuggled out of the mines and reselling them to a local jeweler. He received half their going value, but both he and the jeweler maintained their end of the bargain for the next thirty years.

When he died a few months after Emma and Nathan had visited, Toku's possessions included £60,000 Pounds Sterling, the deed to the Norton estate, a walking cane with the words *His Majesty* carved into it, and one neatly framed Ten-dollar Norton.

*

"Bet I can beat you to the buoy and back," said Nathan, "what do you say?"

"...I say you still owe me that half-dollar," said Emma.

"Ha," joked Nathan, "how about I give you ten Nortons instead."

*   *   *

THE END

Epilogue

Charles Purcell (Nathan) branched out into a variety of civil engineering projects throughout California, even working in Peru for a few years. In 1930, he was appointed chief engineer on a large project, commissioned to design and construct a bridge which would span 8.2 miles from Oakland to San Francisco. The bridge was completed three years later, some sixty years after Emperor Norton's proclamation. **It has yet to be named in his honor...**

The character of Heston Montgomery is based loosely on John Berrien Montgomery (1794 – 25 March 1872), an officer in the U.S. Navy who was sent to Sonoma after foreigners (mostly white Americans) revolted against Mexican authorities in what became known at 'The Bear Revolt.' Montgomery entered Sonoma, lowered the Bear Flag, and raised the American Flag. The Bear Flag eventually became the offical flag of California.

Harry "Slug" Heilmann (August 3, 1894 – July 9, 1951) went on to be inducted into the Baseball Hall of Fame in 1952. His nickname was actually derived from the slow pace with which he ran. He was a close friend of Babe Ruth, and may have been the only contemporary companion of both Ruth and Ty Cobb, who were said to have been bitter enemies.

Made in the USA
Charleston, SC
15 March 2012